Murder Most Sweet

Also available by
Laura Jensen Walker

Phoebe Grant Series
Dreaming in Black and White
Dreaming in Technicolor

Getaway Girls
Daring Chloe
Turning the Paige
Becca by the Book

Other Novels
Reconstructing Natalie
Miss Invisible

Murder
Most
Sweet

A BOOKISH BAKER
MYSTERY

Laura Jensen Walker

CROOKED
LANE

NEW YORK

Published in the United States by Crooked Lane Books, an imprint of The Quick Brown Fox & Company LLC.

Crooked Lane Books and its logo are trademarks of The Quick Brown Fox & Company LLC.

Library of Congress Catalog-in-Publication data available upon request.

ISBN (hardcover): 978-1-64385-502-8
ISBN (ePub): 978-1-64385-503-5

Cover illustration by Rob Fiore

Printed in the United States

www.crookedlanebooks.com

Crooked Lane Books
34 West 27th St., 10th Floor
New York, NY 10001

First Edition: August 2020

10 9 8 7 6 5 4 3 2 1

In memory of my sweet Grandma (Florence) Jorgensen and those blissful after-school afternoons in Racine, eating her scrumptious baked goods. Best. Baker. Ever.

And for my Renaissance-man husband Michael, the current best baker in the family.

Chapter One

I miss my breasts. Occasionally. Back in the B.C. (before cancer) day, I had a nice pair. In fact, they were my best feature—small but perky, even just shy of forty, when some of my more busty girlfriends' boobs were beginning to feel the pull of gravity. Now, five years later as I glanced down at my flat, slightly concave chest with its pale scars marking the place my breasts used to be, my hands reached up to the hollow area and rested there a moment, paying homage to my gone but not forgotten bosom.

Then, like Taylor Swift, I shook it off.

I'm alive-with-a-capital-A, doing what I love, and being paid for it. How many people can say that? Who cares that I am now flat as a pancake? Besides my mother. Flat is how I entered the world and how I will leave it—many years from now, hopefully. Meanwhile, I offered up my daily thank-you to God and the universe for beating cancer and for cancer compelling me to follow my dreams. Dreams that began when I was a little girl but that I did not have the guts to follow until I was slapped upside the head with my own mortality.

In the mirror, a streak of white fur flashed behind me, followed by plaintive barking.

"Good morning, Gracie-girl." I pulled on my favorite boho cotton dress and turned to my eager American Eskimo, ruffling her creamy fur. "Is someone ready for breakfast?"

My rescue dog jumped off the bed and sprang to the doorway, where she stood upright on her hind legs, pawing the air frantically with her front feet. "Okay, since you said please." Grabbing a turquoise silk scarf from the coat rack I had repurposed to hold my myriad scarves, I wound it loosely around my neck and headed down the hall to the kitchen. Gracie zoomed past me, her nails beating a staccato click-click-click on the hardwood floor.

"Teddie, you're not wearing that to the book signing, are you? Can't you at least put on a bra?" My seventy-three-year-old mother, clad in a sleeveless red linen column dress that snugged her trim frame, raised a perfectly waxed eyebrow over her shiny Botoxed face as she sat at my pine kitchen table covered with a crazy-quilt tablecloth.

"Good morning to you too, Mom, and to answer your question—again—no bras for me stuffed with uncomfortable prostheses. Those suckers are heavy and hot." Not wanting to continue this same tired discussion, I asked, "Are you out of tea again, or is it milk today?"

The woman who brought me into this world, Claire St. John, now widowed, lives behind me in a sleek mother-in-law cottage—no chintz or cozy quilts for her—and is forever running out of groceries. She keeps her gray stainless-steel kitchen stocked with the essentials: coffee, tea, soy milk, fruits and veggies, cottage cheese, the occasional piece of fish or chicken, and a variety of seeds. That way she can keep her trim figure and not be tempted by any "bad" foods. Instead, she regularly drops by my vintage kitchen to steal a cookie and supplement her minimalist stash.

She made a face at me. At least I think she did. It's always hard to tell after she's had one of her Botox treatments.

"Neither. My blender broke, and I need to use yours to make my kale smoothie."

"Knock yourself out." I nodded to the appliances at the end of my vintage fifties–tiled counter as I tossed a dog biscuit onto the yellow-and-black-checkerboard floor for the impatient Gracie. "I, on the other hand, am making chocolate-chip pancakes for breakfast." I pulled down a box of Bisquick from the cupboard of my midcentury-definitely-not-modern bungalow.

"Why don't I make you a smoothie instead? It's much healthier and less fattening."

And tastes like a glassful of grass. "No thanks. I'm good with carbs and chocolate."

She sighed. "You're definitely your father's daughter."

Thank you, Jesus.

"Just remember, men don't like big women. You've already got—"

"A couple strikes against me." I finished the rest of my mother's common refrain. "Yes, I know."

"What can I say? Men are visual. They like breasts." She sneaked a chocolate chip. "It's not too late. You can still get a new pair—the surgeon said so. Otherwise, I'm afraid you'll never get a man."

"I'm not trying to get a man, Mother. I'm quite happy with my life as it is." I pushed my unruly hair behind my ears, but the coffee-colored curls sprang free moments later. My naturally curly hair has a mind of its own, and I had long ago given up trying to tame it. My mother used to spend hours straightening it when I was a kid, but I refuse to spend three hours a day ironing my hair. I hate ironing. Cooking and baking are more my style. As evidenced by the batch of silver-dollar pancakes studded with chocolate-chips I whipped up.

"Don't dawdle." Mom leaned forward, her silver bob framing her taut features, to show me the time on her smartphone screen. "We're going to be late."

"Relax." I forked up a piece of pancake and followed it with cold milk. "The signing doesn't start for a couple hours yet. We've got plenty of time."

"This isn't a local author like you, dear. This is *Tavish Bentley*, a rich-and-famous *New York Times* best-selling author. Like John Grisham and Janet Evanovich. We're lucky he squeezed us into his book tour after that Milwaukee bookstore had to cancel. There will probably be tons of fans coming from nearby towns, and a line around the block. I want to be sure and get a good seat."

My mother had conveniently forgotten that when my first book released nearly four years ago, there had been a line around the block for *my* book signing. Nearly our entire town of Lake Potawatomi, Wisconsin, had turned out for the debut of my novel, *Death by Danish*. The fact that my light and frothy mystery was set in a small town similar to ours at a fictional bed-and-breakfast modeled after the Lake House, my friends Sharon and Jim Hansen's popular B and B, might have had a little something to do with it. Having a best friend—Char Jorgensen, owner of the local bookstore—who plugged my book relentlessly to every customer that crossed the threshold hadn't hurt either.

Mom pulled Tavish Bentley's last five glossy hardcover best sellers out of her tote bag. "I'm going to get him to sign these for me—I got a great deal online."

"Not cool, Mom. We need to support our local bookstore."

"I support the Corner Bookstore all the time. Didn't I buy seven copies of your novel to send to family in Phoenix? Speaking of which, I forgot to tell you, your second cousin Kevin is writing a book and would like you to send it to your agent on his behalf."

I rolled my eyes.

*   *   *

As my mother grabbed a seat in the empty front row at the bookstore, I handed the platters of chocolate-chip–peanut-butter bars and lemon sugar cookies to Char.

"Thanks. You're a doll." She snagged one of the sugar cookies, bit into it, and released a small moan. "Your cookies always melt in my mouth. These are so much better than the ones from the grocery store."

"Homemade is always better than store-bought."

"Unless I make them." Char scrunched up her freckled face. "Remember my blackened chocolate-chip cookies?"

My mouth went dry at the memory, and I gulped a cup of punch. "The taste of burnt chocolate chips is one you don't soon forget."

"Good thing you inherited the baking gene from your Danish grandmother."

"Danish *and* Norwegian," I corrected her. "Grandma Florence was equally proud of the Norwegian side of her heritage." In our small midwestern town founded by Danes, who still account for the majority of the population, we mudbloods have to stand up for ourselves. I'm a mutt myself: Danish, Norwegian, English, French, and a touch of Potawatomi—the first peoples to inhabit our local area.

I glanced at the spread Char had set out for the reception following the signing: *frikadeller* (Danish meatballs), Havarti cheese, a fresh-veggie platter, Door County cherries, my homemade cookies, and of course, several flavors of kringle, Wisconsin's official state pastry. As much as I love to bake, I draw the line at kringle. I made the famous Danish pastry once with my grandma years ago, and that was enough. The painstaking process of hand rolling, folding, and resting the buttery dough to get the requisite number of flaky layers—some say thirty-two, others prefer forty-eight—is a three-day marathon.

Eyeing the platters from Racine, unofficial kringle capital of the world and a mere thirteen miles up the road from Lake Potawatomi, I asked, "What flavors did you get?"

"Apple, pecan, almond, raspberry, and because I love you"—Char flicked the pom-poms at the bottom of my silk scarf—"cherry-cheese."

"You rock. Keep that up and I might dedicate my next novel to you."

"That will be sure to shoot it to the top of the best-seller list."

"From your lips . . ."

While we were talking, the bookstore had filled up. Most of the people I recognized from town, but a dozen or so unfamiliar faces—mostly attractive women—had squeezed into the crowded rows of chairs, clutching copies of *Her Blood Weeps*, Tavish Bentley's latest suspense, and humming with anticipation. Much as I hate to admit it, Mom had called it. Out-of-town fans had made the trek to Lake Potawatomi to see the famous author—the taller-than-me English author who bore a slight resemblance to Colin Firth. The celebrated best-selling author who at this very moment was heading our way. A female hipster clad head to toe in black and intent on her iPad accompanied him, along with Char's boyfriend, Sheriff Brady Wells, and Sharon Hansen, my childhood friend and proprietor of the Lake House B and B.

Sharon, Char, and I have been friends since grade school. Dubbed "The Three Musketeers" by our teachers, Sharon is the petite blonde bubbly one that every boy in high school wanted to date, Char is the slim redheaded brainiac who had her fair share of bookish suitors, and I am the quirky Amazon with unruly hair who towered over most of our classmates and chose to stay home and play Scrabble with her folks on prom night.

Charlie's Angels has nothing on us.

"Here she is," Sharon said proudly, linking her arm with me and beaming, "my friend, famous author, and baker extraordinaire, Teddie St. John. Teddie, this is Tavish Bentley."

"Sharon's biased." I gave her arm an affectionate squeeze before grinning at the renowned author to show him I understood that we played in very different leagues. "My *fame*," I made air quotes with my bush-league fingers, "is confined to Lake Potawatomi."

"Nuh-uh," Char piped up. "We've gotten emails about your books from readers in Maine, North Carolina, and Oregon."

"Well there you have it," Tavish said in a killer English accent. "You're a success from coast to coast, and I'm sure that's just the beginning. I read *Death by Danish* last night and found it quite delightful."

"Care to put that on my next book cover?" I teased, pushing my renegade curls behind my ear.

"I'm afraid Tavish only does a limited number of endorsements," interjected his black-clad companion with the Harry Potter glasses.

"Sorry. This is my assistant and publicist, Melanie Richards," Tavish said. "Melanie, meet Teddie St. John, who in addition to writing fun, lighthearted mysteries—that I'm happy to endorse, by the way—also made the scrummy oat biscuits we had last night."

"Biscuits?" Brady and Char exchanged a confused look.

"That's what they call cookies in England," Sharon informed them with a knowledgeable smirk.

"Awesome oatmeal-raisin," Melanie said, glancing up at me over her glasses and releasing a brief smile. Then she pushed her glasses up her nose and peered at her iPad. "Tavish, it's time."

Brady drifted off as the duo departed, with Tavish saying over his shoulder to me, "Lovely scarf. We should compare writing notes later."

Melanie then led the celebrated author over to his adoring public, who burst into applause as he approached the podium. Tavish Bentley smiled and lifted his hand in a brief wave to the assembled audience. A gorgeous blonde in a red bandage dress who looked like she belonged in the *Baywatch* reboot jumped up and waved back, the sunlight streaming in the window and reflecting off the massive rock on her left hand.

"His fiancée," Sharon whispered. "I met her earlier when she stopped by the Lake House looking for Tavish—she said they'd had a fight and she'd come to make up with him."

Char grunted as she scrutinized the Baywatch babe. "Such a cliché. Rich, hot guy our age hooks up with twentysomething blonde bimbo who's clearly had a boob job."

"We don't know that," I said.

"What? That she's had a boob job?"

"No. That she's a bimbo. The breasts are definitely fake—they didn't jiggle when she jumped up." My close encounter with the silicone kind after my first mastectomy five years ago had given me the inside track on what is natural versus surgically enhanced. Lying down, my real breast, like those of every other woman who has not had work done, flattened out and dropped to the side, while the doctor-constructed one always stood proudly at attention. As a result, I can spot fake boobs poolside at fifty paces.

Case in point: the platinum-spiky-haired giggling millennial sitting next to Tavish's fiancée. Side by side, the two women looked like the Boobsey Twins.

We headed to the seats Mom had saved for us in the front row, but halfway there a hot flash from hell hit that made me

9

want to strip off all my clothes instantly. *Thank you, chemo, for sending me into early menopause.* Deciding that flashing the entire bookstore might not be in anyone's best interest, I made a quick detour to the restroom instead, unwinding my scarf before the door fully closed behind me.

Once inside, I yanked off the constricting turquoise silk and dropped it on the oak top of the long antique dresser Char had converted into a bathroom vanity. Then I hurried to the sink, lifted up my white cotton dress with turquoise embroidery that had all at once become an electric blanket turned on high, and splashed myself with cold water. Repeatedly. Not until the splashing became a drenching did I finally feel some relief. Thankfully, after my second mastectomy I had given up bras and those heavy silicone breast forms many cancer survivors stuff inside their brassieres. Otherwise I would not have been responsible for my actions. I'd have yanked those puppies out in full view of God and everyone and thrown them like a Frisbee. Might have shot someone's eye out, or at least knocked them down for the count.

Hearing the squeaky doorknob turn, I quickly dropped my dress back down and scuttled into one of the two stalls as the door opened. Too bad I didn't have the requisite equipment to enter a wet T-shirt contest—I would have won hands down. My cotton dress clung to my wet body like a second skin, highlighting every curve, lump, and bump, including my concave chest. Not having had time to grab any paper towels before the unknown woman entered, I tried drying myself off with toilet paper, leaving me looking like I had a bad case of TP chicken pox.

It doesn't get any better than this. As I heard the taps turn on, I decided to take the plunge. "Excuse me, could you please hand me some paper towels over the top of the stall?"

The taps turned off.

"Hello? You there?"

A rustle of silk. The faint scent of jasmine.

"Bueller? Anybody?"

The door squeaked again.

"What are you doing here?" an unfamiliar female voice growled.

"I'm here to get Tavish back," an indistinct voice said.

"There's no way he'll take you back. Besides, he's mine now."

"We'll see about that."

"Over my dead body."

The things one learns in the ladies' room. I cleared my throat to make my presence known. The door opened and slammed shut. Then silence.

Waiting a moment, I cautiously exited the stall into an empty restroom. Who were those two women? Sounded like a former girlfriend of the famous author might be trying to encroach on his fiancée's territory.

As I plucked my wet dress away from my skin in a feeble attempt to dry it, a few of the toilet-paper dots dropped to the floor. Grabbing some paper towels, I blotted my dress, trying ineffectively to dry it off. Great. Now I had shredded-brown-paper dots sticking all over me. I flashed back to that gorgeous brown-and-white polka-dotted dress Julia Roberts wore at the polo match in *Pretty Woman*. I checked the mirror. Yeah, not even close. More like a giraffe mated with one of those frizzy-headed goats.

I sighed. The only thing to do was cover as much of my wet T-shirt giraffe dress with my scarf as possible, then unobtrusively slip out the back door and make a run for it. Luckily, my house was only two blocks away. I moved to grab my silk scarf from the end of the antique vanity where I had tossed it in the heat of the hot-flash moment. Not there. I checked the other end of the vanity. Not there either. Had it slipped off and fallen to the floor? I checked, but didn't see any turquoise atop the wide-planked wooden floors. Maybe it had fallen into the wastebasket. Nope. I searched the whole bathroom. Nada. My turquoise scarf with the whimsical pom-poms on the ends had disappeared.

Then I remembered the rustle of silk.

Not disappeared. Stolen. No wonder the jasmine-scented mystery woman hadn't answered my paper towel plea—she was too busy stealing one of my favorite scarves.

*   *   *

Half an hour later I stepped out of the shower, having scrubbed away every trace of my polka-dotted humiliation. When I saw myself in the mirror, I recalled the giraffe image from the bookstore and burst out laughing.

Gracie trotted in and tilted her head at me. *What's so funny?*

"Ah, Gracie-girl, leave it to your mommy to turn a special event into the sublimely ridiculous." I had managed to escape Char's bookstore mostly unseen, with only a few people in the back row catching a glimpse of me, intent as they all were on Tavish Bentley. The spiky-haired platinum-blonde Boobsey twin had turned and stared at me as I left, zeroing in on my concave chest. When I checked my phone, it was flooded with texts from my mom, Sharon, Char, and Brady, which I answered in order.

Mom: *Where ARE you? It's rude to miss the signing, especially as a fellow author. People might think you're jealous.*

Me: *Not jealous. Had a fashion emergency and had to leave unexpectedly. Will explain later.*

Sharon: *Are you okay? After you were gone fifteen minutes, I checked the restroom, but you had disappeared. I'm worried. What's going on?*

Me: *Sorry for causing you worry—my bad ☹ I'm fine. Had a hot flash emergency that turned into a comedy of errors, leaving me unfit for human contact. Please give Tavish my regrets and tell him I enjoyed meeting him.*

Char: *Did you fall in? I know I have good reading material in there, but we're missing you.*

Me: *Hot flash emergency. It wasn't pretty. Long story. Meanwhile, if you see a woman in the bookstore wearing a turquoise scarf with pom-poms that resembles mine, it is. Beyotch stole my scarf!*

Brady my sheriff pal: *Should I send in the cavalry?*

Me: *No need. Girl problems, but all is fine now. Meanwhile, there is a petty thief in town. Have Char fill you in.*

I pulled on one of my vintage bohemian crinkle skirts, a flowing peasant blouse, a red-fringed scarf, and my silver Celtic-knot earrings from Cornwall.

Gracie gave a short bark and scooted her bottom across the rug.

"Someone has flop-bott and needs to go outside." I first encountered the term *flop-bott* when reading about the spoiled Tricki Woo in James Herriot's wonderful veterinary tales set in Yorkshire. Although Gracie is not English, or spoiled (much), I am a die-hard Anglophile, so I appropriated the expression for myself. I clipped on Gracie's leash, and she bounded to the front door.

"Okay, okay, I'm coming."

Once outside, Gracie scampered to the grassy lawn next door, checking her pee-mail. After she had answered all her messages and I had deleted the fragrant results, she wagged her tail and regarded me eagerly.

"Good girl. Yes, you've earned a nice long walk." We set off down the sidewalk, with my Eskie stopping every few feet to sniff her mail, giving me a chance to enjoy my surroundings. June in Lake Potawatomi is one of my favorite times of year, with all the dogwood, wisteria, hydrangeas, and roses in bloom. I stopped to admire Joanne LaPoint's white lacy hydrangeas in front of her neat blue cottage, but my impatient Gracie pulled on the leash.

Sometimes I set the route for our walks; other times I let Gracie lead. Today I followed my canine daughter. She led me a couple of blocks, turned the corner, and sprinted to the alley behind the Corner Bookstore, nose in the air and sniffing madly. Then she began to bark.

I caught a glimpse of familiar turquoise pom-poms on the ground beside the dumpster. "Good girl! You found mommy's scarf." Although why the bathroom thief would go to all the trouble of stealing my silk scarf just to discard it a short time later was beyond me.

Maybe she's a kleptomaniac, my inner snark suggested.

Gracie strained at the leash, barking frantically, as we neared the dumpster, where I spotted a longer section of turquoise silk. A crumpled section with a spilled Coke can atop the silk. Definitely my scarf. Ruined. I sighed, rounded the corner of the dumpster, and screamed.

The Baywatch blonde in the red bandage dress with the huge rock on her finger—Tavish Bentley's fiancée—lay dead on the ground, wafting faint whiffs of jasmine, my turquoise silk scarf wrapped around her neck.

Chapter Two

My legs buckled as Gracie strained forward and continued barking. Sitting down heavily on the hard concrete, I pulled my distressed dog to me. She yelped as her paws caught in the turquoise pom-poms. Leaning over to extricate Gracie from the scarf, I fought down the bile that threatened to erupt from my churning stomach as I averted my eyes from the dead woman's staring face.

Brady Wells burst through the back door of the bookstore. My head snapped up to meet the astonished eyes of our sheriff, my fingers still entangled in the scarf's pom-poms. Gracie barked anew.

"Teddie! What happened?" Brady hurried our way, taking care not to contaminate the area more than I already had, I belatedly realized. You'd think I would have known better, since I write murder mysteries, but this was the first murder I'd encountered in real life.

Another scream rent the air. The sheriff whirled around as a cluster of women spilled out of the bookstore into the alley.

"Oh my God! Kristi!" wailed the Boobsey twin pal of Tavish's fiancée, her heavily made-up eyes wide with horror.

The platinum-haired millennial pointed a shaking sapphire-tipped finger at me. "She killed Kristi!"

The trio of women started to surge forward, but Brady held up his hand in a stop motion. "Stay back, everyone. This is a crime scene."

Another cluster of people exited the back door of the Corner Bookstore, including Sharon, Char, and my mother. The last fluttered her hand to her chest and shrieked. "Teddie, what have you done?"

Seriously, Mom?

Just then, a crowd burst around the side of the brick building. Through my daze, I dimly registered the rest of the bookstore audience, Tavish Bentley, and his publicist Melanie.

"What the—" Melanie began.

"Kristi," breathed Tavish, catching sight of his fiancée. His stunned hazel eyes locked on mine.

Gracie's paws finally broke free from the turquoise pompoms. I hugged my shaking dog to my trembling chest, burying my face in her creamy fur. "It's okay, Gracie-girl. It's okay."

Through a fog—was I in shock?—I heard Brady's voice barking instructions into his phone, then felt his hand on my shoulder. "Can you stand up?"

I set Gracie down as the sheriff helped me to my feet and gently led my dog and me away from the curious crowd.

"You'd *better* arrest her," shouted the remaining blonde Boobsey twin. "I saw her sneak out of the bookstore earlier. She was probably lying in wait to ambush poor Kristi in hopes that with her gone she'd have a shot with Tavish." Her derisive gaze swept me from head to toe, lingering on my flat chest. "As if."

My two Musketeer pals shot daggers at her, and Gracie growled. She took a step back.

Moments later, Brady's young deputy, Augie Jorgensen—Char's baby brother—raced into the alley. Augie shooed the lookie-loos back. Then, squaring his shoulders, he moved toward the body on the ground and, with a face bleached of color, unspooled a roll of yellow crime scene tape.

After a quick consultation with his deputy and Char, Brady gently ushered me into Char's office at the back of the bookstore. At the same time, Char and Sharon led a shaken Tavish Bentley and the assembled guests back inside with promises of coffee and kringle.

Sinking into the leather mission-style armchair across from my best friend's beau, I stroked Gracie's fur and stared at the books lining the walls, always a calming influence.

"Okay, Ted," Brady said kindly, using the nickname he had given me in high school, "you want to tell me what happened?"

I recounted how I had been out walking Gracie when she led me to the alley behind the store, where I spotted my stolen scarf beside the dumpster, which in turn led me to discovering Kristi's body with my scarf around her neck. Flashing back to her still form on the ground, I recalled my earlier conversation with Char and Sharon. Even in death, Kristi's boob job did not let her down.

For all the good it did her. I rubbed my eyes.

Brady's voice intruded on my rueful recollection. "So you knew her?"

"What? No. I never saw her before today."

"But you knew her name."

"That's what her friend and Tavish called her."

Brady scribbled in his notebook. "And how well do you know Tavish Bentley?"

"I don't. I just met him today." I angled my head at him. Brady should know that. Char, excited by the prospect of snagging the famous, wildly successful *New York Times* best-selling author for her store when the Milwaukee bookstore on his tour had canceled days earlier, had been telling everyone in town how much we both couldn't wait to meet him.

A knock on the door interrupted us, and speak of the devil, Char entered with a tray holding two steaming mugs and a plate of Havarti and kringle. Gracie jumped down from my lap, nose twitching, straining toward the tray. Char set the tray down on the desk and removed a dog biscuit from her pocket, which she tossed to Gracie, who caught it in her mouth and retreated beneath the desk to enjoy her treat.

"I thought you could use some sustenance." Char handed me one of the mugs. "Drink this chamomile tea; it will calm you."

I took a grateful sip as Brady scarfed down a piece of pecan kringle and drank his coffee. Char started to leave.

"Hang on a sec, Char. I have a question for you," Brady said, in his sheriff rather than his boyfriend voice. "When did Teddie tell you her scarf had been stolen?"

Char gave him a curious glance, but pulled out her phone and scrolled through the texts. "At eleven forty-three AM. Why?"

He ignored her question and turned to me. "And what time did you actually leave the store?"

I scrunched up my forehead, trying to recall. "I don't know exactly. I was in kind of a hurry to get out of here. Maybe five to ten minutes after the signing started. About 11:05 AM? 11:10?"

Brady's mouth set in a grim line. "Why were you in such a hurry to leave, Ted? You texted me you were having girl problems. Were those problems with the deceased?"

Char and I both stared at him openmouthed.

"Are you kidding me? Do you honestly think I killed that girl? Someone I don't even know?" My mystery-author nature kicked in. "Strangled her with my own scarf and left the evidence behind? That would be pretty stupid."

Char's red ponytail swung as she punched her longtime boyfriend on the shoulder. "What is *wrong* with you? How could you even think such a thing?"

Brady's lips tightened. "I'm only doing my job. These are questions I have to ask." He shot me an unhappy look. "I'll ask you again. What kind of girl problems were you having that caused you to leave the bookstore so suddenly?"

So I told him the whole hot-flash-debacle story—TP dots and all.

"I didn't want to disrupt the author's talk and cause a scene." I pointed to my chest with both hands and said dryly, "And this baby minus its usual scarf camouflage with wet cotton clinging to every feature is far too graphic a scene for most to handle—especially when they're expecting foothills rather than valleys."

The sheriff's face flushed. "Sorry, Ted. So, your scarf was stolen from the restroom vanity while you were, uh, otherwise engaged in the stall?"

"You got it."

"And you didn't see the woman—person—who took it?"

"Nope. I smelled her, though—a faint scent of jasmine." Then I remembered. "The same scent I smelled when Gracie and I found Kristi." I stared at Brady as realization dawned. "Oh. My. Gosh. Tavish Bentley's fiancée stole my scarf!" I was about to tell Brady about the second unknown woman who had entered the restroom when a discreet knock at the door stopped me.

Sharon stuck her head in. "Uh, guys, excuse me, but Tavish would like to talk to Brady." She pushed open the door and the *New York Times* best-selling author strode in, distraught.

Oh no. Did he hear me? Way to kick a man when he's down.

Sharon retreated, gently closing the door behind her.

"I'm so sorry for your loss," Char and I blurted in unison.

Tavish gave us a brief nod, but his attention was laser-focused on Brady. "Sheriff, I think I know who killed Kristi."

I fingered the fringe of my red scarf, remembering how the English author had complimented my turquoise scarf earlier. The scarf now wrapped around his dead fiancée's neck. Was he going to accuse me as well?

"Have a seat," Brady said, indicating the wooden chair beside me.

Tavish sat down and shoved his hand through his dark hair. "Kristi has—had—this ex-boyfriend named Tom in LA. He's a nasty sort—very dodgy, been in jail before—and he's been harassing her for a while. Calling her on the phone at all hours, threatening her, following her, showing up unexpectedly. She had to get a restraining order against him."

21

"How long has this been going on?" Brady asked.

"Months, but it increased when we got engaged a couple months ago."

They've only been engaged a couple of months? I exchanged a glance with Char, recalling the earlier bimbo conversation we Three Musketeers had indulged in about the now-dead Kristi. Our respective cheeks flushed with shame.

Brady asked for Tom's particulars, his full name, where he lived, and any other details Tavish knew about the ex-boyfriend, scratching them down in his notebook. As I watched the sure-to-be-heartbroken author answer, I slunk down in my chair, feeling worse by the minute.

"How long was your fiancée with this Tom guy?" Brady asked.

"Kristi's not my fiancée," Tavish said quietly, staring down at his hands. "We ended our engagement a few days ago. Or, rather, I ended it."

* * *

"So, do you think Tavish Bentley killed his ex-fiancée?" Char mumbled around a mouthful of chocolate-chip–peanut-butter bar in the Lake House kitchen.

Sharon grimaced. "Didn't your mother ever teach you not to talk with your mouth full?"

Char swallowed and took a swig of milk from her glass. "She taught me a lot of things, Blondie," she said, using Sharon's high school nickname, "but that doesn't mean they stuck."

Char loves teasing Sharon, who likes to play the role of "mom" in our Musketeers group, even though there's only a six-month age difference between us. (Char and I are both forty-three; Sharon's forty-four.) Probably because Sharon followed a more traditional path than we did, marrying her high school sweetheart after graduating from community college and giving birth a few years later to twins Josh and Jessica, now away at college.

"Well, we all know sticking has never been one of your strengths," Sharon snarked back.

"Okay, guys." I rapped on the large butcher-block kitchen island our stools were clustered around. "Let's keep to the matter at hand. Um, murder at hand." The three of us had decamped to Sharon's B and B after Char closed the bookstore early upon her sheriff-boyfriend's order. Although we were dying to hear why the best-selling author had ended his engagement to the buxom, now-dead Kristi, Brady had shooed us away and taken Tavish over to his office for further—private—questioning.

"He couldn't have killed her," I said.

"What?" Char took another drink of milk.

"Tavish. He couldn't have killed his ex because he was inside the bookstore, surrounded by a packed house at his book signing. Right?"

"Right," Sharon said.

"Unless, of course, he slipped out back to sneak a cigarette, Kristi followed him, refusing to accept their broken engagement, got loud and hysterical, and he snapped and strangled her with my silk scarf that she'd stolen," I mused in a dramatic voice.

Sharon grinned. "Are you brainstorming your next mystery plot, Sherlock?"

"Why not? I'm always on the lookout for new ideas, no matter how farfetched."

Char's forehead creased. "Tavish *did* leave the store briefly. Said he had to take an important phone call." Her face turned paler than usual, causing her freckles to stand out in stark relief. "And now that I think about it, I didn't see Kristi anywhere."

"Well, the store was pretty crowded," Sharon said. "It would be hard to see everyone."

Char snorted. "Not those boobs in that tight red dress. She's not"—she paused—"*wasn't* someone who'd fade into the background. No. His ex was not there," she said, with growing conviction. "At the same time that Tavish wasn't there either." Char reached for her phone. "I need to tell Brady."

"She could have been in the little girls' room," I said.

"Nope. After you texted me about your scarf being stolen, I kept a close eye on the restroom and never once saw her coming or going."

Wait a minute. The little girls' room. I flashed back to the conversation I had heard earlier while trapped in the stall. One of the women had said she was there to get Tavish back and the other woman had replied that Tavish was *hers* now. I had assumed the second voice belonged to Tavish's fiancée, but now, knowing he'd recently ended their engagement, maybe not. Maybe she was the one who'd said she was going to get Tavish back. Was she also the one who had said, "Over my dead body," or was that the other indistinct voice? I rubbed my head, trying to recall.

Sharon shivered. "Do you really think Tavish Bentley killed that poor girl?"

"I don't know," I said. "I don't know him, but he seems like a nice guy. Although that is what people always say after a murder—*I can't believe it! He seemed like such a nice, quiet guy.* Statistically speaking, however, more than half of female homicide victims are killed by their intimate partners."

"Tavish didn't kill Kristi!" Publicist Melanie barreled through the open kitchen doorway, eyes blazing behind her Harry Potter glasses that had slipped down her nose. "Are you making rash accusations against my author? Not cool. That's called slander."

"Nobody's making any accusations," said Sharon's inn-keeper husband Jim, who had accompanied Melanie into the room. "Right?" he said to his red-faced wife.

"Right. I'm sorry," Sharon said. "We were just—"

"Gossiping." Melanie pushed her glasses back into place. "Isn't that the sport du jour in small towns?"

"Not just small towns," Char said evenly. "My colleagues and I have heard plenty of publishing gossip filter down from New York over the years."

"Whatever. You clearly don't know Tavish. He would never do such a terrible thing. He's not capable of such violence." She zeroed in on me, her kohl-rimmed dark eyes narrowing at the sight of my red-fringed scarf. "Wait. Wasn't it *your* scarf wrapped around Kristi's neck? How do you explain that? You also left the signing before it even began. Where were you off to in such a hurry?"

"Now who's making accusations?" Char said. "Remember, that slander thing goes both ways."

"I'm just asking a question."

"That's okay, Char. I'm happy to answer her. Why don't you pull up a stool, Melanie?" I pushed the plate of homemade cookies her way. "Would you like a cookie bar?"

Always-the-mom Sharon jumped up from her stool to serve her guest. "I have some milk to go with the cookies. Or wine and cheese in the fridge, if you prefer."

Melanie waved her off impatiently. "All I want is an answer to my questions." She plunked her iPad down on the counter top and folded her arms across her chest.

"Okay. I believe you asked three questions." I ticked them off on my fingers: "One: was it my silk scarf around Kristi's neck? Yes. Two: how do I explain that? No idea except that someone who smelled of jasmine entered the bookstore restroom while I was otherwise occupied and apparently took my turquoise scarf, because it was gone when I came out of the stall—as was the mysterious jasmine-scented woman.

"Three: why did I leave the signing in such a hurry?" I gestured to my flat chest. "You may or may not have noticed that I don't have boobs."

Melanie flushed.

"No biggie. Although it freaks some people out, so I wear scarves. Today, though, just before Tavish's talk, I had a hot-flash eruption—something you won't have to worry about for years." I shot the twentysomething woman a rueful smile. "In my frenzied efforts to cool down in the restroom, I went overboard, resulting in what amounted to a wet–T-shirt disaster. A disaster I thought I could hide with the help of my turquoise scarf—the scarf that was no longer there because someone stole it. Hence my quick departure. I was simply trying to spare the public the sight of my soggy breastless form. Does that answer all your questions?"

Before the publicist could answer, I heard someone clearing his throat.

Brady. I would recognize my high school friend's familiar throat clear anywhere. I shifted my laser focus from Melanie and saw Brady Wells and Tavish Bentley framed in the kitchen doorway.

Chapter Three

"So now a famous best-selling author knows you don't have breasts?" My mother covered her face with her hands and groaned at my kitchen table the next morning.

"Apparently," I said, pulling out my grandma's *fattigman bakkels* (pronounced "futtymon buckles") recipe from her wooden rosemaling box with its Norwegian painted-folk-art flowers. I had a hankering for the lighter-than-air Norse cookies usually served at Christmas, and they're one of Brady's favorites. Since I hoped to pump him for information on the murder investigation, it wouldn't hurt to prime the pump with something sweet.

"I don't understand why you always feel the need to announce your flat condition to the whole world."

"I'm not announcing it to the whole world. I was explaining to the publicist—who was wondering if I might have *killed* her author's ex—the reason for my abrupt departure from the bookstore." Opening the fridge, I grabbed eggs, butter, and whipping cream, and set them on the counter next to my Smeg mixer. "I can't help it that Tavish and Brady overheard." I gathered the rest of the ingredients from the pantry, set them on the counter, and began separating eggs.

"If you'd had reconstructive surgery, it wouldn't even be an issue."

"It's not an issue for me, Mom." *Now you, on the other hand . . .* I shook my head. "I still can't believe she thought I killed that Kristi."

"What in the world was that woman doing with your scarf around her neck?"

"I'm pretty sure she stole it when I was in the restroom."

"But it didn't even go with her dress."

Fashion (and looks) have always been important to my mom, which is why I've always been such a disappointment to her. And why she has such a hard time with my breastless state. When I was first diagnosed with breast cancer, my folks were frightened—my dad cried and told me he was terrified he might lose me—but I reassured them the cancer had been caught early. I had the option to go with either a lumpectomy and radiation or a mastectomy followed by chemotherapy and reconstruction. I chose the latter, wanting to make sure any and all possible cancer cells were removed from my body. And then several months later my fake boob popped and I learned I had several precancerous lumps in my remaining breast. That's when I made the choice to go flat. Something my father fully supported, but my mom simply can't understand.

I flipped on the mixer and began creaming the eggs, sugar, cardamom, brandy, and whipped cream, tuning out my mother as I replayed yesterday's events in my mind again. Who was the other woman who entered the ladies' room while I was in the stall? Was Kristi a kleptomaniac? Was that why she had stolen my scarf? I hated to admit it, but my fashionista mother was right—the turquoise did not go with her red bandage dress.

So why steal it? Unless maybe she had something against me? No, that couldn't be. We didn't even know each other. Yesterday was the first time I had ever set eyes on the woman. No, the only thing that made sense was that she was someone who got a kick from stealing. What did *not* make sense was why someone would kill her.

"Karma's a bit—"

Noticing my mother's lips moving, I turned off the mixer so I could hear. "I'm sorry. What did you say?"

"I said karma's a bitch."

"Nice, Mom."

"I'm just saying. What goes around comes around. That girl stole your scarf and then someone else strangled her with it."

"But who would have done such a horrible thing?"

"It must have been one of those out-of-towners at the signing. No one in Lake Potawatomi is a murderer, for goodness' sake."

You never know. *Who knows what evil lurks in the hearts of men?*

* * *

An hour later I knocked on the closed door of the sheriff's office with a yellow-checked tin full of cookies and a thermos of freshly brewed French roast.

"Come in."

Brady was sitting at his cluttered regulation-gray metal desk, mired in paperwork and sporting dark circles under his baby blues.

"I thought you could use a little Norwegian pick-me-up." I extended the tin to him.

His bleary eyes brightened. "Is that what I think it is?" He yanked the top off the yellow tin. A whisper of powdered sugar wafted upward, landing on his sheriff's uniform. "You made *fattigman*? But it's not Christmas."

"Consider this your early present." I unscrewed the lid of the thermos.

"You didn't need to bring coffee." He nodded to the eighties-holdover Mr. Coffee in the corner, which stood next to a ubiquitous red plastic tub of supermarket coffee.

"Oh yes I did. This is *real* coffee." I poured the fragrant brew made from coffee beans I had ground an hour ago into two mugs. Pushing one of the mugs across his desk, I sat down across from him, sipping my coffee and munching on a cookie, leaning forward so as not to drop powdered sugar all over my paisley sage scarf.

Brady bit into one of the airy diamond-shaped cookie twists and lifted his eyes heavenward. He finished it off in three bites and took a greedy drink from his mug. "Not only are you the best baker in town, you also make the best coffee."

"Norwegians are known for their classic black coffee. Grandma Florence taught me how to make it when I was fifteen, the appropriate adult age, according to her, to start drinking it." The memory made me smile.

"I remember having coffee and kringle at your house after we won the basketball tournament sophomore year." Brady grinned. "I was getting ready to chug a glass of milk in the kitchen when your grandma said no, such a momentous occasion called for a good cup of coffee—black." A grimace replaced his grin. "That first swallow was pretty potent. I had to grab a big piece of kringle to counteract that strong brew."

"Nothing better than kringle and coffee."

"Unless it's your cookies and coffee." He scarfed down a couple more *fattigman bakkels*, inadvertently dusting his desktop with powdered sugar.

We reminisced about high school for a few minutes, and then I casually said, "So . . . how's your first murder investigation going? Do you think there's something to what Tavish Bentley said about his fiancée's—ex-fiancée's—old boyfriend?"

"So that's what the cookies and coffee are all about. A bribe for information."

"Not a bribe. Think of it as a little gift between friends. Besides, I have a vested interest."

Brady lifted his bushy left eyebrow.

"Two people have already accused me of killing that poor woman since whoever did murder her strangled her with my scarf. I need to clear my name."

"No you don't. Anyone who knows you knows you are a big cream puff who couldn't hurt a fly. You may write about murder, but you could never commit one."

"Well, thank you for that vote of confidence, Sheriff. It would have been nice if you'd told me that yesterday when you were grilling me so relentlessly."

He lifted his shoulders in a helpless gesture. "Just doing my job. Everyone in town knows we've been friends since grade school and that your best friend is my girlfriend. I have to show impartiality. I need to question anyone and everyone who might have ties to the deceased."

"But that's the whole point. I don't *have* any ties to her."

"Maybe not a tie, but a scarf." He stood up, brushed the powdered sugar from his uniform, and held out the tin of cookies to me. "Nice try, but no cigar, my friend. You know I can't give out any information. This is an official departmental investigation."

"Well, you can't blame a girl for trying." I pushed the tin back at him. "Keep the cookies and share them with your skinny deputy. He needs them more than I do." I screwed the lid back on the thermos and stood up to leave.

Just then, that skinny deputy, Augie Jorgensen, burst into Brady's office, waving a piece of paper. "Sheriff, I got the information you wanted on that Tom Rogers dude! Turns out he was holed up in a motel outside Racine the past couple days. Checked out this morning. So he *was* in the vicinity at the time of the murder!"

As Brady glowered at his deputy, I gave my high school friend a sweet smile. "I'll be going now. Always nice talking to you, Brady. 'Bye, Augie. Stay out of trouble."

* * *

Staring off into the distance, I wondered how I was going to kill off my next victim. Gunshot? Stabbing? Blow to the back of the head? Or that old reliable standby, poison? One thing I refused to do was strangulation. Been there, done that, and a little too close to home for comfort.

I sipped my coffee and stared at my laptop screen on the table. Then I scrolled up and skimmed the last chapter again. That always helped kick-start the creative juices. Yes, a blow to the head would do nicely, and require only a discreet amount of blood. Discretion is the better part of valor for the squeamish, of which I am one, along with my gentle readers. Those tender readers of a certain age do not like blood and gore and prefer their violence off the page, not in their face.

My fingers flew across the keyboard as I continued the latest adventure of B and B owner Kate and her crime-solving canine companion Kallie. *Oh yeah, baby, it is really flowing now. I'll make my daily word count after all.* I did an internal fist pump.

"Are you a plotter or a pantser?"

That internal fist pump deflated, replaced with a silent sigh. That's the problem with writing in public. There is always the possibility of interruption—although most of the locals know my daily routine and know not to disturb me when they see me bent over my laptop and typing away in the back corner of Andersen's Bakery.

I held up a hand without lifting my head. "Two minutes. I need to finish this." Continuing to type until I reached the end of the paragraph, I added in my brief blah-blah notes to jog my memory of where I wanted to go next. I always type in "blah-blah" along with a few key words as a placeholder. Then I typed in the perfect sentence that had come to me mere moments before. The sentence I would later weave into the conflict between Kate and the prime suspect—the sentence that would be lost in neverland if I did not write it down this very minute.

Finally I hit save and pushed my curly hair behind my ears. Then I peered over my tortoiseshell readers to see Tavish Bentley standing before me, a contrite expression on his face.

"My humble apologies," he said in his plummy English accent. "I should know better than to interrupt a fellow author at work."

"Pantser."

"Sorry?"

"You wanted to know if I was a pantser or a plotter." My lips turned up. "I'm a seat-of-the-pants writer all the way. Plotting is not my strong suit. I like allowing the story to unfold organically through the characters. You?"

"A bit of both, but heavier on the plotter. I was an engineer before I became a writer." He nodded to the empty chair across from me. "May I?"

I nodded as I took a bite of cheese Danish.

Tavish pulled out the chair, but before he could even sit down, Bea Andersen had hustled her varicose-veined legs over to the table, coffeepot in hand, agog at the sight of the celebrity author in her shop but trying to play it cool.

"Coffee?"

"Yes, please." He indicated my plate with its half-eaten Danish. "Do you have any more of those delicious pastries?"

"Yeah, you betcha," Bea said, channeling Marge Gunderson in *Fargo*—although I doubt the seventy-five-year-old Hallmark Channel–loving Bea even knew who Marge was. Besides, Wisconsinites had been saying that phrase since long before the movie. "Cherry or cheese?"

"One of each, if that's not too much trouble." Tavish delivered a dazzling smile to Bea.

Her lined cheeks pinked. "No trouble at all, Mr. Bentley. Believe you me."

I watched the plump gray-haired restaurant owner I had known since childhood scurry all aflutter to the pastry case at the front counter, where octogenarian Fred Matson sat enjoying his daily bacon and eggs. "I think you have a fan."

"I hope so." He gazed at me.

"I'm a fan too. Just not your number one. The name's Teddie, not Annie Wilkes," I teased, recalling Stephen King's miserable character.

"Thank God." His bantering tone ceased and his hazel eyes shuttered.

Oops. Had I just stepped in it somehow?

Before I could form an apology, Bea returned, plopping Tavish's flaky Danish duo down in front of him. Then she shyly pulled out a rectangular object obscured beneath her left upper arm. "I'm sorry I missed your signing—I was working. Could I get you to sign *Etched in Blood* for me?"

As I watched Tavish interact with a blushing Bea, I wondered what had caused him to shut down earlier. Was he having problems with some intrusive fans? I hear that can happen when you are famous. Not that I would know personally. My fame is confined to a cozy group of fans usually forty and over who often write to share stories of their dogs' mischievous exploits that remind them of Kallie, my protagonist's four-footed playful partner in crime.

"Thank you!" Bea clutched her autographed book to her chest, a huge smile wreathing her round face. "I'll go get yous guys some more coffee." She hurried off.

"Yous guys?" Tavish said.

"A local expression. Kind of like 'All right, mate'?"

"The *guys* part I understand, but *yous*?"

I shrugged. "The rest of America says *you guys*, but *yous* is distinctly southern small-town Wisconsin among Danes and Norwegians of a certain age. Not sure when or where it originated exactly, but I grew up hearing it from my dad and grandparents. Part of the local lexicon."

He grinned. "Like *me luvver*."

"Excuse me?"

"Sorry," he said quickly. "It doesn't mean lover. It's a Cornish expression for someone you're happy to see—perhaps a customer entering a pub: 'Hello, me luvver.'"

"Oh that's right. I think I heard that on an episode of *Vera*. Or maybe *Doc Martin*."

"You like British TV shows?"

I nodded. "Movies too. I'm a rabid Anglophile going all the way back to childhood when I first saw *The Railway*

Children. Watching *Sense and Sensibility, Pride and Prejudice,* and *Persuasion* in my twenties simply confirmed it."

"Ah, the classic Austen trifecta," he said with a knowing smile. "Are you a huge Mr. Darcy fan as well?"

"Actually, Colonel Brandon appealed to me more. I mean, Alan Rickman?" I fanned myself. "That voice."

"One of our country's finest actors. Such a loss. He made a brilliant Snape."

"My favorite Harry Potter character. Next to Hermione, of course."

"Of course."

"I saw Platform Nine and Three-Quarters at Kings Cross when I visited London a few years ago." I smiled, remembering. "Great city, but this small-town girl preferred the countryside. Like Cornwall." I fingered my silver Celtic earrings.

We rhapsodized about yummy Cornish pasties and ice cream and chatted about the other areas of England I had traveled to on my vacation. Tavish said he was looking forward to returning home to the Cotswolds in a few weeks after his book tour ended and he wrapped up other business.

"Sadly, I didn't make it to the Cotswolds, but I hope to visit someday." I sighed. "I know it's considered the quintessential English countryside, with its bucolic villages and fairy-tale cottages. Maybe I should set one of my novels there so I can go over and do research. That way I can write off the trip."

"Perfect. And when you come, I'll be happy to show you around and take you off the beaten path to the places tourists don't usually see." He offered a warm smile.

Cool. A Brit and fellow author as my tour guide. Doesn't get much better than that.

"You've got yourself a date." Then I kicked myself. Date. "I'm so sorry about Kristi."

Tavish's smile disappeared and a shadow crossed his face. "Thank you." I saw the glint of tears in his eyes. "I still can't believe it. Kristi was so full of life. And so young." He swiped at his eyes and released a shuddering sigh. "I rang her parents and told them last night." His fingers tightened on his coffee cup. "I can't begin to imagine what it's like to lose a child."

I nodded. Sometimes there are no words.

We sat in silence for a few minutes while Tavish composed himself.

Then I said quietly, "I want you to know I didn't kill her. I know it looks bad, since my scarf appears to have been the murder weapon, but I honestly had nothing to do with it. My scarf went missing from the bookstore restroom just before your signing. I think someone stole it."

"Most likely Kristi." He rubbed his forehead and sighed. "She had a habit of taking things that caught her fancy but didn't belong to her, no matter whose things they were— stores, strangers, friends, family . . . That's one of the reasons we broke up. One of the many reasons," he added sotto voce.

"Tavish, by chance did Kristi wear jasmine perfume?"

His eyes took on a pained expression. "Yes. Lotion too. It was her favorite scent."

At least that was one part of the mystery solved. Now the question was, who had killed her? Could it have been someone else she had stolen from, or . . . I fixed my gaze on Tavish. "You mentioned an old boyfriend who'd been harassing Kristi and told Brady you think he could have killed her out of jealousy since she was now engaged to you. Or, rather, had been engaged to you until recently."

Tavish nodded. "Yes. Tom Rogers. He was Kristi's neighbor in LA, and they dated for a couple years. Tom is quite volatile, particularly when he's been drinking. Kristi said he hit her a few times." His eyes widened. "I just remembered. She also said that once when he was drunk and they were fighting, he started choking her. She kicked him and managed to break free. The next day when he was sober, he cried and told her he was sorry. That he loved her and would never do anything like that again." He shook his head. "She took him back several times, until she finally had enough."

"How soon did you two begin dating after she broke up with him for good?"

"Just a few weeks. We met at a Hollywood party where my agent was trying to score me a movie deal. Kristi was the bartender." He released a sigh. "Tom called Kristi constantly, begging her to take him back. She changed her phone number, so then he started following her. She got a restraining order against him, and that seemed to do the trick for a while. After we were engaged, however, he began calling her at work and harassing her again. One night he even showed up at my beach house totally wankered and shouting obscenities. I called the police, and they arrested him for disturbing the peace and violating the restraining order. Last I heard he was in jail, but I suppose he could have gotten out by now."

I wondered if I should tell Tavish that not only had Kristi's ex-boyfriend gotten out of jail, but he had been staying just a few short miles away in a nearby motel as recently as yesterday—or if I would get in serious trouble with Brady for revealing what was supposed to be confidential law enforcement information. I wrestled with the right thing to do. On one hand, my loyalty lay with my longtime friend and boyfriend of one of my best friends. On the other hand, I felt an affinity to Tavish as a fellow writer and mystery author. An author whose ex had been brutally murdered using *my* scarf as the murder weapon. I fingered my paisley scarf as I considered what to do.

"Is something wrong?"

"Sorry." I shook my head and decided to just go for it and take my chances with Brady later. "There's something I need to tell you—"

The door of the bakery banged open, jangling the overhead bell. "Where is that English SOB?" bellowed a hulking tanned surfer type in board shorts and a tank top that made him look like he was fresh off a California beach. "I'll kill him!"

Tavish turned around. When the bulky beach boy saw him, he charged our direction with a roar, black rubber flip-flops slapping the linoleum, wild straw-colored hair flying behind him. "You killed her! She's dead! You killed

41

my beautiful Kristi," he yelled, tears streaking down his red face.

"No, Tom." Tavish stood up and calmly faced the larger man. "I didn't." He cocked his head to one side. "Odd to find you here, however. You are quite a long way from home. I assume you followed Kristi from LA. Perhaps *you're* the one who killed her."

The wild-haired man decked Tavish, who stumbled backward, tripped over his chair, and fell to the floor.

Chapter Four

Waves of alcohol wafted off Kristi's crazed ex-boyfriend. When he bent over to punch the downed author again, I jumped up and yelled, "Hey!"

As I approached the agitated drunk, he straightened up, wiping the snot off his face with the back of his meaty hand. Trying to focus his wet bleary eyes on me, he growled in a deep voice, "You want a piece of this too, lady?"

"Why don't you calm down and take a seat. How about some coffee?" I signaled Bea.

"Don't want any damn coffee and don't want any damn woman tellin' me what to do!" He staggered and raised his snotty fist, but before he could swing, I stepped in close and kneed him.

Hard.

He let loose an expletive that would have made my tender readers blush as he doubled over, clutching his nether regions.

Tavish raised himself to a seating position, rubbing his jaw. "Are all Wisconsin women like you?"

"Not all. My dad taught me self-defense in junior high."

"Way to go, Teddie-girl!" crowed coffee shop regular Fred Matson. He pounded his cane on the linoleum floor. "You really gave that so-and-so what for."

Bea hurried over with ice for Tavish just as Brady Wells and Augie Jorgensen entered the restaurant.

"What's going on here?" Brady's eyes flickered between the bent-over Tom to the still-on-the-floor best-selling author.

"That's the man I told you about—Tom Rogers, Kristi's ex," said Tavish, getting to his feet and holding the plastic bag of ice to his jaw. "He came in here quite sozzled and belligerent, yelling all sorts of nonsense. Then he punched me in the face."

Sozzled? *Must add that to my British slang repertoire.*

"He sure did, Sheriff. I saw the whole thing," interjected the elderly Fred. "The big guy there was going to hit this skinny English feller again while he was down for the count, but instead our Teddie up and kneed him in the you-know-whats."

"Nice one, Ted." Brady high-fived me. "Maybe we should make you an honorary deputy."

Yes, you should. Then you can share your official information.

Augie winked at me. Then, at Brady's direction, the deputy cuffed the sniveling Tom.

"You need to arrest the English dude," Tom said in a high-pitched falsetto, still feeling the aftereffects of my knee. "He killed my Kristi!"

"Is that right?" Brady lifted an eyebrow. "I heard a some-what different story. How 'bout we go on over to the jail and you can tell me your version?"

"Jail?" Tom blinked. "I'm not going to no stinkin' jail."

"Yes you are." The sheriff flanked his deputy and took hold of the drunken man's arm as he read him his rights. "Now let's move."

"You're arresting me?" Tom stared dumbfounded at Brady as the sheriff led him to the door. "On what charge?"

"Drunk and disorderly to start with. Possibly assault. Possibly more." The trio exited the building.

"Well don't that beat all," Bea said, fanning herself. "My goodness!"

"First that murder yesterday and now this," Fred said, his eyes wide. "Most excitement we've had in Lake Potawatomi since Vern Jones reeled in that big ole lake sturgeon twenty years ago. That sucker was huge! Seven feet long and almost two hundred pounds. Biggest fish I ever saw. Why, I'll betcha—"

Before he could launch into one of his lengthy fishing monologues that made me want to poke out my eyeballs, Bea linked her arm with his and deftly led him back to his counter seat up front. "I remember that. Whoo-boy, didn't it take him close to an hour to land that sturgeon? You want some more coffee, Fred?"

"Bless you, Bea," I murmured under my breath.

"Is it fishing tales you don't like or fishing in general?" Tavish asked as we returned to my back-corner table.

"Bite your tongue. One does not grow up in a lakeside town and not fish—unless you are my mom and hate *slimy worms*. It's the fish stories—especially those I've already heard at least a dozen times. I prefer stories where I don't know the ending in advance."

"Cheers to that." Tavish raised his coffee cup to mine. He took a drink and grimaced.

"Cold?"

He nodded and set down his cup. Then he pointed to his fat lip. "Not quite the stiff upper lip we Brits are supposed to possess."

"Do you want to go to the doctor? I can take you."

"Thank you, but there's no need. Nothing is broken. Just a little bruised." He offered a wry smile. "Including my pride. I'm not used to a woman fighting my battles for me."

"Seriously? Well, get over that. I'd have done it for anyone—no matter their sex." I shook my head. "Growing up, I hated those movies and TV shows where women stood helplessly by doing nothing—other than crying or screaming—while the man got beat up. I vowed then never to be one of those helpless females."

"You're certainly not that." Tavish flashed me a wide grin. "Rather than making a sexist statement, however, I should be thanking you." He inclined his head. "Thank you for coming to my aid, Wonder Woman."

"You're welcome. Too bad I didn't have my Golden Lasso of Truth on me. I could have used it on that guy to find out if he killed Kristi."

As the words left my mouth, I thought of how Tom had reacted when he saw Tavish—how he had accused him of Kristi's murder. Was it a ploy to draw suspicion away from himself? Then I recalled the tears on Tom's face and the genuine pain in his eyes. Could it have been drunken guilt over what he had done? Or did he truly believe Tavish had killed the woman he loved? "His" Kristi? Now gone forever. If that was the case, then Tom was innocent.

The question was, was Tavish guilty?

* * *

Curled up with Gracie and my laptop on my shabby chic floral couch later that afternoon, I tried to focus on *A Dash of Death*, the latest installment in my small-town mystery series, due to my editor next month. My thoughts, however, kept returning to the real-life mystery right here in Lake Potawatomi.

Finally, I gave up. I saved and closed my work-in-progress file. Then I opened a new Word document, typed in KRISTI KILLER at the top, and began making notes. Tom Rogers, Kristi's neighbor and former boyfriend, seemed like the ideal prime suspect—the abusive alcoholic jealous stalker ex-boyfriend who kept harassing his ex and would not leave her alone, until she finally had to file a restraining order against him. The boyfriend who once choked her and was clearly possessive and obsessive about her, referring to her as "his" Kristi—the same boyfriend who had spent time in jail, lived across the country, and just happened to have been in the area when she died.

On paper, Tom was perfect. Yet as I knew from watching TV mysteries and writing a few myself, the first, most likely suspect rarely turns out to be the murderer. As I recalled Tom's grief-stricken face that I had seen up close and personal, it was hard to reconcile such grief with his murdering the object of that grief. Maybe he was just a good actor. He had certainly delivered his lines convincingly. What was it he had said about Tavish again? "He killed my Kristi!" What made him think that? Hopefully, I would know more after Brady finished questioning him.

Yeah, in your dreams. Brady is not going to share investigative information with you.

I sighed and added another name to my list of possible suspects, as much as I did not want to: Tavish Bentley.

Then I typed out what I knew about Tavish and Kristi. They had become engaged only a couple of months ago, but Tavish had cut it off with her recently. Just a few days ago, in fact. Why? Besides the fact that he realized she was a klepto. Earlier at the bakery, he had said there were many reasons they had split up. Whatever those reasons, Tavish did not seem broken up about the engagement—or Kristi's death, for that matter, unlike Tom with his tears. People grieve differently, however. Not everyone wears their heart on their sleeves. It could simply be a case of classic British reserve. Besides, Tavish had teared up over Kristi at Andersen's.

Thinking some more, I added one more name to my list: Melanie Richards, Tavish's publicist, who had vigorously come to his defense when she overheard us speculating about whether Tavish might be the killer. Was that just a matter of loyalty to her employer, or something more? It would not be the first time a young, impressionable employee had fallen for her older, attractive, and famous boss.

Don't forget rich. The man has at least half a dozen best sellers under his belt.

Perhaps Melanie had decided to eliminate the competition, leaving her an open field for her boss's affection.

No, that did not make sense. The efficient Melanie, who kept close track of Tavish's calendar, would have known he and Kristi had broken up. Probably not the details, since that famous English reserve would have prevented Tavish from sharing them, but at a minimum he would have informed his publicist of the broken engagement, simply for the sake of scheduling. After Tavish ended things with Kristi, he was back on the market again—no need to kill his ex-fiancée to have a chance at him. Besides, both Sharon and Char had separately remarked how well Tavish's assistant had managed his book signing, expertly moving along long-winded fans, helping Char set out more copies when the stock ran low, and maintaining a constant, professional presence throughout the event. No one had said anything about her being absent from the signing at any point. I crossed out Melanie's name.

That left only two suspects: Tavish and Tom.

Aren't you forgetting the mystery woman from the restroom?

I added Unknown Bookstore Babe to the list.

Gracie poked her head beneath my elbow. *Pet me! Pay attention to me! Get off that stupid 'puter.*

"Aw, are you feeling neglected?" I scratched my Eskie behind the ears. "Does someone want some loving?" Closing my laptop, I set it on the antique steamer trunk that served as my coffee table. Then I stretched full out on the couch, laying my head on my "Home Is Where the Dog Is" pillow. Gracie stretched out on top of me, her sweet white face inches from mine. I stroked her fur and stared into her beautiful dark eyes. Woman's best friend stared back at me adoringly.

* * *

Growing up, I had always wanted a dog, but my minimalist mother, who prided herself on an immaculate, clutter-free home, refused to consider it. "Not in my house. Too high maintenance. Dogs shed and make a mess. Hair everywhere."

Instead, I would go get my dog fix over at Grandma Florence's house. Grandma always had at least two or three dogs running around her home. For a brief period she even had five dogs at once after taking in two senior, ailing golden retrievers from the pound to save them from the kill list.

Once I moved out into my own place, I got my first dog, Atticus, a tawny spaniel-mix rescue named after one of my literary heroes. Atticus lived up to his name—a finer, more noble creature I have never known, and he was a far better and more loyal companion than most of the men I have dated. When my beloved spaniel died, I could not imagine ever getting another dog again.

My dad knew better. Although he knew that no dog would ever replace Atticus, he also knew that a new puppy would be healing. Three months after I said good-bye to my first dog, I came home from work one day to find Dad sitting at my kitchen table.

"Hi, sweetie," he said. "How was work?"

"Same old, same old." I kicked off my heels and flexed my cramped toes. "Just another day in cubicle paradise." I kissed him on the cheek. As I did, I heard a noise. "What was that?"

I glimpsed a white ball of fluff in my father's hands. A ball of fluff that moved. "Dad?" I placed my hands on my hips.

He offered a sheepish grin as he slowly opened his large hands to reveal a white fur ball with three black spots in the center. Two of those black spots stared at me.

"Dad, no." I stepped back. "I said I didn't want another dog."

"I know, sweetheart, but I couldn't resist her."

"Great. Then take her home. Explain that one to Mom."

"Just give her a chance."

"C'mon, Dad, how could you do that to Atticus?"

My father gave me a tender look. "Atticus wouldn't want you to be lonely."

I blinked away the rush of tears.

The puppy whimpered.

"It's okay," Dad said in a soothing tone as he cradled the tiny fur ball against his chest. He stroked her fluffy head. "You're okay."

She licked his hand and wagged her tail.

Dad set her down, and she scampered straight to me, wagging her white tail that curved over the top of her back and rubbing against my ankles.

I craned my neck at the ceiling, staring hard at a small spot I had missed when I painted the month before.

The fur ball licked my toes.

My head snapped down to see two big black eyes gazing up at me adoringly.

That did it. I reached down and scooped the puppy up in my arms.

"Hello, sweetheart. I'm your new mom."

* * *

I ruffled Gracie's fur and kissed her on the nose as we snuggled on the couch. She licked my cheek. Then we both took a little snooze.

Half an hour later, the doorbell woke us up. Gracie jumped off me and raced to the front door, barking loudly.

51

"Okay, girl, settle down. I'm coming."

Gracie continued to bark. She always does whenever anyone comes to the house or even simply strolls by our little bungalow. Best alarm system ever.

"It's okay, Gracie," a familiar feminine voice called from the other side of the door. "It's just us."

I opened the door to find the remaining two Musketeers grinning on my doorstep.

"Is it true?" Char asked. "Did you really kick the guy in the cojones?"

"Not kicked. Kneed. This town needs a more accurate grapevine." I ushered my friends inside.

"Well, I've got the fruit of the vine." Char raised a bottle of red.

"And I've got the grapes and cheese." Sharon held up a covered plate. "So spill."

After letting Gracie into the backyard, I brought my Musketeer pals up to date on what had really gone down with Tom in the coffee shop, telling them how he had barged in yelling crazy things while Tavish and I were talking.

"Wait." Sharon held up her hand. "You and the drop-dead gorgeous celebrity author with that yummy English accent were hanging out?"

"No. He just happened to come into Andersen's while I was working, and we got to chatting."

Sharon exchanged a knowing glance with Char. "Uh-huh."

"Chatting about what?" Char asked.

"What do you think? Writing. We are both writers, after all."

"True. Is that all you talked about?"

"No." I helped myself to some cheese and crackers. "We briefly talked about England too. He said if I ever came to the Cotswolds, he'd show me around."

"Ha! He likes you! I knew it!" Sharon crowed. "I could tell when he first met you."

"No, he doesn't. Don't be ridiculous."

"Teddie, you can be so clueless sometimes." She took a sip of her wine.

"And you watch too many Hallmark movies."

"Teddie's got a boyfriend! Teddie's got a boyfriend!" Char said in a singsong voice, reverting to fourth grade. "Teddie and Tavish sitting in a tree, *k-i-s-s-i-n-g*."

"You guys are nuts." I shook my head. "Time to swap out those romance novels you're always reading for a good spy story or whodunit. Maybe even a self-help book. Can't a man and a woman—who happen to be in the same profession, incidentally—have a friendly conversation without it being considered romantic?"

"Depends," Sharon said.

"On what?"

"On whether one of them has the hots for the other."

"I don't have the hots for Tavish Bentley."

"Well then, you must be dead. The man's pretty darned swoon-worthy." Sharon fanned herself. "If I wasn't happily married, watch out." She fixed her bluebell eyes on mine. "Besides, I'm not talking about *you*."

"Oh for goodness' sake." I left the room to let Gracie back into the house.

My girlfriends are always trying to find me a man, even though I tell them I am perfectly happy without one. It's not as if I've never dated or had a boyfriend—just none that stuck. I am not the girly-girl type who giggles, flirts, and plays the dating game. Never have been. Even in high school. And that's fine by me. More than fine. I have my sweet little house, my beloved Gracie-girl, good friends and family, my health, and work that I love. I am grateful for the life I have now. I am grateful for *life*.

I thought back to my pre-cancer world when I worked at my government-cubicle job. Yes, it was a "good" job in the sense that I had great benefits and earned a decent salary— enough to buy my thousand-square-foot 1950s bungalow more than a decade ago, for which I'm thankful. However, after my breast cancer diagnosis five years ago—and beating it, *thank you, God*—I viewed the world through different eyes. Life is short and things can change in a heartbeat. Breast lump. None of us knows how much time we have on this planet. While I am here—for however long that may be—I want to spend my time doing things I love. Things that bring me joy. Things that matter.

That's why once I recovered from surgery and chemother- apy and my oncologist gave me the all clear, I took early retirement and spent six blissful weeks in Europe seeing the famous sights I'd only hungered after in books and movies before then. Char tagged along for the first twelve days in Italy, where we devoured as much art, pizza, and pasta as our bellies would allow, but after that, I was on my own exploring my heritage in Denmark and Norway, where the beauty of the fjords knocked me out. I spent my final two world-traveling weeks in England and France, where I wept at the D-day beaches in Normandy and fell in love with the pictur-esque English countryside, thatched-roof cottages, and deca-dent cream teas.

When I returned home, I picked up my pen and began writing my first novel. I've been writing ever since. Although my sweet cozy mysteries about Kate Kristiansen and her canine companion Kallie will never win a Pulitzer, I have a blast writing them and my readers love them. They send me cards and letters saying my books provide a delightful escape from the hard things in life. Like a breakup, the loss of a job, cancer, the death of a loved one.

In my book, that's better than being on the best-seller list. *Yeah, keep telling yourself that.*

I wondered if Tavish ever got such letters. Then I thought about what Sharon had said about Tavish liking me. Could there be anything to that? Of the three of us, Sharon is the oldest, the one who has dated the most, and the only married Musketeer, so she probably has the most insight into the male mind. Then I remembered Kristi, Tavish's dead ex-fiancée—Kristi of the surgically enhanced bazoombas. I dropped my head to take in the flatness that is my chest.

Nah.

Returning to Sharon and Char, I set down a plate of *fattigman bakkels* on the hassock between us. "Have some cookies, and let's drop this whole imaginary romance discussion.

Chapter Five

As I picked through my collection of scarves the next evening, trying to find one that would work with the green batik dress I was wearing with its cascading swirls of fuchsia and teal, I heard my mom's voice calling from the kitchen.

"Teddie, I need to borrow some milk."

"Help yourself," I called back, praying she would just take the milk and leave.

Please, God.

Unfortunately, the man upstairs never seems to answer my prayers when it comes to my mother. Her kitten heels clicked down the hall to my bedroom. She appeared in my doorway in black capris and a formfitting leopard-print top, holding a small ceramic milk jug.

"Where are you going?" Her waxed eyebrows lifted. "Do you have a date?"

"No." I selected a long fuchsia silk scarf from the back of my scarf rack and wound it loosely around my neck. "I'm just having dinner with one of my writing friends."

"A male friend?"

"No." I crossed my fingers beneath the scarf. *Sorry, God.* I don't like lying and only do so occasionally to my mother. It's called self-preservation. "You don't know her. She lives in Racine and writes feminist fiction."

"Oh." Mom's collagen-enhanced lips turned down. "Well, have fun." As she turned and headed back down the hall, I heard her mutter, "If feminists can have fun."

Half an hour later I pulled into the parking lot of Caldwell's, a popular lakefront restaurant in Racine known for their seafood and prime rib. Tavish had wanted to pick me up, but since I preferred not to give Sharon or Char any more ammunition for their overheated romantic imaginings, I'd told him I would meet him at the restaurant instead.

When I walked in, Tavish was seated at the bar, having a drink. His eyes widened when he saw me. "Wow! You look stunning. Those are great colors on you."

"Thanks." He wasn't too shabby himself in his crisp black jeans and a white button-down, but as his colleague on one of the bottom rungs of the writing ladder, I didn't want him to think I was sucking up to him, so I didn't return the compliment. "Do you mind if we go right in? I'm starving."

"Of course." He picked up his drink, and the compact maître d' with salt-and-pepper hair led us to a table with a great view of Lake Michigan. Diners stared at the famous author and a ripple of recognition and whispers spread through the restaurant, but I did my best to ignore it, choosing to focus on my dinner companion instead. We ordered a calamari appetizer to tide us over until Tavish's prime rib and my fresh perch dinner arrived.

"So how long have you been writing?" Tavish asked as we ate our calamari.

"Personally, all my life, but professionally only a few years." I took a sip of wine. "I'm a late bloomer. My first book wasn't published until I turned forty."

He clinked his glass with mine. "Great way to kick off the fabulous forties."

"How about you? How old were you when your first book came out?"

"Twenty-seven. I had been working as an engineer since university—miserably, I might add. I hated my job but couldn't afford to quit, so I spent my nights and weekends doing what I loved. Six months later I finished my first manuscript and began sending it round to publishing houses."

"And?"

"They all rejected it." He offered up a wry smile "Thirteen altogether. Happened again with my second effort—except *fifteen* publishers rejected that one. Luckily, one of the literary agents I had queried took a chance on me and offered to represent me. Under his brilliant editorial guidance, my third try became my first published book. The first two publishers rejected it, but the third offered me a contract, and I've been with them ever since."

"Was your first novel a best seller?"

"No. *Etched in Blood* had only modest sales. It wasn't until my third book, *Blood-Soaked Flowers*, that I hit the best seller list."

"And how old were you when that happened?"

He blushed. "Thirty."

"Ah, a boy wonder."

"Not compared to these days," he said. "I keep reading about these eighteen- to twenty-year-olds with huge YouTube and Twitter followings scoring great book deals and releasing instant best sellers."

"So that's my problem. Guess I'd better start my own YouTube channel."

We discussed books and the vicissitudes of writing. As we chatted, I thought how nice it was to have a fellow writer to talk to in person. Other than my mom's yoga instructor Helen, who has self-published a beginning yoga book, I am the only author in Lake Potawatomi. I've made a few writing friends at some of the writing conferences I've attended in the past couple of years, but none of them live nearby.

Neither does Tavish.

True, I told my inner nag, *but we're talking now and I'm enjoying the moment, so stuff it.*

The waiter delivered our meals, and we focused on the food. The lake perch melted in my mouth, and Tavish declared his prime rib the best he had ever had. After the waiter brought the dessert menu, Tavish leaned in and said, "This has been a lovely evening. I've really enjoyed talking to you."

"Me too. I mean, I've really enjoyed talking to you too. It's not often I get to talk to another writer."

"I'd like to do this again. Are you by chance free tomorrow evening?"

"You want to talk writing some more?"

"No. I'd like to get to know *you* more, not just the writer." The corners of his eyes crinkled. "I'm asking you out."

"On a date?"

"I believe that's what they call it."

"Seriously? You remember I don't have breasts, right?"

"Breasts are overrated."

Well, I know that, but most men do not. "I don't think I'm really your type, Tavish."

"What is my type?"

"Well . . ." I lifted my shoulders. "Kristi, for instance." Recalling the Boobsey twin in the tight bandage dress, I said, "I'm nothing like her."

"I certainly hope not." He expelled a sigh. "I don't mean to sound cavalier or speak ill of the dead. Kristi's death is a terrible thing. I still cannot believe someone killed her." He closed his eyes and rubbed his forehead with a trembling hand. "Nor can I begin to imagine how awful it must be for her family and those who loved her." Opening his eyes, he held mine with a steady gaze. "But I am not one of those people. At this age—I'm forty-one, by the way—it is embarrassing to think oneself in love and then to realize it was simply infatuation. I confess, Kristi's youth and beauty blinded me initially." He pressed his lips together. "As a result, I acted rashly and impulsively. I knew the proposal was a mistake almost before the words were out of my mouth."

"So why didn't you say something?"

"I did."

"Oh."

His eyes locked on mine. So did someone else's. Off to my right a few tables away, a middle-aged woman with neon-copper hair, a color not to be found in nature, and clad in a pink floral muumuu glared at me.

"Um, Tavish, do you happen to know that lady?" I slid my eyes in her direction.

He followed my gaze. "Oh no," he groaned. "What is *she* doing here?"

Once the woman realized Tavish had seen her, she beamed, patted her bad dye job, and jumped up from her seat. She hurried over, her pink muumuu slapping against her sturdy calves, clutching a copy of *Her Blood Weeps*.

"Hello, Tavish," she gushed, ignoring me. "So nice to see you again. You look so handsome tonight."

"Annabelle, you know you're not supposed to be here."

"I won't stay long. I just have a teensy-weensy favor to ask." She set the glossy hardcover on the table in front of Tavish with her manicured hand—a dimpled hand sporting a small white appliquéd daisy atop her pink-polished pinkie. "Would you autograph this for me? I have every one of your books, you know. All signed first editions."

Tavish carefully placed his hands in his lap. "You know I can't do that. You're not supposed to have any contact with me."

"Oh, what do those police know? I'm not doing any harm. And I haven't made *physical* contact." She sent him a suggestive smile. "It's not like I touched you."

I could tell she wanted to, however, by the way her blue-eye-shadowed eyes devoured him. Then I realized. *Misery*. This woman was Tavish's Annie Wilkes, only with makeup.

"Excuse me," I said gently. "Annabelle, is it? Perhaps it would be best if you left. I know you don't want to cause a scene."

"You shut your pie hole, missy!" She shot me a venomous glare. "I wasn't talking to you!"

"Whoa." I drew back.

Tavish scraped his chair back and stood up, cell phone in hand. "That's *enough*, Annabelle." His mouth set in a grim line. "You need to go. Now. Or I'm calling the police."

"All I want is for you to sign my stinkin' book for my collection," she screeched, her round face flushed and her massive bosom heaving. "Is that too much to ask, Mr. Highfalutin New York Author?"

Diners turned and stared. Several pulled out their phones and snapped pictures, including a scruffy millennial male whose lips pursed in distaste. Those pursed lips and scruffy clothing seemed familiar . . . then it clicked into place—the millennial was a reporter for a regional newspaper.

The diminutive maître d' hurried over. "Madam, I'm going to have to ask you to leave."

She snorted. "Yeah, shorty? You and what army?"

I considered pulling out my Wonder Woman cape again, but I wasn't sure I would be as successful this time. My knee would not have the same effect on Lady Muumuu. Thankfully, Brady and Char entered the dining room just then, saving me from having to find out.

"Brady!" I waved. "Over here."

Annabelle leaned over and said in a harsh whisper meant for my ears only, "You think you're so smart, don't you, scarf lady? Well don't your worry; you'll get yours, sweetheart." Her eyes glittered with hate. Then, moving quickly for one so big, she flounced out the nearby side door.

The middle-aged maître d' pulled out his handkerchief and patted his forehead.

Tavish, still standing, addressed the dining room. "Please accept my apologies for that unfortunate incident. I hope it didn't spoil your evening and that you'll allow me to make amends with a round of drinks." He nodded to the maître d' as an appreciative murmur swept through the room, along with nods of thanks.

"Thank you, sir. I'll inform the servers." The maître d' left as Char and Brady arrived at our table.

"What was *that* all about?" Char asked. "We heard some lady yelling."

"That lady," Tavish said grimly, "was my stalker-fan Annabelle Cooke, whom I have a restraining order against." He held out his hand to Brady. "Thanks, Sheriff, for scaring her off."

Brady gave him a halfhearted handshake and said quietly, "Actually, I need you to come down to the station with me, please."

Tavish's forehead creased. "Why? I already gave you my statement." Recognition dawned. "Did Tom confess?"

"No. Actually, Tom Rogers has been released."

"Released? You're kidding!" I said. "How come?"

"He's no longer a suspect. Tom couldn't have killed Kristi, because at the time of her death he was passed out drunk in Larsen's Tavern, as confirmed by the bartender and several patrons."

"Then why do you need me to come down to the station?" Tavish asked.

Brady's eyes swept the nearby tables, where the diners were hanging on every word. He frowned at them, and their attention quickly returned to their plates. "I understand that during your book signing, you left the bookstore for about ten minutes," he said quietly.

I shot a glance at Char, who affected an absorbed interest in her bracelet.

"Yes. I had to take an important phone call from my agent."

"Is that all?"

Tavish did not respond.

"You were seen having a heated argument with Kristi Black behind the bookstore shortly before she died."

*   *   *

"Does Brady seriously think Tavish killed his ex?" I asked Char as the author accompanied Brady down to the station, after first apologizing to me and settling the bill. "Couples have arguments all the time. That doesn't mean anything."

"But they were no longer a couple."

"Exes have fights too." I quirked an eyebrow at my best friend. "I seem to recall a couple doozies after your many breakups with Brady—including just last year."

Char and Brady had been dating on and off since high school. They broke up the first time when Char went out of state to college, but a dozen years later when she quit her librarian job in Cleveland and returned to Lake Potawatomi to buy the Corner Bookstore, they got back together. Three years later they broke up again after Brady proposed—as a child of divorce, Char wasn't a fan of marriage. Less than a year later they were back together. Then they did the same break-up-and-make-up dance all over again. And again. My friends just couldn't quit each other.

"The difference is we're both still alive," Char said.

There was the rub. Why hadn't Tavish spoken up about his quarrel with Kristi when Brady gave him the opportunity? What was he trying to hide? Was it simply his classic British reserve kicking in again?

That was probably it. The English are more private and circumspect than we are. He was likely embarrassed that their fight had become public. Maybe even being chivalrous and not wanting to cast aspersions on the now-dead Kristi.

"Teddie?" Char waved her hand in front of my face, interrupting my ruminations.

"Sorry. I was just thinking."

"About Tavish. Why are you defending him? You don't even really know him. Yeah, you have that colleague connection thing, but that's it. Right?" Char gave me a sly look. "Or is there some other kind of connection going on? A *loooove* connection, maybe? Is that why you didn't tell us you had a *date* with him tonight?"

I could feel my cheeks turning pink. "It wasn't a date."

Not tonight, my don't-lie-to-yourself voice of reason reminded me. *He did ask you out, though—right before his stalker rudely interrupted. You never got a chance to answer him. Would your answer have been yes?*

Let's see. Nice, gorgeous, English, *New York Times* best-selling author. Interested in *me*—even though some of my lady parts are missing. Definitely not your typical male. My lips curved upward.

"You're holding out on me, best friend." Char's voice cut through my reverie.

The only strike against Tavish Bentley that I could see was that he might have strangled his ex with my scarf.

Nobody's perfect, my inner snark said.

Wait. Was that why he asked me out? To try to distract me? And how would that work, exactly?

I don't know, my right brain retorted to my snarky left brain. *I'm just trying to see this from all sides.*

"Earth to Teddie. Come in, please."

Come in . . . My head snapped up. "Hey, how did you and Brady know to come here to find Tavish?"

"Melanie, his assistant-slash-publicist, told us," Char said. "She knows all."

"Exactly." I downed the rest of my wine and stood up. "Let's go."

"Where are we going?"

"To talk to Melanie."

* * *

Half an hour later, I sat across from Melanie in the sunroom of the Lake House, a plate of my lemon sugar cookies between us and cups of Lady Grey tea in front of us. Melanie had asked Sharon if she had any kombucha, and Sharon and I exchanged a blank look. Color us old.

"So what's up?" Melanie bit into a cookie. "These are really good, by the way."

"Thanks." I studied the twentysomething hipster over my china teacup. During the fifteen-minute drive back to Lake Potawatomi, Char had quizzed me to try to find out what was going on, but I'd put her off, saying I'd tell her after I'd talked to Tavish's publicist. I had my suspicions, but wanted to be sure. I tilted my head at Melanie. "I was just wondering how long you've been providing Annabelle Cooke with your boss's whereabouts. Is she paying you, or is it strictly for the publicity?"

Melanie choked on her tea. "I don't know what you're talking about."

"Really? Then how did Annabelle find out where Tavish would be tonight? You're the only one who knew, besides the restaurant and me. I know I didn't tell anyone, and Racine has a lot of restaurants. I doubt his stalker could hit up every single fine-dining establishment in the city trying to find out if he was eating there. Aren't you the one who keeps Tavish's calendar and makes his reservations?"

"Yes, but—"

I sipped my Lady Grey, recalling the scruffy millennial with the pursed lips. "It's interesting that a reporter from the *Wisconsin Spectator* just happened to be at Caldwell's when Annabelle accosted Tavish—a reporter who happens to be a passionate vegan. So passionate, in fact, that he disdains—and refuses to frequent—restaurants that serve meat." I regarded her over the top of my teacup. "How strange to see him tonight in a place that prides itself on its prime rib."

Melanie's face whitened. Her teacup rattled in its saucer as she set it down with a shaking hand.

"I know this because that same reporter interviewed me for my last two books and would only meet me at the lone vegan restaurant in Lake Potawatomi—since closed."

"Are you going to tell Tavish?" she squeaked.

"It's not my place to say anything. That's up to you, don't you think?"

Melanie nodded, eyes downcast.

"Why did you do it? You know Tavish has a restraining order against that woman."

"For the publicity." She lifted her chin. "Sales were down for Tavish's last book, but when that crazy Annabelle showed up at his Atlanta event a couple months ago proclaiming her love for him and tried to kiss him, it went viral. Sales skyrocketed. I thought another Annabelle encounter might replicate that success." She expelled a sigh that sounded like a balloon losing its air and looked down at her hands. "Pretty dumb idea, huh?"

A knock sounded on the French door of the sunroom. Sharon poked her head in. "Sorry to disturb, but Tavish is looking for you, Melanie."

Melanie's head snapped up.

I handed her the plate of lemon sugar cookies. "Maybe he'll want some of these. We didn't get to have dessert."

Melanie accepted the plate with a trembling hand, and we followed Sharon out of the sunroom.

In the century-old living room that Sharon had decorated in soothing tones of cream and sage, we found Tavish, Jim, Brady, and Char sitting around talking, laughing, and munching on cookies.

Seems your boy Tavish is in the clear.
He's not my boy.

Char gave me a discreet thumbs-up.

"There you are, Mel," Tavish said. "I wanted to tell you—" He broke off midsentence upon seeing Melanie's pale face. "Are you okay?" His eyes moved from her to me. "What's going on?"

"I need to talk to you," Melanie said, setting the plate of cookies down on the coffee table.

"Likewise. There are some things we need to chat about."

My cue to exit. I lifted my hand in a half wave. "'Night, everyone. See ya tomorrow. I'm heading home."

"So soon?" Sharon asked.

"Yeah, so soon?" Char cast me a meaningful look.

"Sorry. It's been quite an eventful day, and I'm bushed. Besides, it sounds like Tavish and Melanie have some business to discuss."

"That we do," Tavish said, "but you and I have some unfinished business as well, Teddie. She-who-shall-not-be-named rudely interrupted us before you could answer my question. Do we have a date for tomorrow night?"

Behind him, Sharon and Char high-fived each other.

*   *   *

"Theodora St. John, why did you lie to me?"

Startled, I woke up from where I had fallen asleep on the couch with Gracie after returning home from the Lake House— I blinked at the oversized clock above my mantel—twenty-five minutes earlier. My frowning mother stood over me in her ice-blue silky robe, hands on her nonexistent hips.

I really need to get that key back from her.

Gracie bounded off the couch, giving my mother a wide berth.

"You said you were having dinner with a feminist writer friend tonight. Why didn't you tell me you were out with Tavish Bentley instead?"

I sighed. "Maybe because you'd read something into it that wasn't there."

Ah, but there was something there, my call-a-spade-a-spade self reminded me. *You* just did not recognize it.

"Cheryl and Michelle from book club were at Caldwell's tonight having dinner, and guess who they saw enjoying a cozy tête-à-tête?" She whipped out her smartphone and showed me a photo of Tavish smiling and clinking his wineglass with mine. "Can you imagine how I felt when my friends texted, 'Claire, how come you didn't tell us your daughter was dating a famous author! So exciting!'"

"I'm not dating him." Yet. "It was just a casual evening discussing writing, Mom. No big deal."

She swiped her index finger across her phone and showed me the next picture. "You call this no big deal?"

Lady Muumuu's florid face, contorted in anger, filled much of the screen—except for a small section on the lower left, where I could be seen recoiling away from her.

*   *   *

I lay in my antique white iron double bed, eyes wide open, unable to sleep. Who would have guessed when I woke up this morning that so much would happen over the next twelve hours? Quite a difference from the low-key daily routine I've grown accustomed to in our sleepy little town. As Fred Matson had said, it was the most excitement Lake Potawatomi had seen since Vern Jones reeled in that record-size lake sturgeon several years ago. That excitement all stemmed from Tavish Bentley. The best-selling author's visit had really stirred things up.

I felt my lips turning up in a smile as I recalled my dinner conversation with Tavish—easily the most enjoyable part of my day. The smile dissolved when I remembered crazy Annabelle and the venom she had aimed at me. I shivered in my cotton nightgown. No one had ever directed such hatred my way.

I sat up suddenly. Wait a minute. If crazy Annabelle, aka Lady Muumuu, could hate me so much simply because I was having an innocent dinner with Tavish, imagine how much more magnified her hatred would be for someone engaged to him.

Enough to kill that person?

Chapter Six

Whoa, slow down there, Sparky. Reaching a bit, aren't you?
No. Someone had killed Kristi—strangled her with my scarf. It wasn't me. It wasn't Tom Rogers, and it wasn't Tavish Bentley.

Before I left the Lake House tonight, Tavish had told me—repeating what he and Brady had already told the rest of my friends while I was busy confronting Melanie in the sunroom—that yes, he and Kristi had argued outside the bookstore. Tavish explained that he had just finished his phone call with his agent when Kristi appeared. She tried to kiss him, but he rebuffed her. She then began touching him and making suggestive comments, saying she missed him and wanted to show him how much. His face reddened as he recounted this to me. Tavish said he told her, again, that it was over—they weren't a good match. Kristi then began screaming obscenities at him, saying he had made a big mistake and was going to pay. Then she spit in his face.

Wilma Sorensen, Lake Potawatomi's biggest busybody, witnessed the entire scene from her kitchen window, which faces the back of the bookstore, and informed Brady.

Seventy-eight-year-old Wilma is always spying on all the comings and goings at the Corner Bookstore, Char says. My Musketeer pal has even spotted Wilma using binoculars to zero in on the book titles customers choose—including the racier novels eighty-something Lew Hobbes frequently buys.

What Wilma failed to see—when she apparently left her prime gossip perch to answer the call of Mother Nature—was Tavish reentering the Corner Bookstore, leaving behind a still very much alive and fuming Kristi. Courtney Peterson, who teaches kindergarten at Lake Potawatomi Elementary, happened to be jogging past the bookstore at the time and caught the aftermath of the argument. Courtney remembered distinctly, she told Brady when he questioned Wilma's neighbors as to what they might have seen, because she saw Kristi flip a bird at the departing author.

Whoever killed Kristi, it was not Tavish.

I had not expected to feel so relieved. Maybe I was more interested in the English author than I realized. I pushed the thought away. Right now, there were things that were more important. Reaching for the pad of paper I keep on my nightstand in case I wake up in the middle of the night with a great idea or plot twist, I scribbled down names of possible murder suspects. Although I had already begun a list and some notes on my laptop, I was too tired to get up and retrieve my computer from the other room. Instead, I opted for the traditional time-honored writer's tools. Then I studied the list and drew lines through all the names but one—Annabelle Cooke.

* * *

Waking up early the next morning, I pulled on jean shorts and an oversized red T-shirt, which I topped with a red-and-white polka-dotted scarf. Clipping on Gracie's leash for her morning walk, I slipped out the front door, pulling it shut quietly behind me. I did not want to risk waking my mom and facing a repeat of last night's inquisition. Even though Mom lives behind me, she sleeps with the window open, and her radar ears don't miss a trick.

Gracie sprang down the porch steps, tail wagging. She scampered down the sidewalk, stopping every few feet to sniff the grass. Since I'd had time to take her on only a cursory walk yesterday, I decided to give her some much-needed exercise. "Come on, girl, let's go."

We power-walked around the corner, inhaling the scent of my neighbor Margaret Miller's glorious roses that ringed the perimeter of her yard. The rich red of Mr. Lincolns flanked the pretty yellow of her Julia Childs, while the vivid orange-and-pink Mardi Gras tea rose hybrid battled with Rio Samba and Heart of Gold for the honor of most beautiful. Then Gracie decided to pick up the pace. She raced ahead, and I had to run to keep up with her.

Three blocks later we ran into septuagenarians Wilma Sorensen and Barbara Christensen next to Lake Potawatomi, the town's namesake. I pulled Gracie up short, panting a little.

"Good morning, Teddie," Barbara said, smiling and reaching down to pet Gracie. "Beautiful day, isn't it?"

"Gorgeous. Starting to get a bit warm." I wiped a drop of sweat from my eye with my scarf. "You ladies enjoying your walk?"

"Oh yes," the gray-permed Wilma said. "We always take our daily constitutional at this time. The doctor says it's important to get exercise at our age."

"Move it or you lose it." Barbara winked.

"Good advice for all of us."

Wilma zeroed in on my polka-dotted scarf. "You have such a collection of pretty scarves, Teddie. Why, I don't think anyone in town has as many scarves as you."

"Probably not. Just call me the scarf queen."

"It's such a shame one of them was used to strangle that poor girl." She added with false sympathy, "You must have felt sick when you saw that. Why, I can't even imagine!" Her liver-spotted hand fluttered to her chest.

I could help you imagine that if you like . . . "Yes, it was pretty awful."

Wilma peeked behind her and said in a stage whisper, "I'll betcha anything that rich author fiancé of hers killed her. You can't trust those foreigners. Besides," she said, her faded blue eyes gleaming with satisfaction, "I saw the two of them having a terrible fight just before she died. I told the sheriff, of course—my civic duty."

"I heard." I fixed my eyes on hers. "I guess you didn't hear that after the argument you witnessed, Tavish Bentley was seen going back inside the bookstore, leaving his *ex*-fiancée Kristi Black very much alive and making her displeasure known. The sheriff and that 'foreigner'"—I made air quotes around the f-word—"both informed me of that last night." I tugged at Gracie's leash. "Come on, girl, let's go before I say something I'll regret. You ladies have a nice day."

Barbara gave me a thumbs-up behind an openmouthed Wilma's back.

If there's anything I hate more than malicious gossip, it's ignorance and prejudice. I was still steaming by the time we reached the bakery. Maybe a cup of coffee and a Danish would cool me off. After tying Gracie's leash to the iron railing next to the shady spot where Bea always keeps a fresh water bowl for the neighborhood dogs and cats, I ruffled my Eskie's fur as she eagerly lapped up water.

The bell above the door jangled, announcing my arrival.

Fred Matson greeted me from his customary stool at the counter. "Hiya, Teddie! Kneed any more strangers in the you-know-whats lately?" He grinned, revealing his loose dentures. I keep waiting for the day they fall out in a public place. Hopefully not here and not today.

"Not since a couple days ago, Fred, but you never know. The day is young."

I slid into the front booth and turned over the upside-down cup as Bea ambled over with the coffeepot.

She gazed at me. "What's got your panties in a wad?"

"Wilma Sorensen."

"'Nuff said." She poured the strong brew into my cup. "That woman can rattle anyone's cage."

"She's something else, all right."

Fred snorted. "Wilma Sorensen is a nosy old biddy with too much time on her hands, ya know? She needs to get herself a hobby or sumpin'. Like me." He took a drink of his coffee.

Bea winked at me. "You volunteerin' to be Wilma's hobby, Fred?"

Coffee sprayed out his mouth. "Fer cripes' sake! Whatcha tryin' to do to me, Bea? Gimme a stroke?" He wiped his face with his napkin, then returned it to his lap. "Now see what you went and made me do," he said, staring at his plate. "I got coffee all over my eggs."

"You already finished your eggs, you old fibber."

"Did not. I still had a couple bites left."

"All right." Bea sighed. "I'll make you some more. Teddie, you want some eggs too?"

"No thanks. Just a cheese Danish, please, and another one to go." Maybe if I buttered up my mother with her favorite forbidden pastry, she might cut me some slack on the Tavish front.

"I hear tell that author feller up and left town today now that he's no longer a suspect in the big murder," Fred said.

My head snapped up from my cup. "What?"

"I said that author feller left town."

"When?"

"Earlier this morning," Bea said, delivering my Danish and the to-go bag. "That assistant of his that always wears black and is constantly typing on that pad thingamabob came in and ordered a couple Danish to go—said they were on their way to Chicago."

Chicago? What about our date tonight? Had he forgotten? Now that he was in the clear and didn't need to stick around, did he just want to get the heck out of Lake Potawatomi and forget he ever heard of our small town?

Fred shook his head. "Dunno why so many young people these days dress like they're goin' to a funeral. That girl is right pretty, but she would look a whole lot better if she put on somethin' with some color. Like red or mebbe orange."

I pulled a twenty from my pocket and set it on the table. "Bea, I'm going to take both sweet rolls to go." I grabbed the cheese Danish from my plate and stuck it in the paper bag as I stood to leave.

"Okay, honey. Let me get you your change."

"Keep it." I waved her off and headed to the door.

"You sure? That's a pretty big tip."

"You deserve it."

Bea called after me as I opened the front door. "Hey, I got some leftover brats from last night in the back—you want 'em for Gracie?"

"No thanks. Gotta go."

"I'll take those bratwursts if you're givin' 'em away," I heard Fred say as the coffee shop door closed behind me.

I couldn't believe Tavish had just left like that. He hadn't even said good-bye. I wondered if something had happened. It didn't make sense—especially after that big buildup he'd given me about wanting to go out with me.

He probably couldn't wait to see the back of this place, my neurotic self snarked. *After all, someone murdered his ex and everyone here suspected him—including you. Face it, he's rich and big-time major league. You play in the minors. The man probably has a line of hotties back in LA just waiting to take Kristi's place.*

He'd seemed so sincere, though, when he said he didn't want another Kristi type.

Focused as I was on my internal back-and-forth, I didn't notice the two bent figures petting Gracie until I almost tripped over them.

"Oh, excuse me, Teddie," said Amy Lewis, the pastor's wife over at First Baptist, as she straightened up. "We didn't mean to block the door but couldn't resist your sweet dog. Noah *loves* dogs." She cast a look of adoration at her newly adopted son.

"My fault entirely—I was daydreaming." I squatted down beside the cinnamon-haired four-year-old gently stroking Gracie's fur. "Hi, Noah. Nice to see you again. Gracie loves when people pet her."

"I love *her*," he declared, giving my Eskie a big hug and kissing her head. Then a look of alarm crossed his delicate features and he raised concerned brown eyes to his mother. "Not as much as I love Chewie, though. Chewie's *our* dog." He puffed out his thin chest. "Mine. And my mom's. And my dad's. We're a family. Right, Mom?"

"That's right, Noah," Amy said, as tears filled her eyes.

My eyes teared too as I recalled Noah's background. The little guy had been born to a drug-addicted mother in Milwaukee and subsequently shuffled through the foster-care system until finding a forever home with Mark and Amy Lewis. The Lewises had been trying to have a baby for a while, but after Amy suffered three miscarriages in four years, they decided to become foster parents instead. Noah came to them a frail, frightened three-year-old and immediately stole their hearts. The couple then spent more than a year jumping through myriad hoops to adopt the child they knew belonged with them. Finally, three months ago, the adoption had been finalized.

Amy knelt down and hugged her son. "Noah, it's okay to love both Chewie *and* Gracie. You love me and you love Daddy too, right?"

He nodded, wide-eyed.

"And I love you and I also love Daddy. There's plenty of love to go around."

"There is?"

Amy nodded.

Noah's pale forehead puckered as he considered this. "Okay," he said, his face clearing. He wriggled out of his mom's arms. "Can I pet Gracie some more now?"

"Sure." Amy straightened and exchanged a smile with me as Noah sat down and returned his full attention to my dog.

"So, how's the new book coming along?" she asked.

"Pretty well. I should be finished in a few weeks."

"I'm dying to read it! I loved the last one. I just wish it didn't take so darned long for the next one to come out in bookstores."

"I know. That's the publishing world. Although"—I winked at her—"I might be able to get you an advance copy so you don't have to wait a whole year. The catch is you'd have to promise to post a review on a few online sites."

"You got it! Thanks." Amy hugged me. "And I'll spread the word at church, too. Now I'd better go in and get Mark's morning Danish before he faints from hunger."

"Me too, me too," said Noah, jumping to his feet and pushing open the bakery door. "I gonna faint from hunger too."

"Don't forget to say good-bye to Gracie and Teddie," his mom instructed.

"'Bye, Gracie. 'Bye, Teddie." Noah rushed inside.

"'Bye, Noah. 'Bye, Amy." I waved as mother and son disappeared into Andersen's. Then I unhooked Gracie from the railing and we resumed our walk. We had barely gone ten feet when a large pink blur rammed into me.

"Ow!"

"Stay away from him! He's mine!"

Gracie growled and lunged at Lady Muumuu, biting her on the ankle.

Annabelle howled and kicked out at Gracie with her other foot, but I blocked it with mine. Grabbing my Gracie-girl by the harness at the same time, I lifted her up out of harm's way and held her against my chest.

Tavish's crazed stalker tottered and nearly fell, hurling obscenities at me all the while. Then she righted herself and delivered a swift kick to my shin before hobbling away to a nearby vehicle and speeding away.

Bea rushed out of the diner, followed closely by Fred Matson.

"Teddie, are you all right?" Bea asked, relieving me of a trembling Gracie. "Who was that crazy lady?"

I rubbed my throbbing shin. "I think she killed Kristi Black."

Chapter Seven

"Did you get her license plate number?" Brady asked as he took my statement.

"No, I was a little busy trying to save my dog from a mad-woman." I hugged Gracie to me.

"What kind of car was she driving?"

"I don't know. Blue, maybe? You know cars aren't my thing."

"I know." He parroted my common refrain whenever any of my friends went into raptures over the brand-new vehicle they'd just bought. "'As long as it runs and has heat, AC, and a player for my audiobooks, that's all that matters.'"

"Well, it is."

"Except this time it matters that we know the type of car so we can find the owner and bring her in for questioning." Brady poised his pencil over his notepad. "Was it a sports car? Convertible? SUV?"

"Wait, I remember now. It was one of those family minivans."

He scribbled in his notepad. "Okay, a minivan, possibly blue. Anything else?"

"You mean other than the fact that I think she's the killer?"

"I'm talking about the vehicle. Is there anything else you can recall about it? Anything distinctive?"

"Nope."

Brady sighed. "I'll check with Bea. With any luck, she's more of a car person than you."

"If not, maybe Fred or Amy noticed something."

"Maybe, although they probably didn't see anything, since they were both inside during the altercation." He set down his notepad and leaned back in his desk chair, balancing it on its back legs as he laced his fingers behind his head. "Now tell me why you think this Annabelle Cooke is the one who killed Kristi."

"Because she's completely obsessed with Tavish. Just like Kathy Bates in *Misery*."

"Never saw it."

"You should watch it. I'll lend you my DVD. Kathy Bates won an Oscar for her role as Annie Wilkes, the 'number-one fan' of a best-selling novelist played by James Caan, whom she holds hostage." I paused. "Annie winds up shooting the local sheriff in the back when he shows up at her house to investigate the mystery of the missing author."

Brady's chair slapped down on the floor. "I'll ask Tavish for Annabelle's details when I see him."

"You won't be seeing him anytime soon."

"Why's that?"

"I hear he already left town for Chicago."

"Yeah, for the final signing on his book tour. He'll be back later today."

Jump to conclusions much?

"He's promised to give me a list of Kristi's friends when he returns, along with their contact information," Brady said.

"Uh-huh." I half listened to my longtime friend as I thought about going out with Tavish tonight. It had been a while since I'd had a date—a long while. I frowned, trying to remember the last time I had gone out with someone. A couple of years, maybe? Or had it been even longer than that?

The dating offers had never come in fast and furious, especially not lately. There are very few single men in town, and those remaining aren't much interested in Amazons in their forties.

Looking up, I found Brady staring at me. "What?"

"You zoned out there for a couple minutes, Ted. Maybe you should go home and take a nap or something."

"Good idea." I set Gracie down on the floor and stood up. "I guess my run-in with Lady Muumuu took more out of me than I realized."

"Make sure to lock your doors. And until we find this Annabelle, maybe you shouldn't go walking around town alone."

"I wasn't alone." I ruffled Gracie's fur. "I had my trusty bodyguard with me."

* * *

My mother pounced on me the minute I walked through my kitchen door. "Theodora Renee St. John, *what* is going on?"

Gracie streaked into the living room—likely to her favorite hiding place beneath my skirted slipper chair, where she often takes refuge when Mom shows up in one of her moods.

Thanks for leaving me defenseless, woman's best friend.

Well, she did protect you against Lady Muumuu. Your mother is a whole other story.

"What do you mean, Mom?" I said.

"What do I *mean*?" Her sculpted brows nearly disappeared into her hairline. "I heard some crazy woman in a hideous polyester muumuu attacked you in town today. Why would she do that, and how do you even know such a person?" Her nose wrinkled.

I'm fine, Mom, really. Thanks for your concern. Leave it to my mother to focus on fashion at a time like this.

Her eyes flickered. "Wait a minute. Was this that same angry woman from the restaurant last night?" She scrolled through her texts, then thrust her purple smartphone beneath my nose, showing me Lady Muumuu's enraged face beneath her neon-copper dye job.

I puffed out a sigh, lifting up my bangs. "Yes. Her name is Annabelle Cooke. She's Tavish Bentley's deluded stalker-fan. She warned me to stay away from him. Apparently she doesn't like any woman getting close to him, even when it's purely professional."

Who are you trying to kid? You know Tavish's interest in you extends beyond the professional.

Yes, but my mother does not need to know that. The longer I can keep that information from her, the better.

Good luck with that. How exactly do you plan to keep tonight's date a secret?

Absolutely no idea.

My mother stared at me, her mouth a round O. "Oh my goodness! I'll bet she killed that Kristi, Tavish's ex!" She began punching numbers into her phone.

"Who are you calling?"

"The sheriff. Who else?"

"No need. Brady's already on it." I filled her in on the basics.

Mom began calling her girlfriends before she even exited my back door. "Cheryl? You will not believe this. Just wait until you hear." She pulled the kitchen door shut behind her.

Just in time, too. Seconds later Tavish Bentley's name flashed on my phone screen.

Walking into the living room, I settled into my chintz wingback. "Hi, Tavish."

"Teddie? Are you okay?" he said in that killer English accent. "I heard what happened. Did Annabelle hurt you?"

Stretching out my legs before me, I glanced down at my purpling shin. "Not really. I've gotten bigger bruises playing softball."

"I'm so sorry." I could hear the distress in his voice. "This is all my fault."

"How is it your fault?"

"If it weren't for me, you'd never have met my crazed stalker and become her target."

"But I wouldn't have met you either, and that would be a shame."

The tenor of his voice changed from concerned to playful. "Are you flirting with me?"

"Oh God no!"

Gracie's white head poked out from beneath the slipper chair opposite me.

"No need to sound so appalled."

"Sorry. What I meant is I don't flirt. I've never been good at those dating games, so I don't bother playing them. I just tell it like it is."

Tavish laughed. "And that, Theodora St. John, is one of the many reasons I'm looking forward to tonight. Where would you like to go, by the way? I'll have Melanie make reservations."

"Um . . ."

"Don't worry, she confessed—although I'd already figured out that she'd informed Annabelle of my whereabouts. Melanie was quite embarrassed and contrite—even offered her resignation. I didn't accept it, by the way. Actually, I'm not sure how I'd manage without her—she keeps everything running efficiently so I don't have to worry about the details and can focus solely on my writing. I did give her a stern talking-to, however, and told her if she ever did something like that again, I'd fire her."

"And rightly so."

"But enough about that," he said. "You still haven't told me where you'd like to go this evening."

"Do you like Chinese food?"

"Love it. Peking duck is my Patronus. I didn't realize there was a Chinese restaurant in town, however."

"There isn't. We're going to go a little farther afield."

"Racine?"

"Farther. After last night's encounter with Annabelle, I think it might be a good idea to lose ourselves in a bigger city."

"Chicago? I'm actually there at the moment."

"Nope. Milwaukee. I know a great hole-in-the-wall Chinese restaurant that your stalker will never find, especially if you don't mind a little subterfuge."

"You're talking to a fellow mystery writer. Subterfuge is our stock-in-trade."

I told Tavish my plan to throw Annabelle—and my mother—off the scent. Then I enlisted my fellow Musketeers' assistance.

Chapter Eight

"We did it!" Tavish clinked his water glass with mine as we tucked into the crab rangoon at Green Jade a few hours later.

I clinked back and grinned. "Yes we did."

It had taken a variety of fibs, outright lies, and assorted machinations to escape undetected from Lake Potawatomi and arrive incognito in Milwaukee, but thanks to the help of Sharon, Jim, Char, and Brady, we'd pulled it off.

I'd texted Char and told her what we needed, and Tavish had discreetly enlisted the aid of innkeeper Jim. That night at five thirty, Sharon and Char showed up at my front door loudly announcing to anyone who might be within earshot that they were taking me on a girls' night to help me forget about the upsetting incident earlier. Before we left, we stopped by my mother's house, dressed for a night on the town. Mom complimented us on our outfits—even remarking on my glitzy black-and-silver scarf—when I asked her to feed Gracie, since the girls were spiriting me away for an evening of fun. Then we

Three Musketeers piled into Char's Honda Civic and took off toward Milwaukee.

Meanwhile, Tavish announced to Melanie, innkeeper Jim, and the other three guests enjoying wine and cheese at the Lake House that he was exhausted from winding up his book tour that day. He excused himself, saying he planned to read in his room for a while and crash early.

An hour later, Jim texted Tavish that the coast was clear and the van was ready and waiting in the garage, keys in the ignition. Tavish slipped down the back stairs wearing a Cubs baseball cap pulled down low, loose windbreaker, and shades— Jim's trademark style. Then Tavish entered the garage through the house, got into the pristine white van with The Lake House stenciled on its side, and drove in the direction of the Milwaukee airport, rockin' out to U2. Seven miles out of Lake Potawatomi, as planned, on a mostly deserted stretch of highway, a cop car with flashing lights pulled the van over while Tavish—as Jim—sang along loudly to "I Still Haven't Found What I'm Lookin' For."

Brady approached the Lake House van, and as he did, he told us later, what we suspected might happen came to fruition, since Annabelle was keeping a close eye on Tavish's whereabouts, including where he stayed. A dark-blue minivan passed by with a large copper-haired woman in bright pink at the wheel. Brady—who's always been good with numbers—memorized the license plate as he raced back to his cop car to give chase. Unfortunately, stalker Annabelle had a head start and eluded him. Brady then returned to the

Lake House van and a waiting Tavish on the side of the highway.

Char received a text from Brady telling us Tavish was on his way. Within moments, the white van exited the now-deserted highway and turned down the side road where we had been hiding around a bend laden with foliage. The van pulled in behind us, and we began the game of musical cars. Tavish, minus the windbreaker and baseball cap, hopped out of the van and ran over to Char's Civic.

Sharon and Char were *supposed* to exit the car simultaneously and head to the van, where Jim was secretly hiding in the back to drive them home to Lake Potawatomi. Char jumped out of the driver's seat, but Sharon struggled in the back of the Honda.

"Hurry up!" Char hissed.

"I am! My sleeve got caught on one of Penelope's buttons!"

Penelope was our fourth passenger—a protective blow-up doll Sharon used as a pretend passenger when she was driving alone at night. Earlier, once the car was parked safely behind the foliage, Char had gotten out, grabbed the blown-up Penelope from the trunk, and thrust her in the back seat. Penelope sported a little black dress and a blonde curly wig in our pathetic attempt to try to make her resemble Sharon.

At last Sharon freed herself from her wannabe doppelgänger. "Have fun yous guys," she whispered, before running after Char and jumping into the van, where the real Jim now sat at the wheel in his ubiquitous Cubs cap.

Tavish, incognito again in case Annabelle doubled back, slid into the driver's seat, buckled his seat belt, and started the car.

I belly laughed.

"What?" Tavish pulled down the visor to check himself out in the mirror. He fluffed the long red wig on his head, sucked in his cheeks, opened his eyes wide, and adopted a Scottish accent. "Am I not a dead ringer for Amy Pond from *Doctor Who*?"

"More like Ron Weasley in Harry Potter with a dash of Reba McEntire."

"I'll take that," he drawled with a country twang. "Reba's hot." Then he belted out the chorus of "Fancy" as we three pretend Musketeers headed toward Milwaukee.

From there we took turns sharing and singing a collection of our favorite hits—mostly from the eighties and nineties—until I took it back to the seventies with the most joyous pop band ever. Thanks to the two *Mamma Mia* movies, the whole world now knows and appreciates Abba. Well, maybe not the whole world. Brady, a classic rocker, turns his nose up at what he calls their "bubblegum sound," yet I've seen his toes involuntarily tapping to "Dancing Queen." Everyone's toes tap to "Dancing Queen" unless they're dead.

Tavish and I finished over-singing the dramatic duet of "SOS" as we pulled up to the restaurant.

"You're a much better singer than Pierce Brosnan," I said.

"Thank you. I'll tell my agent. Maybe he can get me into the next movie."

"I'll buy tickets to that."

Digging into the *moo shu* pork, I asked Tavish if he had any brothers and sisters.

"One of each. Nigel is three years older than me and an IT geek at a technology company in London, and Felicity's turning thirty this year."

"What does Felicity do?"

"Good question." He gave me a wry smile over the pot stickers. "She's still trying to find herself. First she thought she wanted to be a veterinarian because she loves animals so much, but when they required her to dissect dogs and cats as part of her training, she dropped out."

I shuddered, seeing my sweet Gracie's face before me. "I don't blame her. I would have as well." Helping myself to some Peking duck, I asked Tavish, "Do you have any pets?"

"Two dogs. One in New York—Sherlock, a golden retriever I got through a rescue group—and Scout, a spaniel mix back in England, both of whom I'm missing dreadfully. Sherlock doesn't do well on planes, so when I'm traveling, I have a dog-sitter who comes and stays with him," he explained. "Same thing with Scout—although leaving him in England was initially a holdover from the stringent quarantine laws the UK used to have. Thankfully, the laws have relaxed considerably in more recent years. But Scout's not a big fan of flying either and prefers to stay home."

"Scout as in *To Kill a Mockingbird*?"

He nodded as he speared a pot sticker and dipped it in soy sauce.

"My first dog was named Atticus," I said.

"I knew there was a reason I liked you."

We bonded over favorite books and dogs and extended our phones across the table to show off pet pictures. One of Tavish's photos showed a striking, slim young dark-haired woman in snug jeans standing in front of a two-story stone cottage with a cobalt-blue door cuddling a fluffy spaniel.

"Gorgeous dog. Gorgeous house. Gorgeous girl."

"That's my sister Felicity with Scout at our family home. Felicity watches over Scout while I'm in the States—her current job. Before that she was selling beaded handmade jewelry in Portobello Road, but she chucked that." He released a sigh. "The joy of siblings."

"Could be worse. You could be an only child like me—a child who's a constant disappointment to her mother." I grinned and crossed my leg, and as I did, my skirt fell away from my shin, revealing the huge bruise.

Tavish's eyes narrowed at the sight. "Is that Annabelle's work?"

"It looks worse than it is."

"I could kill her for doing that to you."

"Do you think she's the one who hurt—I mean killed—Kristi?" I asked.

"I wouldn't be surprised," Tavish's mouth set in a grim line. "The woman is certifiable. She even sent dead roses to my ex-wife once."

"You were married?"

Embarrassment—or was it shame?—flickered across his features. "For a couple years. We divorced over a year ago, and

I met Kristi shortly thereafter. I think you Americans call it going from the frying pan into the fire." He grimaced. "I'm afraid I don't have a very good track record in choosing the right woman." Tavish delivered a steady gaze to me. "But I'm trying to change that."

"Did you and your wife have any kids?"

"Fortunately, no."

"You don't like children?"

"I love them, actually. I always wanted to be a father, and told Lucinda that when we were dating. We met when I first moved to LA. A couple of my books had been optioned by movie producers, and I hoped living there and establishing a presence among the film community would help ensure the movies actually got made." He gave me a wry smile. "Shows how naïve I was. Lucinda was my realtor. She led me to believe she wanted children too, but after we were married about a year, she made it quite clear that she would never spoil her perfect body with stretch marks."

Perfect body, huh? That seems to be a theme. Shallow much?

"You have a thing for perfect bodies, huh? You must be slumming with me."

Did I really just say that aloud?

Tavish choked on a pot sticker.

I could feel my cheeks grow hot. "Sorry. My mouth gets ahead of my head sometimes."

Tavish coughed and then coughed some more, clutching his hand to his throat.

I jumped up, ready to do the Heimlich.

He held up his hand, grabbed his glass of water, and swallowed a huge gulp and then another. Setting down his glass, he blotted his streaming eyes with his napkin.

"You okay?"

He nodded, and I sat back down.

"You warned me you tell it like it is," Tavish said. "Only this time, you got it wrong—at least half wrong." He examined his hands. "I admit when I first arrived in Los Angeles, I was gobsmacked by the women there—usually blonde, tanned, with fit, hard bodies and blinding white teeth. The quintessential California girls I had only seen in the films, and quite out of my reach. When I became 'famous'"—he used air quotes—"those unattainable women took notice of me, which was quite an ego boost to a country boy from England. Unfortunately," he grimaced, "I allowed that ego to direct my relationships—ones that I eventually came to realize were superficial and empty. That's why I broke up with Kristi and also why I got divorced."

Tavish captured my eyes with his. "Going out with you is not slumming. In fact, it is the very antithesis of slumming. Getting to know you is the most genuine encounter I have had with a woman in years. I like you, Teddie. You're smart, forthright, funny, and unpretentious, and you have an honest beauty those women didn't possess."

"I can't have kids."

"Sorry?"

"You need to know that ship has sailed. I went into early menopause after chemotherapy, so this body won't be birthin' no babies."

You're quoting Prissy from Gone With the Wind *now? Um, not cool.*

Ignoring my inner PC nag, I explained, "I just wanted to put that out there. If you don't want to go out with me again, I totally understand."

Tavish exploded with laughter, causing diners at the other tables to turn and stare. "You're fabulous."

* * *

After I skunked Tavish at a fun and laughter-filled round of miniature golf—his first time playing—we drove back to Lake Potawatomi in Char's car. I dropped my date off at the Lake House a few minutes before midnight, where he gave me a chaste peck on the cheek and said good-night.

What's up with that? Is he going to turn into a pumpkin or something?

Shut up, I told myself. *He doesn't want to rush it. We're taking things slow.*

I'll say. The only thing slower than that is a dead snail. Let me know when you pick up the pace and the good stuff starts.

I drove Char's car to my house and parked in the driveway. To complete the fiction of our girls' night out, we had agreed to tell my mother—if she saw the Honda—that Char and Sharon had both had too much to drink and dubbed me the designated driver. Grateful to see Mom's lights off, I yawned as I approached my back door, keys in hand.

My feet crunched on something. My eyes flicked to the ground—broken glass. Wide awake now, I peered closer at my dark back door. Why was the light off? I always leave it on when I go out. Then I noticed that the bottom windowpane was shattered. Backing up a few steps, I pulled out my phone and punched in the sheriff's number. "Brady?" I whispered. "I think someone broke into my house."

"Where are you?"

"Outside the kitchen door."

"I'll be there in five minutes," he said. "Do not, I repeat, do *not* go inside."

Then I heard it—the faint sound of a whimper. Gracie.

Gripping my purse like a weapon, I rushed the door, shoving it open, and flipped on the light switch. A white furry body lay motionless on its side on the checkerboard floor.

I screamed.

Chapter Nine

"Ted! Ted!" Brady's voice crackled through the phone, but I ignored it as I raced, sobbing, to my fallen dog's side. "Gracie!"

She didn't move. She didn't whimper.

Kneeling beside her, I noticed the remnants of a steak on the floor. I gently placed my head on Gracie's chest to check for a heartbeat. Nothing.

Fighting back hysteria, I forced myself to calm down and recall my doggy CPR training. Placing my fingers on the inner side of Gracie's midthigh, I checked for a pulse. Was that a faint hint I felt? I couldn't tell. Laying my Eskie on her right side, I gently pulled her tongue forward and cleared her airway. Then I placed my hands on her chest and firmly pressed down. I could hear the air moving out. I stopped pressing and listened for the air to move in. Nothing. I pressed down on her chest again, stopped, and listened. Still nothing. *Don't die on me, Gracie-girl. Please don't die on me.*

I repeated the pressure again and again, blinking away tears. Nothing.

Making sure her tongue was in line with her canine teeth, I closed Gracie's mouth. Then I lowered my mouth to her nose and slowly blew into her nostrils, waiting to see her chest rise. I removed my mouth to allow the lungs to deflate. When her chest did not expand, I blew with more force, closing my hand around her muzzle to seal her lips and watching again to see if her chest filled. I repeated this process every ten seconds, checking Gracie's pulse.

The blare of a siren filled the house, followed by the sound of pounding feet. Still I kept blowing into Gracie's nostrils.

I felt a large, gentle hand on my shoulder. "Ted, let me take over. Come on, Ted."

Lifting my head, I stared up at Brady, the tears streaming down my face. "Please save her."

Brady continued CPR, pressing down on Gracie's chest as I watched in abject fear. Then he blew into her nostrils.

Char dropped down beside me and put her arm around me. "Doc Johnson's on her way," she said, over the roaring in my head. "Brady called her. She should be here any minute."

I nodded dumbly, unable to speak or tear my eyes away from my dog.

"What in the world is going on?" My mother's strident voice pierced the crowded kitchen. Then she saw Gracie on the ground. "Oh my God, what happened?"

I ignored Mom because I saw something too—the faintest of movements. "Her chest moved!" I shouted. "Brady, she's breathing!"

He checked her pulse. "She is!"

"Okay, everyone, out of my way," ordered a female voice.

"I beg your pardon," Mom said.

"Move it, lady!" Veterinarian Emily Johnson pushed my mother aside as she hurried over to kneel beside Gracie and Brady. "Everyone clear out and give us some room here."

Char ushered Mom and me out the back door.

"I don't want to leave her," I said, squinting through wet eyes over my shoulder at the trio of figures on the ground.

"It'll be okay," Char said soothingly. "She's breathing now and in the hands of professionals. They'll take good care of her."

Mom led us into her stark minimalist cottage, where she offered us a glass of water. "Sorry, I'm out of tea," she said, "and it's too late for coffee."

But drinks were the last thing on my mind. "Mom, what time did you feed Gracie and what exactly did you feed her?" My voice cracked. "Think carefully."

"I don't need to think carefully. I fed her the canned dog food you left in the fridge, mixed with a few pieces of cut-up chicken breast, per your specific instructions, at seven o'clock."

"And then what?"

"Then she ate her dinner, and when she was finished, I let her into the backyard to do her business." Mom wrinkled her nose. "She left you a present—one I wasn't about to touch."

"And then?"

"Then what?" she said, confused.

"After Gracie pooped, then what did you do?"

"I took her back inside, where I made sure her water bowl was full—also per your quite specific instructions—locked the back door, and went to bingo."

"What time did you get home?"

"Around ten. It was a bad night—I didn't win anything."

"Did you check on Gracie then?"

"No, why should I? I fed her earlier as you asked, took her outside, where I made sure she relieved herself, then brought her back inside, where she curled up in her dog bed fat and happy."

"Gracie's not fat!" I glared at my mother. "And she's certainly not happy right now." Tears splashed down my cheeks. I dashed them away. "Do you not even understand that someone broke into my house and tried to kill my dog tonight?"

Mom's hands clutched at the neck of her silk kimono. "Your house was broken into? Did they steal anything? What about my mother's Haviland china?"

"I don't know and I *don't care*!" I stormed out and hurried back to my house.

Brady met me at the back door. "I was just coming to get you, Ted. Doc Johnson's taking Gracie back to the vet clinic tonight."

"Why? What's wrong? Is she worse?" I pushed past Brady, where I saw my barely moving dog cradled in the vet's arms, an IV inserted in her front left leg. I stroked Gracie's creamy head and stared into her dull, half-lidded eyes minus their usual bright spark. "Did someone poison her? Is she going to die?"

"This sweet baby's not going to die," the vet said, "not if I have anything to say about it. Right, girl?" she cooed to my lethargic dog. Then Doc Johnson turned her attention to me. "I'm not positive because I need to run some tests, but it appears someone fed Gracie a sleeping pill."

"A sleeping pill?"

"Probably to shut her up while they robbed your house," Brady said, in his official capacity. "I'll need you to go through each room and tell me if anything's missing."

"I don't give a damn if it is. I just want to make sure Gracie's going to be all right." I turned to the vet, pleading. "She is, isn't she, Dr. Johnson?"

"I think so. I hope so. That's why I'm taking her back to the clinic—so I can give her some meds and monitor her closely through the night." Her voice tightened with anger. "Animals can have severe reactions to human medications, but thanks to your heroic efforts and the sheriff's, you saved Gracie tonight. However," she added gently, "she's not quite out of the woods yet. Sometimes there can be damage—such as lowered blood pressure, seizures, even kidney failure. I'm taking her to the clinic so I can do further tests, give her any additional medications she might need, and keep an eye on her."

"I'm coming too." I continued to stroke Gracie's fur, murmuring to her all the while.

"That's not necessary."

"It's necessary to me."

"All right then, let's go," Doc Johnson said.

"Hang on a second, Ted," Brady said. "Your house was broken into. They could have stolen something valuable. I need you to walk through it with me, room by room, and let me know if anything's missing."

"I can do that tomorrow." I picked up my purse from where I had dropped it earlier at the sight of my sweet Gracie on the ground.

"Okay, but there's something else you need to know before you go."

"What?" I said, impatient to leave.

Brady's eyes bored into mine. "Annabelle Cooke lives in Calumet City, south of Chicago, with her husband and parents. None of them has seen her in several days." His lips compressed into a tight line. "An hour ago her blue minivan was found here in town over by the high school with a flat tire, and no Annabelle. I have an APB out and we're combing the area. We'll find her."

"You'd better, because if I ever see that crazy woman again, I'll strangle her with my bare hands."

Chapter Ten

I wept with relief when Gracie woke me with a kiss on the nose early the next morning. I hugged her to me atop the rickety cot in the back room of the clinic where I had spent the night.

"She dodged a bullet," Doc Johnson said, ruffling Gracie's fur. "We were lucky. The sleeping pill didn't do any damage." Her face darkened. "I'll never understand humans who hurt animals and treat them as if they're disposable."

"The more I know people, the more I love my dog," I said. "It's a cliché, but that's because it's true."

"Ya got that right, sister." The vet high-fived me, then gave Gracie a dog biscuit and returned to the front office to see her first patient of the day.

I shed the cotton jammies I'd slept in, courtesy of Char, who had brought them over last night along with my toothbrush and a change of clothes for today after Brady filled her in. Once I'd pulled on jeans, a sleeveless cotton blouse, and an Indian-print scarf, I group-texted Brady, Char, and Sharon to let them know Gracie was fine.

"You ready to go home, Gracie-girl?"

She released two excited yips and wagged her tail furiously.

Kneeling down so that we were face-to-face and I was gazing into my Eskie's dark velvety eyes fringed with white eyelashes, I stroked her cheek and said, "I'm so sorry someone hurt you, sweetheart. I promise you they will not get away with it. Mommy will keep you safe."

She licked my nose. *It's okay, Mom. It's not your fault.*

Then I PM'd Brady and told him I was on my way home and he could come do the search of my house.

* * *

I had barely gotten home and started feeding Gracie her breakfast when there was a knock at the back door.

"That was fast," I said, opening the door with the cardboard taped over the broken pane. Instead of the expected Brady, however, Tavish Bentley stood on my doorstep, concern etching his fine features.

"Sharon told me what happened," he said. "I'm so sorry. How is your dog?"

Gracie trotted over, tail wagging.

Tavish knelt down and held out the back of his hand to her. "Hello, girl, aren't you a beauty?"

Gracie preened and promptly licked Tavish's hand, which he then used to stroke the back of her neck.

"You have quite a way with the ladies," I said.

He delivered a slow smile full of promise that made my stomach flutter. "Hopefully not only the four-footed ones."

"Am I interrupting something?" Brady towered over Tavish's kneeling form in the doorway.

Tavish stood up. "Morning, Sheriff. Have you located Annabelle yet?"

"Not yet, but my deputy's still searching. We'll find her. Now if you'll excuse us, Teddie and I need to do a search of her house to see if anything's missing after last night's break-in."

I stared at my old friend. Why was he being so rude to Tavish?

He's doing the protective-big-brother thing, silly. Think about it—none of these problems happened until Tavish came to town.

Gracie started doing her flop-bott routine on the kitchen rug.

"I need to take Gracie out first. You'll have to wait a few minutes."

Brady sighed. "Okay, but please hurry up. I don't have all day."

"Someone got out of the wrong side of bed this morning."

"I could take her for a walk while you and the sheriff do your search," Tavish interjected.

When Gracie heard the w-word from Tavish's mouth, she scooted over to him and gave a short *Yes, please* bark.

I hesitated, not sure I wanted to let my sweet girl out of my sight after last night's trauma.

Tavish offered me a steady, reassuring gaze. "She'll be safe. I promise to guard her with my life."

"Are you sure it won't be too much trouble?"

"No trouble at all. As I said last night, I'm really missing my dogs, so this will give me the fix I need."

"Okay, thanks." I grabbed Gracie's leash from her basket and clipped it on her collar, giving my impatient dog—who was now doing her potty dance—a hug. "You be a good girl now."

She looked up at me as if to say, *Yeah, Mom. Fine. Whatever. Now I really gotta go.*

"Taking her around the block should do the trick—although she may get greedy and want more."

"Not a problem. I could stand a little exercise, especially after all the cookies and pastries I've been eating since I arrived." Tavish patted his nonexistent belly.

Gracie strained at the leash and bounded down the back step, Tavish following. "I think the lady's in a bit of a hurry," he said.

"If you have any problems, just call."

He gave me a thumbs-up and trotted after Gracie.

When I turned around, Brady was frowning at me.

"What?"

"Do you really think it's a good idea to get involved with that guy?"

"I thought you liked him."

"He's okay, but you have to admit his arrival has brought a rash of bad things with it—beginning with the first murder in our town's history."

"That's not his fault."

"Isn't it?"

"Seriously?"

Brady held up his hand and began counting off on his fingers, beginning with his thumb: "The dead woman is his ex-fiancée." Index finger: "The drunk and disorderly guy you brought to his knees is his ex-fiancée's ex-boyfriend." Middle finger: "His crazed stalker-fan verbally assaulted you in a restaurant and then later physically attacked you in the street." Ring finger: "And now someone—most likely that same crazy stalker who's on the loose somewhere in our town—has broken into your house and nearly killed your dog."

I shuddered at his last words.

"And that's all in the space of only a few days. I just don't think it's safe for you to be around Tavish Bentley," Brady said. "In fact, I think the sooner he leaves town, the better. Then maybe all this trouble will leave also."

He has a point, the logical part of my nature said. *If Tavish leaves, crazy Annabelle will likely leave too, and then Gracie will be safe. Wouldn't it be better to end whatever this is now before someone else gets hurt? It's not as if you're in love or anything— you've only had one date, after all.*

I really like him, though, I argued with myself. *It's been a long time since I've liked someone like this. He really likes me too, and we have a lot in common.*

Do you love him like Gracie—your best friend and devoted companion you nearly lost?

Of course not. I sighed. *I guess Brady's right. It would be better for everyone if Tavish left town. Soon. Before anyone else gets hurt. Even though none of this is his fault, his departure will allow things to go back to normal—boring, but normal. And safe.*

"I thought you said you didn't have all day," I snapped at Brady. "Can we do this already?"

"Now who got up on the wrong side of the bed?"

We began our search in the kitchen. I opened cupboards and drawers, even the refrigerator, but nothing seemed missing or out of place—aside from the broken windowpane. Then we moved into the dining room and living room. Same story. Everything was fine and accounted for, including all my electronics—TV, DVD player, and laptop—the last still sitting on the ottoman where I had last left it. I headed down the hall to the bathroom.

"Do you have any opioids?" Brady asked. "Painkillers like Vicodin, maybe? Druggies have been known to break in and steal those from bathrooms."

"Well, they'd be out of luck. The only painkillers I have here are Tylenol and ibuprofen."

After giving my bathroom the all clear, we did a cursory search of the guest bedroom, but everything was still in place, including the vintage record player and my collection of old albums from the seventies and eighties, with a few Sinatra and Judy Garland classics from their heyday tossed in. No one sings like Judy.

At last, we entered my bedroom.

"Aha!" Brady said, surveying the half-open drawers and clothes strewn everywhere. "Now we're getting somewhere. The burglar really made a mess in here. Be sure to check carefully and let me know what's missing."

"No burglar did that, unless you consider Char and Sharon thieves."

"Huh?"

"They came over to help me get ready for my date with Tavish last night—making me try on several outfits before they at last deemed one satisfactory enough for that crucial first date. We didn't have time to put things away before we left on our stealth mission, and obviously when I got home and found Gracie on the floor, that was the last thing on my mind."

I began picking up discarded dresses and skirts and putting them back on hangers, my back to Brady.

His phone buzzed with a text.

"Ted?" Brady said in a strained voice. "Are you missing any scarves?"

"Why?"

"Could you check, please?"

"Okay." I went to my scarf rack and sorted through the myriad colored silks and cottons. "That's odd. The red-and-white polka-dotted one I had on yesterday is missing." I turned to him. "Do you think crazy Annabelle stole it?"

Brady had a strange expression on his face.

"What? What's going on? Oh my God! Is it Gracie?" I grabbed the phone from his hands.

"No, Ted. Don't."

Too late. Annabelle Cooke stared vacantly back at me from the phone screen, my missing red scarf wrapped tightly around her neck.

Chapter Eleven

A nother woman strangled with one of my scarves. *What the heck is going on?*

Oh. My. Gosh. Had Tavish snapped and murdered his crazy stalker? His words from the restaurant echoed in my head. "I could kill her for doing that to you."

Absolutely not, my inner voice of reason said. *If he did, he certainly would not use your scarf as the murder weapon. Unless . . . he's trying to deflect the focus from himself onto you. Maybe he's been playing you this whole time just to get close to you and make you the fall guy for his serial killer proclivities.*

"Ted? You with me?" Brady's voice interrupted my wild imaginings. "You want to give me my phone back?"

My eyes slid to the picture again. I shuddered before surrendering the phone, recalling Kristi's same vacant stare.

"Let's have a glass of water and sit down." Brady led me out of the bedroom and down the hall. His phone blared out Aerosmith's "Dream On."

"Hey, Augie, what's up?"

Laura Jensen Walker

As Brady and his deputy conferred in the background, I focused on the two murdered women—one young and beautiful, the other not so much. On the surface, they seemed like total opposites. They did have one thing in common, however: a mutual desire for Tavish. A desire he didn't return. Would that be reason enough to kill them? I recalled the other voice I had heard in the restroom. Could that have been Annabelle? Were Annabelle and Kristi fighting over Tavish?

I considered the facts. Tavish had broken off his engagement to Kristi only a few days ago—a breakup she obviously hadn't accepted, or why else show up at his signing? To save face, maybe? Particularly to her friends? The former couple had argued behind the bookstore, as both Wilma Sorensen and Courtney Peterson had observed. Courtney, however, had seen Tavish go back inside, leaving behind an angry but still very much alive Kristi. Who was to say that Tavish hadn't doubled back a few minutes later when the prying eyes were otherwise engaged and done the dirty deed?

Really? Now you've turned against Tavish too, my conscience nagged me. *I thought you liked him.*

I do. I'm just trying to take the facts into account. We have never had a murder in Lake Potawatomi's history, and now in the space of less than a week, we've had two. It's only logical to consider the common denominator. Even if it is a common denominator I don't like seeing.

Brady ended his call with Augie. He poured me a glass of water, and we sat down at the kitchen table. As I drained my glass, he pulled out his notebook.

"I'm sorry, Ted, but I need to ask you a few questions."

114

"Ask away."

He shifted uncomfortably in his chair. "Do you remember what you said last night about Annabelle?"

"About Annabelle? No. What?"

"You said if you ever saw her again, you'd strangle her with your bare hands."

"Good thing my scarf was found around her neck then." I waggled my fingers. "That puts these lily-white hands in the clear."

But Brady missed the waggling, intent as he was on his notebook and fulfilling his sheriff role. "When was the last time you saw Annabelle Cooke?"

"Yesterday morning, when she attacked me in front of Andersen's."

He scratched a note in his pad. "And last night when you left here with Doc Johnson, did you stay at the vet's all night, or did you go out at any time?"

"Out? Where?"

"I don't know. For a walk? To the store?"

"Nope. All the stores in town close by seven. You know that."

He nodded, still bent over his notebook. "So you didn't cross paths with Annabelle anytime last night or this morning?"

Why is he asking me that? I already told him yesterday morning was the last time I saw her. Wait . . . My jaw dropped like Macaulay Culkin's in *Home Alone. Does he suspect me of murder?* "Are you serious? Brady Wells, look at me."

He raised his head reluctantly.

I stared at him. "We've been friends for years. You *know* me. Your girlfriend is my best friend. Do you honestly think I killed that woman? Why? What in the world would be my motive?"

"Revenge for nearly killing Gracie," he said in his detached sheriff-doing-his-job voice.

"Seriously?"

"You'd be surprised what people will do when someone they love is hurt or threatened."

Gracie announced her return with two short barks.

Saved by the bark. I jumped up from the table, scooped up my fur baby, and snuggled her to my chest as I unclipped her leash.

"We enjoyed our walkies." Tavish grinned and chucked Gracie beneath her chin. "This girl was full of energy, so I let her take the lead. She got so excited at one point, she was hopping down the street on her hind legs." He shook his head. "Quite extraordinary. I've never seen anything like it."

"She's an extraordinary dog," I said, nuzzling Gracie close.

Tavish continued, "We wound up in a lovely park by the lake, where we met some of her canine pals. Everyone there seemed to know Gracie, both four-footed and two-footed."

"That's life in a small town," Brady said. "Everybody knows each other."

"Or *thinks* they do," I said in a clipped tone.

Tavish's eyes swiveled from Brady's to mine, his forehead creasing. "Is something wrong?"

"You could say that," Brady muttered.

I set a squirming Gracie down on the checkered linoleum. "They found Annabelle."

"Brilliant. Is she in jail?"

Brady shook his head.

"Whyever not?" Tavish said, sounding remarkably like *Downton Abbey*'s Lord Grantham.

"Because she's dead."

I watched Tavish's face closely as Brady delivered the news, checking for any signs of guilt. All I saw in his eyes was shock and surprise.

"Annabelle? How? When?"

"I don't know the exact time yet, but according to my deputy, the coroner says it likely happened late last night or early this morning." Brady's sheriff eyes drilled into Tavish. "Where were you between, say, midnight and five AM?"

"Asleep in my room at the Lake House," Tavish answered without hesitation. "I went straight to bed after Teddie dropped me off from our date." He sent me a warm smile. "A fun and lovely date, I might add, and one I hope to repeat soon."

I turned away.

"Teddie? What's wrong?"

The concern in Tavish's voice sounded genuine—or was that simply his plummy English accent? Could I be blinded by that accent?

Not just his accent. How about that book-loving, dog-loving connection you share? And that he finds you attractive—with an "honest beauty"—and doesn't seem to care about your lack of breasts. If that's even true. My mother's voice intruded upon my inner neurotic. "Men are visual. They like breasts."

Of course they do, my practical inner voice agreed. *You have to admit, Kristi was pretty boobalicious, and it sounds like his ex-wife was too. Didn't he say she had a perfect body?*

Yessss, I answered my pragmatic devil's advocate. Was it only last night that we had talked about his wife—a woman who was also blonde and superficial like Kristi? Tavish had said he was trying to change his dating type to someone real and genuine. Like me.

Yes, but think about it logically. Isn't it possible that everything Tavish said to you was a crock to get you on his side and to divert attention away from him? You have to admit it's more than a little suspicious that the only two murders to have ever occurred here in town coincided with Tavish's visit. Face it, girl. You've been played.

A sour taste filled my mouth.

"Teddie?" Tavish's voice interrupted my inner battle. "What's wrong?"

I whirled on him. "Besides the fact that yet another woman you know is dead? And not only dead, but strangled with one of my scarves. Again."

"What? Bloody hell! What the devil is going *on?*"

"That's what we're trying to figure out." Brady stuck his notebook in his shirt pocket. "Tavish, I'd like you to come with me to the station to answer some questions."

"Of course." The response was automatic, as Tavish focused his attention solely on me. He reached out and touched my arm. "I'm sorry, Teddie. I cannot believe this has happened again. It makes no sense. I thought Annabelle killed Kristi. Who would have killed Annabelle? And why?" His eyes widened. "Unless—" His head whipped around to Brady. "Could Annabelle have committed suicide and used Teddie's scarf to try and implicate her?"

Brady raised a skeptical eyebrow. "I suppose . . . although death by strangulation is rarely suicidal." He fixed Tavish with a steady gaze. "It's usually homicidal."

At those words, I moved away from the man I had hoped to kiss a mere twenty-four hours ago, causing his hand to drop from my arm.

Tavish's face shuttered, but not before I glimpsed the hurt in his hazel eyes. "I'll accompany you to the station now, Sheriff, and answer any questions you might have."

My mother chose that moment to make an entrance. "Good morning, everyone," she trilled. "Why didn't anyone tell me we were having a party?"

Chapter Twelve

After Brady and Tavish left, Mom took a seat at my kitchen table and began bombarding me with questions, while I brewed coffee and cut a couple pieces of almond macaron kringle—a sliver for her, a normal-size piece for me.

"Why were Tavish and Brady both at your house so early?"

"Eight o'clock isn't early, Mom," I said. "Lots of people start work at that time."

"Never mind that." She took a bite of kringle. "Why were they here?"

There was no way around it. I had to tell her about Annabelle's murder.

"What?" My mother's eyebrows rose so high on her Botoxed forehead that they nearly disappeared into her hairline. "That crazy lady in the hideous muumuu who yelled at you at dinner, then attacked you in front of Andersen's?"

"The one and only."

"Where was she killed?"

"Near the high school."

"*Our* high school?"

I nodded.

"Oh my God! There's a killer running loose in Lake Potawatomi!" She jumped up from the table and locked my back door.

"A lot of good that will do with the broken window."

"You need to get that fixed right away."

"Already on it."

Her gray eyes narrowed. "Is that why Brady and your author friend were here? Does the sheriff think Tavish Bentley killed that Annabelle creature?"

"I don't know, Mom. You'll have to ask Brady."

"Well, Tavish Bentley is the only one around here who knew her, so that makes sense."

"Maybe. Maybe not. Just because she died here doesn't mean the person who killed her is staying here or even from around here."

Then the words I had uttered to distract my mother from her guilty-Tavish assumptions registered. Why hadn't I thought of that? Tavish was a famous author with readers *all over the world.* Who was to say Annabelle was his only stalker? There could be another obsessed fan out there knocking off the competition so she—or he—could have a better shot at Tavish.

And that crazy fan is using your scarves to commit the murders why exactly?

No idea. I ignored the logic of that question as I zeroed in on one word. *Scarves.* Plural. I'd neglected to mention to my mother the tiny little detail that the second victim had also been strangled with one of my scarves. Maybe I didn't need to tell her.

Yeah, like that's an option. It's probably all over town already. You better tell her before someone else does.

I did. And as expected, she freaked.

"Theodora Renee St. John! What will people think?"

"Oh, I don't know. Maybe that I suddenly went berserk one day and decided to start strangling women I don't know for some inexplicable reason. Or"—I adopted a sinister tone—"maybe it's *not* so inexplicable. Maybe it's because they have something I want."

"Tavish?"

"Breasts." I took a bite of kringle with a chaser of coffee.

"Very funny. You don't have to be so sarcastic, young lady." Mom rubbed her forehead. "All this is giving me a headache."

My phone buzzed with a text from Char.

Char: *OMG! Brady just told me about the dead Annabelle and your scarf. WTF??*

Me: *Can't talk. Mom's here. Will call you later.*

Char: *Good luck with that.*

"Someone must have it in for you," my mother mused as she popped a couple of ibuprofens.

"Huh?"

"I said someone must have it in for you."

Was that a note of concern I detected in her voice?

"What in the world did you do to tick someone off?"

Ah, there it is. Her tendency to think the worst. Mom always played bad cop to Dad's good cop during my childhood, and she was still playing that role. Even though I'd left childhood behind decades ago and my good cop had been gone three years.

My good-cop dad died suddenly of a heart attack while out jogging around the block one day. And life as I knew it changed forever. Dad had always been my biggest champion. When I got the news that a publisher had bought my first book, Dad had almost been more excited than me, proudly introducing me to everyone he met (including grocery store clerks and gas station attendants) as "my daughter, the author." He'd also bought fifty copies of *Death by Danish* from Char's bookstore when it first released and handed them out to everyone he met.

I blinked back tears and stood up to pour another cup of coffee.

Before I got the chance, Gracie trotted into the kitchen, making sure to skirt a wide path around the section of linoleum where she had lain unconscious last night, which made my stomach clench. When she reached my side, Gracie pawed at my foot and gazed up at me, her liquid-chocolate eyes full of concern.

I scooped her up and nestled her against my chest, all the while making the kinds of ooey-gooey noises and baby talk I used to roll my eyes at in my pre-doggy days. As my canine daughter and I indulged in a mutual love fest, my phone buzzed with another text. I checked the screen and saw a message from Sharon.

Just heard about Tavish's dead stalker and YOUR scarf! Again?? WTH???

Sharon, like Char, would just have to wait. Right now, my hands were full of something more important.

Mom gave my Eskie an awkward pat on the head. "I'm happy to see Gracie is back to her normal self today." She turned her wrist to view her vintage Rolex. "I must dash. My book club is having brunch at Cheryl's this morning, and I'm helping her set up." She paused at the door, her hand on the knob. "Make sure you get this glass replaced today."

"I will."

"And Teddie?"

"Yeah?"

"Be careful." She held my eyes for a moment before slipping out.

I stared after her retreating figure. What had just happened here? Had aliens appeared and replaced the woman who gave birth to me with a kinder, gentler mom-clone while I was spending the night at the vet's?

Gracie appeared as confused as I did.

I feel the need. The need to bake. Whenever things are chaotic, stressful, or just plain do not make sense, baking is my go-to cure. Some people do yoga, practice meditation, or see a therapist; I bake. I do my best thinking when I bake, and afterward I always have something delicious to show for it. There is a comfort in the familiarity of ingredients, especially recipes from past generations. I inherited all my Grandma Florence's recipes when she died. My Dad's too. Although my father enjoyed baking, he absolutely *loved* to cook, which is a good thing, since Mom has always been a lousy cook and has zero patience for it. Dad's roast chicken is still the best I've ever had, and his lasagna remains legendary around Lake Potawatomi. Today, however, I wanted to make some of my father's yummy muffins.

Growing up, I loved sitting in the kitchen watching my dad as he cooked and baked. We would talk about everything as he measured, chopped, and stirred. School. Books. Boys. Travel. And food. Always food. We both loved to eat (unlike my mom, who was forever dieting and determined never to gain an ounce on her slim frame). Dad taught me how to crack eggs and measure ingredients when I was five, and at six I baked my very first cake—Grandma Florence's fruit-cocktail cake from the fifties, dad's favorite. (Which I immediately recognized when Truvy mentioned it as the "cuppa, cuppa, cuppa" cake the first time I saw *Steel Magnolias*.) I've been baking ever since.

I set Gracie down, and she trotted over to her doggy bed in the corner, turned three times, and curled up on her soft blankie. Gracie loves her naps. So do I, but not this early.

Flipping through my recipe box, I pulled out the one for Dad's famous carrot-cake muffins. Instead of muffins, however, I decided to make mini loaves to give as gifts to friends. I pulled out flour, sugar, baking powder, soda, and cinnamon. As I mixed the dry ingredients together, I kept seeing the hurt in Tavish's eyes after I stepped away from him earlier. The same hurt I'd felt when Brady, one of my oldest friends, even entertained the thought that I might be capable of taking a life. The difference was that Brady had known me for over three decades, whereas I'd met Tavish only a few days ago.

Longevity isn't the only friendship factor, however. Sometimes there is an instant connection with a person. I recalled how Tavish's eyes had softened when he talked about his dogs and how he had shown up on my doorstep that morning as soon as he heard about Gracie. I also remembered how Gracie had immediately taken to Tavish—the polar opposite of how she'd responded to Annabelle. Dogs see a person's true heart and soul. If Gracie responded negatively to someone, there was a reason for it, and I needed to pay attention. And if she liked and trusted someone, I needed to pay attention to that also.

Hmmm. Does that apply to Tavish? You may have really screwed up there.

The ceramic sign on the wall above Gracie's food corner, which I had found years ago at a garage sale, caught my attention—"To err is human, to forgive canine"—and I realized I *had* messed up. The hurt in Tavish's eyes wasn't fake. I had jumped to conclusions based on the way things appeared— Tavish seemed to be the only connection between the two dead women, ergo, Tavish was the killer. Yet someone who didn't know me—the platinum-haired Boobsey twin at the signing, for instance—and saw my scarf wrapped around Kristi's neck might jump to the conclusion that *I* was the killer. Especially once a second woman showed up dead with another one of my scarves as the murder weapon.

I hadn't killed Kristi or Annabelle—someone just wanted to make it appear that I had—and Tavish hadn't killed them either, contrary to how it appeared. Deep down, I knew in my bones that my fellow author and dog lover wasn't a killer, but how could I prove it?

Figure out the identity of the real killer.

Exactly. Not while grating carrots, though. Blood doesn't go over well in carrot cake.

After I finished shredding the carrots, I mixed in eggs, crushed canned pineapple, canola oil, vanilla, and orange extract. Then I beat all the ingredients together, poured the batter into several small greased and floured aluminum loaf pans, and stuck them in the oven.

Setting the timer, I grabbed the yellow-lined legal pad I always keep handy in case a great plot point or killer sentence for my work in progress pops into my head while cooking. Call me old school, but I like writing on a yellow notepad, especially with a black rollerball pen—medium point, not fine. There is something about the feel of the pen in my hand and the sight of the free-flowing ink spilling onto the heretofore blank page. The letters form fluidly one after another, creating a waltz of words.

I poured myself another cup of coffee and sat down at the table. As I started to make notes on the legal pad, I reminded myself to think like a cop—like Brady—and to base my investigation solely on evidence, possible motives, and relationship to the victims.

The evidence showed that two women—polar opposites—had been strangled with scarves. Scarves belonging to yours truly. Therefore, Brady had to question me and consider me a possible suspect. As the town's peace officer, he was compelled to pursue that line of investigation, much as he probably didn't want to.

My hurt and anger at my longtime friend receded.

The sheriff also had to examine the connection between the two victims. That connection was obviously Tavish. Finally, he had to come up with a motive.

I scribbled the question: *What could Tavish's motive be for killing Kristi?*

To rid himself of an unwanted fiancée who didn't understand the meaning of "It's over."

And Annabelle?

To rid himself of a crazed stalker who was intruding on not only his professional but also his personal life. By murdering both women, Tavish could kill two birds with one stone.

Bird as in the English slang for *chick*? Ba-dum-bum. Although the expression doesn't quite fit middle-aged Annabelle.

Annabelle. As I thought about the deranged Lady Muumuu, I recalled the hate in her blue-shadowed eyes when she stared at me, simply a new friend of Tavish's. Just because she was now dead didn't mean she hadn't killed Kristi. In fact, it was quite likely that Annabelle *had* killed his ex-fiancée, a gorgeous young woman whom Tavish had had a much more intimate relationship with than he had thus far with me. The fact that he had recently broken up with Kristi was not common knowledge, so Annabelle would probably have thought the two of them were still engaged. As obsessed as she was with Tavish and as insanely jealous as she was of any woman who came near him, Annabelle would have viewed Kristi as a roadblock in her quest to possess Tavish for herself. What does a bulldozer do when it encounters obstacles in its path? Plows right through them and then discards them.

No, even though she was dead now, crazy Annabelle was still at the top of my list for murdering the unlucky Kristi.

Which meant there were two murderers. And one was still on the loose.

Chapter Thirteen

The timer dinged, and I pulled the carrot-cake loaves out of the oven, setting them on baking racks to cool. Gracie jumped up at the sound of the ding and trotted over, tail wagging and smiling up at me expectantly.

"Sorry, that's too hot and also too sweet for you, Gracie-girl."

Her ears flattened, and she sent me a mournful look.

"Well, I guess we know who the alpha female is in this house." I opened the fridge and tossed her a baby carrot.

Sucker. That dog plays you like a violin.

I know. Good thing I don't have kids—they would probably be spoiled brats. In my defense, however, the vet says carrots are good for dogs' teeth, so I'm only watching out for Gracie's dental health.

Keep telling yourself that.

Oh, shut up.

Returning to the table, I chewed on the end of my pencil, trying to decide what to do next. Maybe it would be good to write down everything that had happened since the day Tavish arrived in town and Kristi was murdered. Perhaps if I saw it all laid out on paper, I might discover some kind of pattern or clue that could lead us to Annabelle's killer. That always works with my books when I'm stumped about what to do next or the plot is sagging and I need to figure out how to get the story moving again—usually with another murder. I started writing.

- A woman smelling of jasmine stole my scarf from the bookstore during Tavish Bentley's signing. She also had a Tavish-focused encounter with a mystery woman in the restroom. Two hours later the jasmine-scented woman, Kristi, Tavish's ex-fiancée, was found dead with my silk scarf around her neck.
- Kristi's drunken ex-boyfriend Tom accused Tavish of murdering Kristi and decked the author, whereupon I promptly kneed him.
- During my writing-colleague dinner in Racine with Tavish, his crazy muumuu-loving fan Annabelle Cooke went all Annie Wilkes on us and threatened me.
- I confronted Tavish's assistant Melanie about revealing Tavish's whereabouts to stalker Annabelle. She admitted it was for publicity and apologized to her boss.
- Annabelle, aka Lady Muumuu, showed up in town and warned me away from Tavish. Gracie lunged at her, and Annabelle kicked out, hitting me in the shin.
- Tavish and I sneaked to Milwaukee to have our first official date, where we discovered we were kindred spirits in many ways and I learned Tavish had an ex-wife with a perfect body. Just like Kristi.

- During that out-of-town date, someone broke into my house and fed a steak laced with sleeping pills to my unsuspecting dog, leaving Gracie unconscious while the burglar stole one of my scarves.
- Thankfully, Gracie rebounded from being drugged, and the dog-loving Tavish showed up to take her for a walk while Brady and I searched my house and discovered another one of my scarves missing.
- Stalker Annabelle was found strangled with my red polka-dot scarf.
- Brady questioned me, and then took Tavish in for questioning.

As I read over my notes and saw the mention of Tavish's ex-wife, I wondered what she looked like. What had he said her name was again? Lucille? No, Lucinda. Tavish had mentioned she was a realtor in LA. I powered up my laptop and did a Google search for Los Angeles realtors named Lucinda. Several popped up. I wondered . . . would she have kept Tavish's last name? I typed in Lucinda Bentley.

Bingo. A sun-kissed blonde in an icy-blue business suit that perfectly matched her eyes filled my screen. I made her face larger and had to shield my eyes so I wouldn't get snow blindness from her megawatt smile. Wow. Those teeth. They had to be veneers. No one has teeth that white or that straight. Unless they're a movie star.

Well, she does live in Hollywood.

Examining Lucinda's smiling fortyish face, I recognized the telltale signs of Botox. As I skimmed through her website, however, I realized she wasn't a blonde bimbo Kristi clone. Lucinda's high-end real estate listings and testimonials from satisfied clients showed that she was a successful professional. A professional who didn't want kids.

My phone buzzed with a group text from Sharon and Char.

Teddie, what the hell is going on??

Crap. I hadn't called the Musketeers. I closed my laptop and did so now, putting them on speakerphone as I pulled out the cream cheese and butter from the fridge to soften.

"Sorry, guys, I got busy baking and totally forgot to call you."

"You're baking at a time like this?" Sharon asked.

"Of course she is," Char said. "That's what our Teddie always does in times of stress or confusion."

"Guilty as charged."

"Speaking of guilty, do you know that Brady has Tavish down at the jail right now and is questioning him about the murder of his mad stalker?" Sharon asked. "Can you believe it?"

"Yep. Brady questioned me too, only at my house."

"Why did he question you?" Char asked, her voice rising on the last word.

"Well, my scarf was found around Annabelle's neck. That makes two women strangled with my scarves in less than a week. Seems more than a little suspicious."

"Only to people who don't know you," Char said. "Is Brady suggesting that *you* might have killed those women? How dare he?"

"Yes, how dare he?" Sharon echoed. "He knows you could never do such a terrible thing."

"Calm down. I was upset at first too, but the man's gotta do his job. This is his first murder investigation, after all."

"Actually, second," Char said, "now that there's two dead bodies."

"Exactly. This is uncharted territory for Brady, so he's probably trying to do everything by the book."

"He needs to read a different book, then," Sharon said, "one that doesn't include throwing his friends under the bus."

Even though we weren't FaceTiming, I could see Char's hackles rise on behalf of her boyfriend. "That's not what he's doing. But I am glad that he's moved on to the person who's likely the real killer."

"Tavish Bentley isn't the murderer." I began opening the packages of cream cheese. "Of that I'm certain."

"How do you know?" Char said. "Do you have proof?"

"Not yet, but I will. And I'm hoping you two will help me."

"All for one and one for all," pledged Sharon, echoing the motto of the original Three Musketeers that we'd adopted as kids.

Char, who had been a librarian for years before buying the Corner Bookstore, offered to connect with her librarian pals to research Tavish's past to see if anyone might have a possible grudge against the best-selling author. Sharon agreed to spend more time with her B and B guest Melanie, Tavish's assistant and publicist, and discreetly grill her about Kristi and any other girlfriends Tavish had had, including his ex-wife.

And me? I planned to make a little trip to Calumet City to visit Annabelle Cooke's family and learn more about the recently deceased stalker. First, however, I had a few humble pie deliveries to make.

*   *   *

Half an hour later I entered the sheriff's office with my peace offering, where I found Augie, Brady's young deputy, doing paperwork at the front counter.

"Hiya, Teddie, how's it going?" He whistled. "That's sure a pretty dress."

"Thanks." I smoothed down the peppermint-striped sundress I had finally settled on along with a pink gauzy scarf after discarding four other outfits for my jailhouse visit. I had started to feel like Goldilocks trying on dress after dress: Too hot. Too dressy. Too bulky. Too sexy. At last, this dress was just right. I had also scraped my curly hair back into a high ponytail to keep it off my neck, but already I could feel tendrils springing loose.

Augie sniffed the air appreciatively. "Whatcha got there?"

Setting the box of individually wrapped carrot-cake loaves on the counter, I pulled out two for my best friend's baby brother. "I remember how much you love my carrot cake, so thought I'd drop off a couple loaves."

His eyes lit up when he saw the frosted loaves topped with a whimsical iced carrot. "You got that right. Especially that dope cream cheese frosting. Are you ever going to tell me the mystery ingredient?"

"Then it wouldn't be a mystery. A girl's got to keep her secrets, you know."

Augie lifted one end of the plastic wrap, flicked his finger across the corner of frosting, licked his finger, and closed his eyes in bliss. "Thanks, Teddie. You rock. My sister could take lessons from you."

"Baking is not Char's thing."

"That's for sure."

Raised voices from Brady's office punctured the air.

Augie quickly removed the two baked loaves from the counter and set them on his desk. The young deputy then adopted a formal, businesslike tone. "So what can I do for you today?"

"I brought some carrot cake for Brady too, and Tavish Bentley." I nodded toward Brady's closed office door. "Is that who's still in there with him?"

"I can't answer that, but I do know Brady doesn't want to be disturbed. If you want to leave the carrot cake with me, I'll make sure the sheriff and the suspect—" Augie's face flamed. "I mean I'll make sure they get it."

"Thanks, but I'd rather deliver it personally." I smiled and sat down on the wooden bench opposite the counter. "I'll just wait here until they're finished."

"Uh, I'm not sure the sheriff would like that." The deputy lowered his voice. "He's not in a very good mood right now, so it might be better if you come back later. Or even tomorrow." His eyes brightened as he walked around the counter. "Yeah, tomorrow would be the best bet, Teddie. Why don't you come back then?" He opened the front door to usher me out.

Sorry to do this to you, Augie, but it can't be helped. I fanned my face and puffed out a breath to lift my bangs. "Is it hot in here, or is it just me?"

"It's not that hot."

"Not for you, but then you're not a postmenopausal woman."

Augie's ears turned pink.

I fanned myself with both hands and blew out another puff of air. Then I started flapping my scarf against my flat chest. "I'm dyin' here, Augie. I want to rip all these stupid clothes off. Can you get me a cold glass of water?"

"Sure." He backed away, his face beet red, and scuttled behind the counter. "There's some in the fridge. Hang on, I'll be right back." He hurried to the back room.

The minute he was gone, I headed straight to Brady's closed door. I knocked lightly and pushed the door open without waiting for an answer.

"What the hell do you think you're doing?" Brady said in a raised voice as he scowled at me. "I'm conducting an interview here."

"Yes, I know. The whole town knows, in fact. Surprise, surprise." My eyes flicked from Brady's angry countenance to Tavish's set, unsmiling face and eyes that refused to meet mine. "I come in peace." I held up the box of carrot-cake loaves. "Actually, I came to apologize. To both of you."

"This is not a good time, Ted."

"It's the perfect time, Brady." I faced my longtime friend. "I'm sorry I got mad at you for questioning me and thinking there was a possibility I might be a suspect in Annabelle's death. You had every right to question me—in fact, you would have been remiss not to, since both murder weapons belonged to me. You *are* the sheriff, after all."

His scowl dissolved and his voice softened. "Thanks, Ted. I appreciate that."

"However," I plowed on, "you're making a big mistake thinking Tavish is the killer. Tavish didn't kill Annabelle. He didn't kill Kristi either."

Brady's scowl returned, while Tavish appeared uncertain. Did I detect a glimmer of hope in those hazel eyes?

"And how do you know that, Ted?"

I lifted my bare shoulders. "I just know." *Actually, Gracie's the one who made me realize that in her inimitable dog fashion.* Wisely, I didn't say that aloud, however. "Something else I know that I keep forgetting to tell you, Brady, is the morning of the signing when I was in the bookstore bathroom stall, I overheard two women in the restroom staking their claims to Tavish."

"What?" Brady yelled, as Tavish's eyes widened. "Who were the women?"

"No idea. I didn't recognize their voices, but I know for sure they weren't from Lake Potawatomi. No Wisconsin accents. I *think* it may have been Annabelle and Kristi."

"You've heard Annabelle's voice up close and personal now," Brady said. "Did one of them sound like her?"

I closed my eyes and tried to recall the voices I'd heard. "Maybe . . . one sounded a bit growly and threatening, which would be right in Annabelle's wheelhouse." I shook my head. "But I can't say for sure."

Augie appeared, pink-faced, in the doorway. "I'm sorry, Sheriff, I told her you didn't want to be disturbed. I left the room for just a second, and when I got back she was gone."

"That's okay, Augie." Brady sighed. "I know more than most that nothing can stop Ted when she's on a mission. Except"—his eyes took on a speculative gleam–"maybe handcuffs. We'll keep that in mind for next time." He waved his deputy off.

"Sorry, Augie," I called after his retreating back.

"Guess this is my day for apologies." I turned to my fellow author and locked my eyes on his, feeling a flutter in my chest that I quickly tamped down. "I'm sorry I jumped to conclusions and thought the worst. You're not the kind of man who could or would strangle a woman—no matter how obnoxious she is." Lady Muumuu's rage-contorted face filled my head. "You simply don't have it in you. I mean, you write a great murder, but no way could you commit one. I know that. As sure as I know the sun will rise tomorrow, my mother will continue to bug me, and you will never taste a carrot cake as good as this." I reached into the bakery box and extended two of the iced loaves to him.

Tavish's mouth twitched as he accepted my peace offering.

"Friends again?"

His hand lingered a moment on mine, his mouth curving upward. "Friends."

"Okay, good." I turned back to Brady. "So, are we done here?"

"*You* are." The sheriff took hold of my elbow and escorted me through the door. "I'm still conducting an investigation. 'Bye, Ted." Brady shut the door behind me with a deliberate click.

Chapter Fourteen

T wo hours later, I pulled up in front of a ramshackle ranch
house on the outskirts of Calumet City. "You have
reached your destination," my smartphone announced in the
crisp British accent I had programmed into it.

The run-down seventies ranch took me by surprise. I had
expected Annabelle's home to be a bit more colorful—perhaps
even pink—not the boring beige before me. But Brady had
said she lived with her parents, and when I looked up Annabelle's address online and cross-referenced it with county
records, it had shown the homeowners to be Darlene and
Floyd Grubb. Perhaps the Grubbs weren't as colorful as their
daughter.

Ya think? With a name like that?

I plucked out the fake business card I'd printed that identified me as a reporter from the *Lake Potawatomi Times*, adjusted
the knitted knockers inside my bra, and smoothed down the
navy blazer that completed my journalist's disguise.

After leaving Brady's office and beginning my journey to
the Illinois city bordering Indiana, I had stopped at a roadside

gas station and changed clothes. Inside the restroom, which could have benefited from an entire package of bleach wipes, I removed my scarf and sundress and strapped on my bra stuffed with the lightweight knitted knockers I'd ordered online. I had first seen the handmade breast prostheses for women who have had mastectomies on social media—the invention of a fellow breast cancer survivor and knitter who wanted a lightweight alternative to the usual heavy silicone breast forms. Deciding I might want boobs every now and then—or at least the option to wear them if I felt like it—I had ordered a pair of the soft, comfortable, and breathable knitted prostheses after my first breast was surgically removed five years ago.

Today, since I wanted to fly under the radar and be inconspicuous, I decided against going flat, my preferred state. After donning the flesh-colored pair of fake B-cup boobs that wouldn't make me sweat, I covered them with a businesslike white blouse and blazer and finished off my member-of-the-press costume with oversized reading glasses, pale-gray slacks, and comfortable flats in case I needed to make a run for it.

During the two-hour drive, I rehearsed what I planned to say to Annabelle Cooke's grieving family. When I initially called them to ask a few questions under my reporter's guise, I had expressed my condolences to her mother and said I didn't want to intrude during such a difficult time. However, I told her, I would like to paint a true picture of her daughter in the story I was (not) writing for the local newspaper. "No one here knew Annabelle," I said, hands poised over my laptop to take notes, "so I was hoping you or one of your family members could tell me more about her."

"Shoot, honey, why don't you just come on out here and interview us in person," Darlene Grubb had suggested. "That way you can talk to all three of us. My husband doesn't get out much these days and he doesn't like talking on the phone, so if you want to hear from him, you'd best come on over."

That's why I now found myself standing on the front porch of the Grubbs' run-down ranch.

You sure this is a good idea, Anderson Cooper? What if cray-cray runs in the family?

My hand closed around the container of pepper spray in my purse. Then, taking a deep breath and adopting my objective journalist stance, I rang the doorbell.

Nothing.

I waited a minute and rang again. Still nothing. Were they not home?

I checked my phone to make sure I was on time. Yep. In fact, a minute early—punctuality is one of my strong suits. I double-checked my screen. No texts or missed calls. As I started to tap in the Grubbs' phone number, the front door opened to reveal a paunchy white-haired man in a burgundy nylon tracksuit, gripping a walker and breathing heavily around the large lump in his lower cheek.

"Sorry. Takes me a while to get where I'm goin' these days," he said.

"That's okay."

"My wife's still puttin' on her face, and there's no tellin' where my no-good son-in-law disappeared to." He scowled, revealing nicotine-stained teeth and a wad of chewing tobacco.

"No problem." I'd intended to shake his hand, but the brown spittle that he wiped away with the back of his age-spotted hand stopped me. Instead, I settled for a bright smile. "Hello. I'm Brooke Starr. I spoke to Darlene on the phone?"

"Yep. You're that reporter from Lake Whatchamacallit." He shuffled a few steps backward. "I'm Floyd. Come on in."

I followed Floyd's lumbering frame into the cluttered living room, where a massive flat-screen TV blaring *Judge Judy* dominated an entire wall. A sagging sectional and two brown recliners faced the boob-tube behemoth. Floyd sank into one of the Naugahyde recliners and swigged a beer from the overflowing TV tray table beside him. After spitting a stream of tobacco into a second beer can next to an open bag of Doritos, he gestured for me to sit on the sofa.

Surreptitiously brushing away crumbs and trying to avoid the multiple stains that polka-dotted the beige corduroy fabric, I perched on the edge of the couch and pulled a pen and notebook from my purse. As I adjusted my reading glasses, a stray curl escaped the slicked-back bun I'd scraped my rebellious hair into at the gas station. Tucking the curl discreetly behind my ear, I leaned forward. "I'm so sorry about your daughter, Mr. Grubb. Please accept my condolences on behalf of our town."

He jerked his head in a nod, having just crammed a fistful of nacho Doritos into his mouth. "Annabelle was always doing somethin' stupid," he mumbled around a mouthful of the chips, leaving a halo of orange dust above his wrinkly lips. "I always knew one day she'd wind up in deep kimchi, as they said back in my Army days. I tried to tell her, but she didn't listen." He took another swig of his beer. "Girl had a mind of her own." Floyd picked up his beer can spittoon and spit another stream of tobacco into it.

My stomach roiled. What happened if he mixed up his cans? I threw up a little in my mouth.

"Why hello!" a high-pitched voice behind me squeaked. "Sorry to keep you waiting." Cheap perfume smelling like Febreze wafted over me as a massive woman in a striped poly-ester caftan rounded the couch and pumped my hand. "I'm Darlene Grubb. Nice to meetcha, Ms. Starr."

"Please, call me Brooke," I said faintly, as I stared up into a lined face that resembled a Kabuki doll, with its bright-red lips and white-powdered skin topped off by thick, shoulder-length, stick-straight jet-black hair—obviously a wig.

Darlene plopped into the recliner next to me, which creaked under her weight. Adjusting the shiny gold-and-brown-striped caftan—now I knew where her daughter had gotten her fashion sense—she leaned toward her husband. "Floyd, did you offer our guest a drink?"

"Nope." The male Grubb kept his eyes glued to *Judge Judy* as he spit more tobacco juice into his empty Budweiser can.

"You'll have to excuse my husband, Ms.—I mean, Brooke—a billy goat has more manners than him. The only way he'd commit to learning manners is if Judge Judy sentenced him to being neat and orderly." She reached down and opened a large plastic picnic cooler on the floor beside her chair. "You want some Coke? Mountain Dew?" She fished through the ice. "I got regular and Diet Coke. I also got me some Red Bull."

"Diet Coke would be great. Thanks."

Darlene plucked a Diet Coke from the cooler, wiped the can sweat on her caftan, and handed it to me. Then she popped open a Mountain Dew and glugged it down.

"You hungry, honey?" She nodded to the end table beside me. "Help yourself to some Cheetos or M&M's—unless you want some Doritos?" She reached for the bag on Floyd's TV table, almost knocking over his spit can in the process.

All of a sudden, my mother's modern sterile home looked awfully appealing. "Thanks. I'm good." I took a sip of my Diet Coke and set it down on the only available space on the crowded end table, nestled among the Cheetos, a Tupperware bowl full of M&M's, a jumbo bottle of Tylenol, and a plastic purple pill organizer marked with each day of the week. "I appreciate your invitation to come and talk about Annabelle. I know this is a difficult time."

The dead woman's mother raised a tissue to her eyes—eyes that remained curiously dry. "Yes it is. Thank you." She scarfed down a handful of M&M's.

"Can you tell me about your daughter?" I said gently. "What was she like?"

Darlene dabbed daintily at her mouth with a tissue before releasing a heavy sigh. "Annabelle was my child and I loved her, but Lord love a duck, that girl didn't have the sense she was born with." She snorted. "Take the loser she married. Harley. What a catch. He was stocking shelves at Walmart when she met him and living in his parents' basement. Now he's living in our basement and hasn't worked for the past five years. No wonder she took such a shine to that English author."

Now we're getting somewhere. Tread lightly.

"Was Tavish Bentley the only man Annabelle"—I hesitated—"um, had a crush on?"

Floyd grunted and began hacking.

"If you didn't chew that filthy tobacco, you wouldn't cough so much," Darlene said to her husband. "Don't blame me when you choke to death on that chaw one of these days." She cackled and sent me an exaggerated wink. "Just make sure your life insurance policy is up to date."

Her husband grabbed some brown fast-food napkins from his TV table and spit into them. Then he took a long pull of his Budweiser. "Shut your pie hole, you silly woman." He faced me. "Annabelle had more crushes than you could shake a stick at—mostly Hollywood actors. Like those bachelor guys on TV."

"I keep telling you, those men are not actors," his wife said. "They're real people like you and me. That's why it's called reality TV."

"Well, they seem like actors to me," he said stubbornly, "staying at that fancy California mansion and kissing all those beautiful women in bikinis and such. I don't see folks like you and me living like that."

Score one for Floyd.

Darlene sighed.

Floyd ignored her. "I know for a fact that Annabelle had the hots for the Rock and that guy who played Wolverine."

"Hugh Jackman?" I asked.

"Yep."

Well, who wouldn't?

"She'd go to all his movies the day they opened and bought the DVDs as soon as they released. Had his pictures taped all over her wall too and kept sending him love letters. Until she got a cease-and-desist letter from the cops."

As he leaned over to spit again, I averted my eyes.

"Then she started watching all those fancy English shows and took a cotton to everything British—especially their accents," Floyd said. "They just primed the pump for her to fall for that English author."

A door slammed at the back of the house and a dog yipped.

"Shut up, you stupid mutt," yelled a male voice.

"Here comes Annabelle's Prince Charming," Darlene sneered.

Floyd swiveled his head back to *Judge Judy* as a balding giant in baggy sweat shorts and a shapeless T-shirt entered the room carrying two six-packs.

"Where you been?" Darlene asked.

"Seven-Eleven. We were out of Dr. Pepper." The sweaty giant shambled to the ice chest and shoved the six-packs inside after first removing one of the plastic bottles.

"Seven-Eleven?" Darlene screeched. "That's too expensive! I told you to always buy soda at Walmart."

"Walmart's too far on my bike." He plopped down on the other end of the sectional and unscrewed the cap of his Dr. Pepper. "Some of us don't have cars, remember?" He swigged his soda.

"Well, if someone hadn't totaled his wife's Mary Kay Cadillac while driving under the influence, they might still have a car."

Annabelle had sold Mary Kay? That accounted for the pink addiction.

"It wasn't my fault. That SUV came out of nowhere." Noticing me for the first time, he sucked in his potbelly. "Who's this?" he said with a leer.

"This is the newspaper reporter I told you about." Darlene shot daggers at her son-in-law. "Come to talk to us about your *dead wife*."

Never complain about your mother again.

"I'm so sorry for your loss," I said, extending my hand to him. "Brooke Starr."

He lowered his head in feigned sorrow. "Harley Cooke, Annabelle's husband." As he raised his head back up, I noticed his eyes were a faint blue. Almost colorless. Empty of feeling.

I shivered.

Harley clasped my hand in his meaty paw and shook it, his fingers lingering on mine.

I felt a frisson of unease. Casually extricating my hand, I said, "Your father-in-law was just telling us about some of the celebrity crushes your wife had. I understand she was a bit of an Anglophile."

"Huh?"

"Someone who loves England and all things English."

"You can say that again." He grimaced. "Especially that Tavish dude."

"Do you know when Annabelle first met Tavish Bentley, and how?"

"Yep. Couple years ago when he came to town. Jewel, my little sister, loves his books, so she dragged Annabelle along to his book signing in Chicago. And that was that," he said, snapping his fingers. "My wife was a goner. She became obsessed with the dude."

As I scribbled the details in my notebook, I felt a couple more curls spring free from my slicked-back bun. Absent-mindedly I tucked them behind my ears and continued writing. "And how did you feel about that?"

"What is this? An interrogation?" Something in Harley's voice made me pause. "You a shrink or something?" His colorless eyes narrowed. "Or maybe a cop?"

Careful. "Neither. I'm sorry; I didn't mean to make you uncomfortable. I'm just trying to get a clear picture of Annabelle and her relationship with Tavish Bentley."

"*Relationship?*" Harley guffawed. "The only relationship my wife had with that dude was the one in her head."

"That's what we heard. And you weren't jealous?"

"Nope," he said matter-of-factly. "Annabelle and I had what you might call an open marriage."

Floyd grunted. "In my day they called it an excuse to mess around."

"But we're not in your day anymore, are we, Gramps?" Harley said, turning his cold empty eyes on his father-in-law. "That day is dead and gone."

"The only thing dead and gone around here is Annabelle," Darlene exclaimed, her voice rising. She pointed a shaking finger at her son-in-law. "And *you're* the one who killed her!"

Chapter Fifteen

"Make sure you write that in your paper," Darlene said to me, her face flushing red under her white makeup. "This lowlife murdered our daughter!"

Slowly and quietly, I slipped my hand into my purse and fumbled for the can of pepper spray.

"Why would I kill my wife?" Harley tipped his bald head at Darlene.

"For a couple reasons: to be with that skinny chippy you have on the side, and for the insurance money. Annabelle told me a while back that you convinced her to get the two of you matching insurance policies."

"It's called being fiscally prudent," Harley said, sounding like a commercial for life insurance while conveniently ignoring the "chippy" accusation his mother-in-law had lobbed at him. He laced his fingers behind his head and splayed out his pasty tree-trunk calves before him. "Insurance is protection for those you leave behind. That way the remaining spouse or family member isn't on the hook to pay funeral and burial expenses during their time of grief." He added in a mock-innocent tone, "I'm sure you and Floyd have insurance policies, right?"

Darlene flushed. "Never you mind about Floyd and me. That's our business." She turned to face me. "Ms. Starr, as a reporter, have you ever heard of funeral expenses costing *a hundred grand*?"

Floyd released another grunt. "That'd have to be a gold-plated casket."

Sounds like the perfect motive for murder, I thought.

Annabelle's mother inclined her head to me expectantly.

"No," I said, "but then I haven't had much experience with funerals." Just deaths. By strangulation.

I scratched the back of my neck, where drops of perspiration had formed at my hairline, causing more curls to spring loose from my tight, unfamiliar hairstyle.

"Starr," Harley said with a speculative gleam as he pinned me with his colorless eyes. "That's funny. You have the same name as Brenda Starr, the redheaded reporter in my comic books."

I knew I should have come up with a more original alias.

"I know," I said weakly. "I get that a lot. But as you can see, I'm not a redhead, nor is my name Brenda."

"That's right," Darlene said. "Her name's Brooke. Now stop changing the subject, Harley Cooke, and confess. You know you killed Annabelle."

"Did not." He scowled at her. "You're as crazy as your daughter." He chugged down the rest of his Dr. Pepper and belched.

"And you're a freeloader and a loser." Darlene whipped out her cell phone from the pocket of her caftan. "And a murderer! I'm calling the cops right now."

"I wouldn't do that if I were you." Harley rose in a smooth, fluid motion for such a big man and advanced menacingly toward his mother-in-law.

I jumped up, can of pepper spray in hand. "Stop right there or I'll shoot." I pointed the can at him, my trembling finger poised on the nozzle.

"Yeah, right." He took a step toward me. I pressed the nozzle.

Harley howled and clutched at his face, eyes streaming. Then he dropped to his knees. As he did, Floyd heaved himself to his feet and trapped Harley between his walker and the couch.

"Way to go, Brooke!" Darlene held out something to me. My glasses. "These fell on the floor when you jumped between me and that good-for-nothing son-in-law of mine."

"Thanks." I blew my sticky bangs off my face and unconsciously shoved my curls behind my ear. That's when I discovered my rebellious curly hair had at last completely escaped its confining bun. Oops.

Darlene considered me. "You know . . . with your hair down and no glasses, you seem kind of familiar."

I shrugged and placed the plastic oversized glasses back on. "I guess I just have one of those faces."

"No." A frown creased her forehead. "You remind me of someone. I just can't think of who."

"Julia Roberts in *Pretty Woman*?" I sucked in my cheeks and struck a pose. "Katharine Hepburn in *Bringing Up Baby*?"

Darlene shook her head. Then she scrunched her eyebrows together and leaned in closer. Her brown eyes grew wide. "Oh my gosh!" Digging excitedly in the pocket of her voluminous caftan, she yanked out a paperback and held up the back cover next to my face. "You're Theodora St. John!" she squealed.

Busted.

Sirens wailed out front.

Great. That's all I needed—getting arrested for impersonating a reporter. Then I remembered Harley. My gaze slid from the still-writhing widower to the phone in Darlene's hand. "I thought you didn't have a chance to call the cops."

"She didn't," Floyd said, wheezing. "But I did."

*   *   *

Two and a half hours later after the police had questioned all of us—and placed a call to Brady to confirm my story—they released us. All except Harley, who had a record for DUI and assault in his background, as well as an outstanding warrant for unpaid parking tickets. The cops placed Harley in a holding cell while they investigated him for his wife's murder.

The Grubbs wanted to take me out to an early dinner at Outback to celebrate, but I begged off, eager to get home and back to Gracie, whom my neighbor, Joanne LaPoint, was dogsitting. Before I left, however, Darlene had me sign *Death by Danish*, *The Macaroon Murders*, and *Pineapple Upside-Down Death*. She also made me promise to send her an autographed copy of *A Dash of Death* as soon as it was released.

"My friends will be so jealous when they find out I'm friends with Theodora St. John," she said, proudly examining the personal notes I'd written in her books. "We just love your

Kate and Kallie mysteries. That dog is so smart, the way she always figures out the mystery and saves the day."

Too bad Gracie can't do the same. "Kallie's a clever girl," I agreed, inching toward the front door. "Well, I'd better get going."

"You come back and see us again," Darlene said. Her face lit up. "Or . . . I could always visit you in Lake Potawatomi."

"I'm not sittin' in a car for no two hours," groused Floyd.

Thank God. The last thing I need is my own stalker-fan.

Darlene walked me to the door. "I'll just leave Floyd behind when I come to see you," she whispered. "There's a lady from the county who comes in and helps out a few days a week. I'll get her to watch him."

I gave Darlene a weak smile and a wave good-bye, hoping she didn't hear my stomach growling.

Leaving the Grubbs' neighborhood, I grabbed a granola bar from the emergency stash I keep in my glove box and inhaled it. Then I patted myself on the back for getting Annabelle's murderer off the street and clearing Tavish.

Aren't you forgetting something? my inner nag asked.

Like what?

Your scarf around Annabelle's neck? How did Harley know to strangle his wife using the same murder weapon—albeit a different color—as the one that killed Kristi?

He must have read about it online. I dismissed my pragmatic second-guessing. *Several online news venues have run stories about Kristi's murder.*

True, but didn't you notice that they left out the details of who the owner of the scarf is? Brady's been keeping that information quiet.

Well then, Annabelle must have told her husband details about Kristi's murder and he replicated it, I argued with myself.

That's possible. But you know what that means then, don't you?

Ew. Harley Cooke has been inside my house.

I shuddered at the thought. If Harley had broken in and stolen my scarf, that meant . . . he was also the one who'd poisoned Gracie! I nearly flipped a U-ey to drive back to the police station and deck the creep who had hurt my dog, but I doubted the cops would let me near him. Plus, I didn't want to get arrested for assault and battery. Instead, I pulled into the nearest drive-through and ordered a burger, fries, and an industrial-sized iced tea for sustenance. Checking my phone as I waited for my order, I discovered eleven text messages, seven missed calls, and four voice mails. Yikes. I'd told my neighbor and occasional dog-sitter Joanne I had a business appointment out of town and would be gone for five or six hours, but I hadn't told her where I was going or what the business was. My friends and family I had purposely left in the dark.

I skimmed the texts.

Char: *Guess what? I found someone who has it in for Tavish. Call me.*

Sharon: *Had an interesting talk with Melanie. Much to tell. Talked to Josh and Jessica too. They're both loving their summer jobs (although I still wish they'd come home and work with their dad and I at the Lake House again, but that's just me). They said to say hi to Aunt Teddie.*

Joanne LaPoint: *Kelly's having the baby! Gotta go. Left Gracie with your mom. Sorry* ☹

Mom: *Joanne brought Gracie home. She left another present in the back yard for you.*

Tavish: *You're right. Best carrot cake ever. I'd like to thank you in person. Are you free for dinner?*

Mom: *Where are you? I left you three messages! I have to leave soon for Bunco.*

Char: *Did you get my voicemail?*

Mom: *Why even have a phone if you don't use it?*

Brady: *WTH possessed you to go to Annabelle Cooke's house?! By yourself?*

Group text from Sharon and Char: *ARE YOU INSANE? Don't EVER do something like that again on your own! Remember: all for one, and one for all.*

Tavish: *Are you all right? Please ring me.*

My thumb hovered over the voice mail button. I really wasn't up to listening to everyone scold me.

"Eight seventy-nine, please."

Saved by the fast-food worker.

Chapter Sixteen

Opening my back door two hours later, I called out, "Gracie-girl, Mommy's home!"

The door hadn't even fully opened before Gracie flung herself at me, begging for a hug. I scooped her up in my arms, nuzzling my face in her creamy fur as she planted ecstatic doggy kisses on my neck and nose.

"Good girl. Mommy missed you. I'm sorry I was gone so long." When I lifted my face from my dog, I saw them: Sharon, Char, Brady, Tavish, and my mother all crowded around my kitchen table with coffee mugs in front of them, glaring at me. All except Tavish, who wore an expression of concern.

"What is this, the Inquisition?" I joked as I set Gracie down and plopped my purse on the counter.

Mom stiffened in her seat. "Don't you take that cavalier tone, young lady! Not after what you put us through."

I glanced at my fellow Musketeers, expecting the familiar discreet eye roll that usually accompanies my mother's criticisms. No eye roll, discreet or otherwise. Not even a quirked lip as they tried to hold back a smile. Sharon and Char weren't smiling tonight.

That's when I knew I had messed up.

"Dammit, Ted, what were you thinking?" Brady exploded. "Going to a stranger's house in an unfamiliar city without telling anyone or having any kind of backup?"

"A stranger who turned out to be a *murderer*," Sharon said, her lip quivering.

"An *alleged* murderer," Brady, ever the proper lawman, corrected her.

"Alleged, schmelleged, I don't care about that." Char's eyes blazed at me. "But if you ever do something like that again, Theodora St. John, I will personally strangle you with one of your own scarves."

"Not if I get there first," my mother muttered.

"Teddie," Tavish said in a conciliatory tone, "no one knew where you were, and when you didn't answer your phone or respond to repeated messages and texts, we grew concerned."

"I told Joanne I had an out-of-town appointment."

"Yes, but she didn't know *where* you were or when you'd be back," my mother said in a clipped voice. "We've all been trying to reach you, and no one could get ahold of you."

"We thought something might have happened," Sharon added. "There is a killer running loose, you know."

"I know. I'm sorry. I didn't mean to make you worry. And I did text you on my way home—belatedly, I know, but I was focused on trying to learn more about Annabelle from the people who knew her best. The reason I went to Calumet City and met with her family was to get proof that Annabelle killed Kristi, since I knew Tavish didn't, and neither did I." *And Brady, if I'd told you—or Char—my plan in advance, you'd have stopped me.*

"What about the person who killed Annabelle?" Brady said quietly. "Did it ever occur to you that maybe one—or more—of her family members might have killed her?"

Had that occurred to me? It must have on a subconscious level; why else had I brought the pepper spray?

"It's not like I went unprepared. I had protection." I reached into my purse and pulled out the can of pepper spray. "See? I was well armed." I lifted my chin. "I know how to take care of myself, Brady, and am quite capable of doing so."

"She certainly is," Tavish said. "I can personally attest to that."

I felt my face flush. Even more so after glimpsing the knowing glance Sharon and Char exchanged. I rushed out the words "Anyway, all's well that ends well. The murderers are gone, and now things can settle down and get back to normal around here again."

Did I really want normal, though? I wondered. Normal can sometimes be boring, and the past week in Lake Potawatomi had been anything but.

You know what else normal means, don't you? I asked myself. *Tavish will be leaving soon to return to his exciting jet-setting life in New York, LA, and England.*

Tavish's hazel eyes met mine, and my stomach did a strange flutter.

Don't even go there, my practical self said. *He'll be gone soon.* This was just a brief diversion. Time to return to the real world.

"I hope things do settle down," Brady said, with a sigh. "I'd like to close the book on this whole case and move on, but there are still a few loose ends to tie up. The police chief in Calumet City will keep me informed on the Harley Cooke investigation, and once it's wrapped up, I'll let you know." He wagged his finger at me. "Meanwhile, Ted, from now on please confine your sleuthing to your mystery novels and leave the true crime to the professionals."

Sharon giggled.

My mom scraped back her chair and stood up. "And perhaps you could select at least one person here to keep apprised of your whereabouts in the future." She walked up to me and arched an eyebrow as best she could. "And I don't expect it to be me," she said softly. Mom gave my arm a brief squeeze, then checked her watch. "Now I'm going to see if I can catch the end of Bunco night. Good night, everyone." She reached down and petted Gracie on her way out. "Good night, Gracie."

Gracie licked the back of Mom's hand.

Char and Sharon sent me an incredulous stare as the door shut behind my mother. Then Sharon jumped up from her chair. "That's my cue," she said. "I need to get back and relieve Jim." She flung her arms around me and hugged me tight. "I never thought I'd say this," she whispered, "but please listen to your mother. Promise me you won't go off again without letting someone know exactly where you are."

I hugged her back. "I promise."

Char and Brady approached next, and we did the awkward group-hug thing. "And from now on, answer your flipping phone," Char growled, punching me none too gently on the arm as they departed.

That left Tavish.

"Aren't you going to read me the riot act too?" I asked.

"No need. I think everyone else covered that quite thoroughly already." He tilted his head, a puzzled expression on his face as he regarded me. "You look different. Not yourself."

"It's my reporter's disguise." I removed the blazer and kicked off my flats. "I had to play the part." Lifting the tie-dyed scarf hanging from the kitchen hook where I kept my aprons, I wound the scarf loosely around my neck with one hand while nonchalantly plucking out the knitted knockers with the other. "Plus"—I dropped the yarn-covered breast substitutes on the table—"you've never seen me with boobs."

Tavish threw back his head and guffawed. He laughed so hard he snorted—something I'd never expected from a well-bred Englishman. Then he snorted again, which made him laugh even more.

I joined in. It would have been rude not to.

We laughed and laughed until the tears came. Then we laughed some more.

Tavish swiped at his eyes. "Teddie St. John, you are bloody marvelous. I have never known anyone like you."

"What can I say? I'm an original."

"That you most certainly are." He stopped laughing and got an odd look in his eyes. A look I'd never seen before, a look that took my breath away. He stepped tentatively toward me, raising his eyebrows in a question mark. I closed the distance between us until we were face-to-face. Then I closed my eyes. Tavish tenderly cupped my face in his hands and kissed me.

I kissed him right back.

Chapter Seventeen

The next morning I slept in—as much as is possible with a dog. Gracie had tried to wake me at seven thirty, our usual morning walk time, but I shooed her away. She tried a second time at eight and I put her off again. Finally, at eight thirty, she bounded on top of me, landing on my T-shirted stomach and urging me out of bed. Then she jumped back down to the floor and stood on her hind legs doing her cute begging routine as she pawed the air with her front feet.

"Okay, okay, just a minute." I shoved my feet into my fuzzy slippers, then followed her to the kitchen, yawning. When I opened the back door, she shot into the yard like a kid on the last day of school.

I sat down at the kitchen table in my oversized T-shirt and cotton sleep pants, chin in hand, thinking back to last night, which caused me to break out in a blissful smile. Tavish and I had talked into the wee hours, squeezed up next to each other on the couch—although Gracie chaperoned herself between us. As we talked, I gave Gracie her nightly tummy rub and

Tavish scratched her behind the ears, earning himself a friend for life.

"Now that these dreadful murders have been solved," Tavish said, "we can get to know one another properly and not have to worry when the next shoe will drop."

"Or the next scarf will be found," I said dryly, flicking the ends of my silk scarf.

"I like your scarves." Tavish ran his hand up the tie-dyed fabric and lightly stroked the back of my neck. "Just not around other women's necks."

"That makes two of us." I tried to ignore the delicious shiver his touch sent down my spine.

Easy, girl. I took a sip of wine and brought my mind back to the murders. "Tavish," I said thoughtfully, "do you think Annabelle planned to kill Kristi, or did she just suddenly snap and strangle her in a moment of jealous rage?"

He frowned and stopped petting Gracie. "I don't know. If she had planned it, that would be premeditated murder, which would be rather chilling. However, I don't think Annabelle was clever enough or cunning enough to pull that off."

Gracie nudged his hand with her nose. Tavish resumed his doggy affections.

"I think you're right," I reflected. "From what I saw and have since learned, Annabelle had an intense obsession with you, but she wasn't calculating. With her it was all emotions." I took another sip of my Cabernet. "My guess is she killed Kristi in the heat of the moment—assuming she was still your fiancée. She was jealous that Kristi had what she wanted." I angled my head. "Did Kristi ever meet Annabelle?"

"Once." Tavish's neck reddened. "Kristi was at an event in Atlanta with me a couple of months ago when Annabelle showed up, proclaiming her love for me, and tried to kiss me."

"And?"

"And what?" he asked.

Gracie jumped down from the couch and stretched out at our feet.

"And how did Kristi respond to Annabelle's attempted kiss and declaration of love? Did she get angry and tell your stalker off?"

Tavish steepled his fingers and rested his chin on them. He closed his eyes, remembering. "No. Kristi laughed at Annabelle and said, 'In your dreams, fatty.'"

"Ah."

He couldn't meet my eyes. "Kristi wasn't an especially kind person."

Ya think?

I set my hand lightly atop his. "And what did Annabelle say to that?"

"It wasn't what she said." Tavish laced his fingers with mine, his eyes downcast. "It's what she did. Annabelle shrieked and lunged at Kristi, yelling, 'I'll kill you.'"

"Whoa."

"Yes. And in the end, that's what she did." He stared off into the distance. "Perhaps if I'd lent more credence to Annabelle's threat at the time, Kristi might still be alive."

"You can't think that way." I squeezed his hand. "You had no way of knowing Annabelle would actually act on those words."

"No, but if I hadn't dismissed them as so much rubbish, my former fiancée's parents wouldn't be burying their daughter next week."

"And how did everyone else—including Kristi," I asked gently, "react when Annabelle yelled at her?"

"No one took her seriously." Tavish raked his hand through his hair. "It was just crazy Annabelle being Annabelle."

"Well, okay then." I lightly touched his cheek with the back of my hand. "You are not to blame, so don't put that on yourself." I brushed his lips with mine. "No *if onlys* allowed."

Later, as we stretched out side by side on the couch, Tavish's long legs dangling over the end, he played with my hair. "I love your curls—they're so springy." He gently tugged on a ringlet in front of my ear and then released it. The curl snapped back, softly slapping against my ear. "See what I mean?"

"Just like a yo-yo."

"Wasn't that a song or something?"

"Before our time." But not my father's—he loved the Osmonds.

Tavish's forehead creased. "Do you think Annabelle's husband knew she killed Kristi?"

"I'm not sure," I said slowly. "I've been thinking about that. If he did know, perhaps he thought if he committed a copycat murder, no one would suspect him and he could get away with killing his wife. That would make sense." I sat up as I pictured the scenario. "Maybe Harley followed Annabelle to Lake Potawatomi—perhaps even the day she assaulted me in front of Andersen's." My words tumbled over each other eagerly as I imagined how the scene unfolded. "Harley would have seen that

I have a dog and he could have easily found out where I live. That night when we were on our date in Milwaukee, he could have come back here and broken into my house with the sole purpose of stealing one of my scarves to mimic Kristi's murder."

My stomach clenched and my eager imaginings ended as abruptly as they began as I remembered the rest of the story. "But first he had to feed Gracie the sleeping-pill steak." I leaned down and scooped my sleeping white fur ball into my arms, hugging her tightly to my chest. "Worst day of my life." Next to my dad's death.

Tavish put his arm around my shoulders and hugged me to him.

Gracie released a comforting woof. *Don't worry, Mom. I'm not going anywhere.*

I stared at my dog and frowned, as I recognized the fallacy in my imagined scenario. "Except . . . Gracie would have barked her head off when Harley broke in, and Mom or Joanne would have heard her. Gracie always barks at anyone who comes to the door, and she would have raised a ruckus at someone entering her home—especially a stranger—as Mom has complained about on more than one occasion." Like the pizza delivery guy. Repairman. Even sweet Girl Scouts hawking cookies.

"Scout does the same," Tavish said. "Sherlock too." He gave Gracie an affectionate pat on the head. "Our four-footed friends are quite protective of their turf. That's what makes them such brilliant guard dogs, on top of everything else."

"Uh-huh," I said absently, my mind on other things. I had just realized another flaw in my re-creation of the night in question. "Harley doesn't have a car," I said softly. I turned to face Tavish. "How did he get from Calumet City to Lake Potawatomi to kill Annabelle?"

"Uber?" Tavish suggested.

"For that distance? Way too expensive."

"Right. Perhaps he borrowed a friend's car?"

"Maybe," I mused. "Or stole one. Having met Harley, the latter seems more likely."

"Bit dangerous, that," Tavish said. "The owner of the car would have reported it stolen, and if Harley was stopped driving a stolen vehicle, he wouldn't have been able to carry out his deadly plan."

"True . . ." More and more holes kept opening up in my theory. I sighed. "Could it be I've got this all wrong? Maybe it wasn't Harley who broke into my house at all but Annabelle, as we originally thought." I rubbed my head. "Which still begs the question of how Harley got here in the first place."

"Not to mention Gracie's barking," Tavish reminded me. "After her run-in with Annabelle in the street earlier that day, I would imagine Gracie would bark up a storm if she dared even approach your house, never mind actually break in."

"You're right." I pressed my hands against my temples. "This is giving me a headache."

"Why don't we leave it to the police to figure out?" Tavish gently removed my hands from my head and brought them up to his lips. "We've got more important things to think about."

"Exactly," I said innocently. "If I don't meet my deadline for *A Dash of Death*, my editor will kill me."

Chapter Eighteen

G racie scampered back into the kitchen, interrupting my remembrances of last night.

After Gracie answered all her mail within a two-block radius, I settled into my wingback with my laptop, ready for a day of writing the latest adventure of Kate and Kallie and beefing up my paltry word count. Recent events had put me way behind schedule, and I seriously needed to make up for lost time.

Before I began composing the next chapter, however, I sent a group text to Sharon and Char: *Incommunicado today—hunkered down in writing cave.*

Char: *Hunker away. Just don't run away.*
Sharon: *Have a productive day! Want to hear all though after you come up for air.*

I'll bet you do, my friend. I had a lot to tell my fellow Musketeers—later.

My fingers flew across the keyboard as my crime-solving duo followed the Danish butter cookie trail of their latest murder. As Kallie pursued the probable suspect through the cobblestoned streets of the fictional Wisconsin town with Kate hanging on to her leash for dear life, I couldn't wait to discover what was going to happen next. As a classic seat-of-my-pants writer, I don't plot my books out in advance. Though I know the beginning and usually the ending, the middle is always a surprise to me as I allow the story to unfold organically. It's as much fun for me to uncover the twists and turns of my mysteries as it is for my readers.

A knock at my back door interrupted Kate and Kallie's exciting chase. *Are you kidding me? Can you not read, Mother?*

I had hung my Do Not Disturb: Genius at Work sign bearing Einstein's face on the doorknob—a necessity after one too many times of my mom barging in on me over the years while I was trying to write—and still she persisted. I ignored the intrusion and tried to regain my train of thought.

Another knock.

"Aaarrgh!" I hit save, slammed my laptop shut, and stalked to the back door. "What?" I snarled, flinging it open. "Did you *not* see the sign?"

Tavish stood there holding a pastry bag. "Sorry," he said, contrite. "I thought you could use some sustenance before you begin your writing day."

"I began an hour ago."

"Right. I, ah, didn't realize you were a morning person." He sent me a lazy smile. "Particularly after last night."

"I'm the one who's sorry." I sighed and moved toward him. "I didn't mean to yell at you. I thought you were my mom. I was right in the middle of an important scene."

"No apologies necessary, except from me. I should know better." He handed me the bag, planted a quick peck on my forehead, and gently pushed me back inside. "Now get back to work, Theodora St. John. I'll ring you later."

A distinctive sound reached my ears—Mom's sliding-glass door opening—before I could make a quick getaway. I groaned inwardly.

"Why good morning, Tavish," Mom trilled as she approached. "What a lovely surprise to see you still here. I thought you'd be on your way back to New York already."

"Not yet." He turned to face my mother. "Actually, we mustn't disturb Teddie, as she's on deadline and writers get quite cranky when they're in deadline mode, as I can personally attest. Best leave her to it." Tavish linked his arm with Mom's and steered her away. "May I take you to breakfast?"

I'd known there was a reason I liked that man.

* * *

Seven hours later I closed my laptop and stretched, satisfied that I had created enough red herrings to throw my readers off the scent of the actual killer. *And* I'd more than doubled my daily word count. Another few days at this pace and I should be caught up.

Gracie ran up to me, wagging her tail. *Finally, you're off that stupid 'puter! Can we go play now, Mom, please?* My dog angled her creamy head at me and fastened her dark eyes on mine, indicating I could use some fresh air too.

"All right, Gracie-girl. Give me time to shower and change and then we'll go." I headed to the bathroom, where I shucked off my sleepwear and took a quick shower. Ten minutes later, my hair still wet from the shower, we were on our jog to the park as we passed Joanne LaPoint, two houses over, deadheading her roses. "Hey, Joanne, how's that new grandbaby?"

She beamed. "Most beautiful baby ever." She pulled out her phone. "I have pictures—"

Gracie strained at the leash, refusing to stop. "Sorry"—I tossed her a regretful smile—"I'll have to see them on the way back. Gracie's on a mission."

Joanne grinned and waved me on.

At the park, Gracie and I did a couple of laps around the perimeter, and then I pulled out her favorite toy. Unclipping her leash, I threw the ratty tennis ball as far across the park as I could. She zoomed after it and raced back to me moments later, proudly dropping the ball at my feet.

"Good girl." I picked up the ball and stretched my arm back, preparing to throw it again. Gracie tensed, ready to run. Then I faked flinging the tennis ball. Gracie ran in the direction I had supposedly hurled it, then pulled up short, examining the ground around her. She ran a few feet and stopped, turning her head from side to side, searching for her beloved ball.

I whistled and held up the faded felt-covered orb. Glimpsing the yellow from across the park, Gracie sprinted back. She sat upright on the grass before me, panting and never taking her eyes off the ball. I raised my hand and threw with all my might. Gracie raced after the yellow sphere.

"Dogs sure do love their balls, don't they?" a familiar voice said behind me.

I turned to see Barbara Christensen, accompanied by town gossip Wilma Sorensen, smiling at me.

"They sure do."

"Robert used to love coming to the park with Duke and playing fetch," Barbara said wistfully, brushing away a tear.

"I remember that," I said gently. "Duke was such a sweet, beautiful dog. He sure loved his dad."

"Robert was Duke's person," Barbara said simply, lifting her shoulders. "When he died, Duke's heart broke. That big, soft, golden heart of his couldn't bear to go on beating without his person. Duke's heart gave out a week later."

My eyes filled. "I remember."

Gracie returned with the tennis ball and dropped it at my feet, wagging her tail.

Barbara reached down and patted Gracie's head. "Good girl. You're smart as well as beautiful."

Wilma smoothed down her gray perm and cleared her throat. "Word around town is they caught the man who murdered that stalker lady." She pursed her lips in a satisfied smirk. "What did I say? It's almost always the husband. That's why I—and everyone else in town—thought that famous author killed his fiancée. They may not have been married, but they were awfully close to it, seein' as how they were engaged and all."

"Actually, Wilma," I said sweetly, "don't you remember? We talked about this before. Tavish and Kristi had recently broken off their engagement."

Wilma's wrinkled face flushed. Then she cast me a knowing glance. "Ah, that explains why his fancy rental car was parked at your house all night last night." Her eyes gleamed with malice. "You want to be careful there, Teddie. A man doesn't need to buy the cow if he's already getting the milk for free."

"Wilma!" Barbara said.

"That's okay, Barb, Tavish and I were just saying last night how much we love milk—both straight and in our tea. That's how they drink their hot tea in England, you know." Tilting my head, I sent her gray-haired companion an appraising look. "Calcium is good for you. Wilma, you might want to start adding more milk to your diet. At your age you can't be too careful about brittle bones." Clipping on Gracie's leash, I winked at Barbara as we left. Barb gave me a discreet thumbs-up behind Wilma's back.

Gracie and I ended our play date at the Corner Bookstore, where Char gave my Eskie a bowl of water and her favorite peanut-butter dog biscuits behind the front counter. Then my fellow Musketeer sat down across from me with a gleam in her eye. "Okay, now, spill. I want all the details of last night."

"All?"

"There's no need to get graphic, but as your best friend, I think I'm entitled to know the basics." She fixed me with a knowing gaze. "Did you and Tavish spend the night together?"

My eyes darted around the bookstore.

"Don't worry, there's no one here except Fred Matson, and he's snoozing in sci-fi at the other end of the store."

"Well . . . in that case . . . Tavish didn't leave until about five this morning, so I guess that means we spent the night together."

Her eyes widened. Then Char broke into a huge smile and hugged me. "Good for you! It's about time you had some romance in your life. Nothing wrong with a little fling—you're both consenting adults. And it's not like you need to worry about getting pregnant."

"That would be what they call a miracle."

She sighed. "Sometimes I envy you your early menopause—it makes things so much easier."

I flapped my scarf against my face. "Tell me that again once you get your first hot flash." Then I leaned into my friend and whispered in her ear, "We didn't sleep together."

"You didn't?"

"Nope."

Her face fell. "Well, crap. I thought for sure I sensed heat between you."

"You did. We're just keeping the flame down low and taking things slow." Fred Matson appeared from behind the sci-fi bookshelf and began shuffling our way. "Can we change the subject now, please?"

"Okay, but just tell me one thing," Char whispered as Fred approached. "Did you at least kiss?"

"Oh yeah."

* * *

Sharon and Jim invited a few of us—including my mother—to dinner at the Lake House that night to mark the end of the murders and a return to normalcy in Lake Potawatomi. "Be sure and dress up," Sharon instructed when she called. "This is a celebration."

As Adele sang in the background, I stood in front of my closet, trying to decide what to wear. Unlike my mother, I am not a clotheshorse. Formfitting designer clothes from high-end stores have never appealed to me. I prefer my simple boho style—or hippie chic, as some call it. I just call it comfortable. Most of my clothing comes from thrift stores or quirky shops off the beaten track. I love color, however, as evidenced by the rainbow of scarves hanging from my repurposed coatrack.

I pulled out the green batik dress I'd worn the first time Tavish and I had dinner—a dinner I'd thought was simply two colleagues getting together to talk writing. I thought back to last night. We were definitely more than colleagues now. We had spent the entire night talking about so many things—after giving up trying to solve the Harley-versus-Annabelle break-in puzzle. We'd talked about families, childhoods, our beloved canine children, travel, art, and of course, writing. Tavish shared that he had been playing around with an idea for a quieter, more introspective standalone novel, but his agent had advised him against it because it would not fit with his blood series "brand" and his readers would not accept it.

"So write it under a pseudonym," I suggested. "That's what J. K. Rowling did after Harry Potter." That led into a twenty-minute discussion of Harry Potter, with both of us admitting we wished we had come up with the brilliant idea of a boy wizard and the magical world of Hogwarts.

"Teddie?" my mother's voice called out from the kitchen. "Where are you?"

"In my bedroom," I yelled. I really need to get that key back.

Mom appeared in the doorway moments later, pink cheeked and with windblown hair, her arms full of shopping bags from Nordstrom's and other chichi clothing stores.

"Someone's had a busy day," I said.

"You can say that again." She dropped the bags on the floor and sank onto my bed, removing her shoes and rubbing her feet. "It was fabulous! Such fun. Tavish and I spent the day shopping on Michigan Avenue."

I turned and stared at her. "Say that again? You did what?"

"Spent the day in Chicago with Tavish Bentley, shopping." She grinned and started rummaging through the bags. "Just wait until you see what we got you."

We?

"While we were having breakfast at Andersen's, Tavish said he had to run to Chicago for a business appointment." Mom continued searching through her shopping bags. "I happened to mention I'd been planning to do a little shopping in the Windy City today, so he offered to take me with him. He said it would be a good chance for us to get to know each other. Although"—she jutted her chin toward me—"I think what he was really trying to do was keep me out of your hair while you wrote. Tavish explained that authors need concentrated writing time free of distractions."

If I'd had a brick wall in my room, I would have banged my head against it. *I've only been saying that for years, Mother. But then again I'm not male, nor do I have an English accent.*

"Ah, here it is." Mom pulled out a flat narrow box and handed it to me with an expectant gleam in her eye.

"What is this?"

"Open it and find out."

I removed the lid and parted the tissue paper to reveal a rectangle of turquoise silk. As I lifted the silk from the box, the light caught the iridescent scarf, spotlighting shimmering shades of turquoise swirling from light to dark. "It's beautiful," I breathed. "Thank you."

"Don't thank me. Read the card."

For the first time I noticed an envelope at the bottom of the box. I opened it and pulled out a card penned in beautiful calligraphy. *This is to replace the scarf my ex stole. I couldn't find one with pom-poms, but I hope this will be a suitable substitute. I think it will look lovely against your dark curls.—Tavish*

Raising my head from the note, I saw my mother grinning broadly and extending another bag to me. A large one. I held up my hands, palms out. "That's too much. I can't accept that from Tavish."

"I know. That's what I told him. This one's from me." Mom studied her French manicure. "Don't worry, it's not from Barneys or Bloomie's. I know you wouldn't be caught dead in one of those stores." She lifted her shoulders in a shrug. "I found it in a little Indian boutique on a side street. Tavish spotted the store and suggested we give it a try."

Were pigs flying overhead? Opening the bag, I pulled out a coral-colored flowing maxi dress detailed with exquisite turquoise embroidery at the bodice and hem. *Am I in an alternative universe or what? Did my mother really just buy me the best dress ever?* I stared at her, words failing me.

Who are you and what have you done with my mother?

"Well?" she said, uncertainly. "Do you like it or not? If you don't like it, you can always exchange it—although you're the one who will have to go back to that store." She wrinkled her nose. "Too much incense and strange smells for me."

"I love it." I held the cotton dress up against me before the mirror. "It's so me."

"That's exactly what Tavish said." Mom added casually, "I thought it might go well with the turquoise scarf he got you."

I wound the silky scarf around my neck, letting the ends fall against the coral cotton. "It's perfect," I said softly. "Thank you, Mom." Attempting to maintain the tenuous, unfamiliar mother-daughter clothes connection, I asked, "What are you going to wear tonight?"

"Oh, I'm not going." She began collecting her bags. "I'm too exhausted. I'm going to take a long bubble bath and curl up with a glass of Pinot Noir and *Her Blood Weeps*." As she slipped her shoes back on and stood up, Mom caught sight of herself in the mirror and yelped. "My goodness, I'm a fright." She smoothed her hair. "Why didn't you tell me my hair was a mess?"

Chapter Nineteen

When I arrived at the Lake House an hour later, everyone was drinking wine and noshing on appetizers in the living room. Tavish's eyes lit up when he saw me. "Wow." He strode over and kissed me on the cheek. "You look gorgeous."

Melanie did a double take from across the room.

"Thank you." I lowered my voice. "And thank you so much for the gorgeous scarf. I absolutely love it."

"It goes perfectly with that dress—I thought it might."

"Thanks for that too—for steering my mom to a shop she wouldn't normally be caught dead in." I grinned at him. "I still can't believe you took my mother shopping—you deserve a medal."

"Actually, I had a good time. Your mom's not so bad." He chuckled. "Although she does give new meaning to the words 'Shop till you drop.'"

Char and Brady approached. "Whoa, Ted," Brady said. "You look really hot."

"Careful," Tavish teased, putting his arm around me.

Melanie materialized next to Tavish in her ubiquitous black, her eyes inscrutable behind her Harry Potter glasses. "You two are together?"

Brady's eyes sought Char, who lifted her shoulders and shrugged.

Before Tavish or I could confirm or deny, a beaming Sharon appeared at my elbow with a tray of appetizers. "I take full credit," she said. "I'm the one who introduced them. The minute I met Tavish, I knew he and Teddie would be perfect together. They have so much in common."

Yes, I realized, *we do.*

Jim, Sharon's other half, winked at me and handed me a glass of wine. He raised his glass. "Well then, here's to Teddie and Tavish."

Everyone raised their glass except Melanie, who was busy shoving a stuffed mushroom into her mouth. She chugged her wine and choked. Her hand flew to her chest, and she got a panicked expression as she continued choking.

"Are you okay?" Tavish rushed to his young assistant's side and slapped her on the back.

Her face turned red and she coughed.

"Raise your arms," Jim ordered.

Brady strode over to Melanie, but Char beat him to it. She quickly stepped behind the choking girl, wrapped her arms beneath her chest, crossed them tightly, and executed a swift Heimlich thrust. The mushroom flew out of Melanie's mouth and slid across the hardwood floor. She gasped and coughed, eyes streaming.

Tavish led her over to an easy chair, Brady following close behind. Jim snagged a glass of water from the table and rushed it over to his guest.

"Someone isn't happy about her boss's new relationship," Char said to me sotto voce.

"Ya got that right. I think someone may have a little crush."

"That's what I wanted to tell you," Sharon said quietly. "You asked me to grill Melanie, so I plied her with cookies and coffee and asked about her job. Then I got her talking about Tavish's ex-wife and Kristi. That's when I realized Melanie has a little crush on Tavish."

Jim motioned for his wife.

"We'll talk later. I still need to tell you about Tavish's ex-wife," Sharon whispered. She hurried over to the men around Melanie, leaving me alone with Char.

"Well, someone is certainly smitten." My best friend grinned at me.

"Is it that obvious? I was trying to be discreet."

"You can forget that noise. Besides, I was talking about Tavish."

His head angled in our direction.

Had he heard? We rejoined the group.

"How are you doing, Melanie?" Char asked.

"Fine—thanks to you. How did you learn to do that?"

"First-aid training—I'm a small business owner and my boyfriend's a cop." Char winked at Brady. "He says it's always good to be prepared in case of an emergency."

"Well, then thanks to both of you for coming to my rescue." Melanie turned to Sharon with a wry smile. "I hope you don't mind if I skip the rest of the stuffed mushrooms."

Everyone laughed.

Conversation flowed easily over the perch and grilled vegetables. As we talked books and publishing, Brady chimed in to say he'd known back in second grade when I wrote the story of Wendy the Wriggly Worm I would wind up being an author someday.

"Wendy the Wriggly Worm?" Tavish grinned at me.

"Don't ask."

Sharon raised her glass. "Well, I for one would like to make a toast to things getting back to normal around here." She shook a playful finger at Tavish and me. "No more murders, thank you very much, except in the pages of one of your books."

"I'll drink to that," Tavish said.

"Me too." I raised my glass. "Here's to normalcy."

"Amen," Brady said. He clinked his glass with mine.

For dessert, Sharon served Danish layer cake from Andersen's Bakery. All talk ceased as we concentrated on the deliciousness that was three layers of moist yellow cake filled with ribbons of custard and raspberry jam and topped with buttercream icing.

"This cake is scrumptious," Tavish said. "A bit like Victoria sponge, only on steroids."

"Danish layer cake is a local staple that originated in Racine and made its way here," Sharon informed Tavish and Melanie. "We always have it on special occasions."

Brady licked frosting from his fork. "Andersen's cake is good, but it can't compare to Ted's."

"Ya got that right," Char said. "Teddie makes the best Danish layer cake around." She smacked her lips. "She made me one for my fortieth birthday. Yum."

Tavish grabbed my hand and beseeched me. "If I promise you the world, will you please make me this luscious cake for my birthday?"

"I might be able to do that. When's your birthday?"

"Wednesday," he and Melanie said in unison.

"Jinx." Tavish grinned at Melanie, and she blushed.

Sharon kicked me under the table, and Char slid me a discreet knowing gaze.

"Can you send this kind of cake through the mail?" Melanie asked. "We won't be here for Tavish's birthday. By then we'll be back home." She smiled at her boss. "I don't know about you, but I can't wait to get back to New York." She darted a glance at Sharon. "No offense. There is nothing like the city. Right, boss?"

"Right. There is no place like New York." Tavish shifted in his seat. "Actually, Mel, I'm not going back home quite yet," he said apologetically. "Sorry. I meant to tell you this afternoon and ask you to change my flight, but my Chicago business today took longer than expected and I didn't catch you before dinner." He laid his hand atop mine and gave me a warm smile. "I've decided to extend my stay."

Sharon and Char exchanged a satisfied smirk.

Tavish turned back to Melanie. "I know you're eager to get home to Brandon, though. I'm sure he's missing you and vice versa."

"Who's Brandon?" Sharon asked.

"Melanie's boyfriend," Tavish said. "He's a great bloke."

"Yes he is," Melanie said with a pride-of-ownership smile. "And I do miss him."

So . . . just your average garden-variety boss crush, not the crazy-stalker kind. Thank God. One Annabelle was more than enough.

"How long have you two been together?" I asked.

"Since high school. We started dating junior year."

"Sounds familiar." Char gave Brady's shoulder an affectionate bump. "So have you guys—"

A loud crash from the foyer interrupted her. "Hey, where is everybody?" a man's voice yelled.

"Excuse us." Sharon and Jim both jumped up to hurry out front. Before they reached the doorway, however, a well-dressed older couple, obviously under the influence, stumbled into the dining room and collided with the buffet, nearly tipping over a crystal vase of flowers. Quick on his feet, Jim grabbed Sharon's beloved Waterford before it fell.

"Whoops-a-daisy," the petite woman in purple said. "We could have used you in the other room. That poor plant wasn't as lucky."

"We'll pay for the damages," said the man, who was not much taller than her.

"I jus' love flowers, don't you?" The woman hiccupped. "'Scuse me. I think I may have had one too many old-fashioneds." She giggled.

Sharon led her to an easy chair. "Why don't you sit down?"

Jim approached the seersucker-suited man, who had opted to support himself against the wall. "May I help you?" he asked politely.

"Yep. We have reservations."

Jim frowned. "I'm afraid we don't have any reservations for tonight."

"Sure do. I booked it myself online—two nights for our anniversary. Jack and Rhonda Hellman."

"Ah, Mr. Hellman." Jim's frown was replaced by an apologetic expression. "Actually, your reservation is for tomorrow and the next night."

"What?" shrieked the woman. She glared at her husband. "Leave it to you to get the date wrong. I knew I should have done it." The couple traded colorful insults back and forth as we all watched transfixed from the peanut gallery.

Brady sighed, pushed back his chair, and walked up to the combative couple. He flashed his badge and introduced himself. "Now you two need to settle down." He steered the suddenly docile husband to the chair beside his wife. "I'm sure we can work this all out." Brady inclined his head to innkeeper Jim.

"Actually, we do have another room available," Jim said. "It's not the Lake Michigan suite you booked—I'm afraid that's occupied until tomorrow—but our Lake Superior room with a queen bed and claw-foot tub has a great garden view. You could stay there tonight and we can move you to your suite tomorrow. How does that sound?"

"Well . . . it's okay with me," Jack Hellman said, "but I don't know about the wife. She had her heart set on that king-size bed and spa tub."

"I'm not going in a Jacuzzi tonight," she said. "Not in my current condition. Tomorrow's soon enough."

"There, you see," Brady said, "it all worked out. Let's have some coffee before we call it a night." He nodded to Sharon, who brought over a pot of coffee and cups. Jim followed with milk and sugar.

They're going to need something to absorb all that booze and coffee, I thought. My eyes slid to the half a cake remaining on the table. "Char, can you get a couple plates and forks, please?" I cut two slices of cake.

"Any chance I might have another piece as well?" Tavish winked and held out his plate.

"Someone has a sweet tooth." I cut him a large slice, then carried two cake plates over to the inebriated couple. "Happy anniversary."

"Thank you," said the older woman.

"Yeah, thanks." Her husband crammed his mouth full of cake, spilling crumbs on his blue seersucker.

Mrs. Hellman took a daintier bite and murmured her appreciation. Her bleary eyes met mine and then widened. "Hey, I know you!"

Wow, two fans in one week. Time to ask for a bigger advance.

She zeroed in on my turquoise scarf. "You're that mystery author who's been strangling women with her scarves." Her hand fluttered to her crepey neck.

"That's right." Jack Hellman stared at me. "I *thought* you looked familiar. We read all about you on that blog thingamabob."

"What?" Brady burst out as I took an involuntary step back.

"Teddie hasn't strangled anyone!" Sharon glared at her guests.

I heard movement behind me.

"Well, that's what it said online," Mrs. Hellman said defensively.

"And you believe everything you read online?" Tavish drew himself up to stand shoulder to shoulder with me. He squeezed my hand. "Wherever did you read such rubbish?"

"Tavish Bentley!" she gasped, going all fluttery.

As the older woman stared speechless at the celebrity author, the efficient Melanie appeared beside her boss, iPad in hand. She read aloud. "'What small-town Wisconsin writer popular with blue-hairs and known for funky scarves and doggie-sleuth mysteries is killing women associated with a certain *New York Times* bestselling author and why? Research for her next book, maybe?'" She passed the iPad to Tavish, causing him to drop my hand and stare at the screen in his hands.

I peeked over Tavish's shoulder. I had seen the young, spiky-platinum-haired woman at the top of the page somewhere before.

Tavish's fingers tightened on the iPad. "That's Brittany Maloney, Kristi's friend. We'll sue her for libel."

"She was at your signing," I recalled. One of the Boobsey twins. Although I did not say that aloud.

Everyone started talking all at once. Char's voice cut through the clamor. "She threw out a wild accusation then too."

Glancing up from the iPad, I saw my best friend intent on her phone. Char read aloud. "'And why exactly hasn't local law enforcement arrested this killer yet? Could it be because she's tight with the sheriff?'"

Brady's jaw clenched. "I think it's time to give this Brittany Maloney a call . . ."

Chapter Twenty

Gracie pounced on my bed early the next morning, telling me it was time for her morning walk.

I groaned and buried my head under the pillow. It had been a late night. Nevertheless, my dog would not be deterred.

She swatted my shoulder with her paw.

I pulled the quilt up over me.

Gracie burrowed beneath the quilt and nudged me with her cold nose.

I ignored her.

She nudged me again.

I turned over on my side, presenting my back to her.

Finally, she took a flying leap, landed atop my pillow, and barked. *C'mon, Mom, I really gotta go.*

I yanked my head from beneath the pillow before Gracie smothered me, threw back the covers, and swung my feet over the side of the bed. "All right already. Hang on, Miss Impatient."

Gracie jumped off the bed and wagged her tail, before racing down the hall.

Yawning, I shuffled after her. She scratched at the back door in the kitchen. After I opened it, she shot into the backyard and promptly emptied her bladder. Years ago, I had installed a doggy door for Atticus so he could come and go as needed to answer the call of nature. It had worked for Gracie at first too. After she got skunked for the third time, however, and filled the entire house with the awful fragrance of eau de skunk—including my favorite quilt, which she rolled on in an attempt to rid herself of the smelly oil—I'd closed off the doggy door for good.

Coffee. Must have coffee. Only the coffee canister was empty. I grabbed the bag of French roast, poured the beans into the electronic grinder, closed the lid, and pushed the button.

"Ow!" I clapped my hands over my ears. *Make it stop. Make it stop.*

I hit the button again. "Shh," I whispered. "Not so loud."

There was nothing for it. I pulled down the instant coffee I kept on hand for emergencies, nuked a mug of water, then spooned a heaping teaspoon of the coffee crystals into the hot water, stirred, and took a big gulp.

Yech—should have gone with tea instead. I popped a couple of ibuprofens and rested my throbbing head on the table.

* * *

Last night after the Hellmans had sidled off to their room, the rest of us had stayed up late drinking wine and discussing the best course of action.

"That woman won't get away with slandering you like that, Teddie," Sharon said.

"Absolutely," Jim agreed. "Freedom of speech doesn't include slander. Everyone thinks they can say whatever they want online without any consequences. Wrong."

"Actually," Melanie corrected her B and B hosts, "slander relates to speech—the spoken word; libel is printed."

"Slander, libel, whatever you call it, she's not going to get away with it." Sharon's blue eyes snapped.

"No, she's not." Tavish pulled out his phone. "I'll ring my lawyer and he'll sort this out. That post will be removed immediately or we'll sue Brittany for defamation of character."

Once upon a time, I would have thrilled to have a knight in shining armor ride to my rescue, but that was back in my fairy-tale reading days. I'd left fairy tales behind decades ago.

"Thanks, Tavish"—I laid my hand on his arm—"but I can handle this. I'll contact my publisher first thing tomorrow, and their legal department will take care of it."

"Um, I don't think you want to wait till tomorrow," Char said. "Her followers have increased a thousandfold in the past few days."

"How do you know that?" Sharon asked.

"Because she humblebrags about it on her blog," Melanie interjected. She read aloud from her iPad, adopting a breathless, girly tone. "'Wow, y'all, thanks so much for following my little beauty blog! Just a few days ago, I had less than a thousand followers, but now I am up to 400,000 and climbing! You guys are the best!!!'" Melanie lifted her head, grimacing. "In addition to the overuse of exclamation points, she ends with two rows of smiley faces and kiss emojis."

I winced.

Tavish shook his head. "I don't believe this. The woman gives makeup tips on a blog—that's how she and Kristi met."

"Online?" Brady asked.

"Yes. They only recently met in person—during my book tour."

Char's eyes widened. "At *my* bookstore?"

"No, in Detroit."

I stared at him. "Wait. This Brittany came all the way here from Detroit? She must be a huge fan." *It's Annabelle Cooke all over again*, I thought.

"Actually," Tavish said, "I think she was more a fan of Kristi's. Kristi told me Brittany had a crush on her. She was trying to make me jealous, but I was actually relieved, thinking it might be a good distraction for her."

Brady lifted an eyebrow. "Distraction?"

"From our breakup—I ended our engagement that evening."

Brady exchanged a quick glance with Char. When Char saw that I had witnessed it, a rush of color stained her pale cheeks.

Looks like a talk with my best friend is in order.

"Well, I don't care if this Brittany had a crush on Kristi, you, or Wonder Woman," Brady said, "but she's making libelous statements about me and Ted, and that's going to stop right now." He pulled out his phone and left the room.

Sharon fanned herself. "Whoo, that Brady is sure something when he's riled up."

Jim peered at his wife over the top of his glasses. "I'm right here, dear."

She winked at him and blew him a kiss. "You sure are, baby."

*   *   *

Gracie bounded back inside and scampered over to me. *Okay, Mummy. I'm done in the backyard. Time for walkies now.*

"Mummy?" I stared at her. "Walkies? When did you start speaking with an English accent?"

Her tail thumped on the linoleum. I clipped on her leash and we headed outside, only to run smack into Mom.

"Theodora!" she said breathlessly. "You've been accused of murder by a platinum blonde with dark roots."

"I know—I saw it last night." I tilted my head. "Question is how do you know?"

"I follow a couple beauty blogs to keep up with makeup trends."

Of course you do.

Gracie strained at the leash. "Don't worry about it, Mom. The post has been removed—she was threatened with legal action."

"But it's already gone viral. It's spreading like wildfire on Facebook."

I knew I shouldn't have introduced my mother to social media. The woman is addicted to Facebook. At least she hasn't discovered Snapchat.

"Well, they say no publicity is bad publicity. Maybe it will increase my book sales." I was not being cavalier. I have just learned not to sweat the small stuff. After going through the cancer mill, I don't waste my time and energy on the negative these days.

She stared at me. "Aren't you worried about this ruining your professional reputation? What will your publisher think? Can they drop you because of this?"

"Of course not. It's just innuendo and rumor—no one loses their job because of a silly rumor that has no basis in truth." I pushed my hair behind my ears. "Besides, someone is already in custody, so once the real murderer is announced, all the people who believed that ridiculous rumor are going to feel awfully foolish."

Gracie released an impatient bark.

"And now I need to take this girl for her walk before she does a number right here."

Mom quickly retreated in her leopard-print flats.

As Gracie and I made our way through the neighborhood, I thought about my mother's concerns about my publisher. I love Baker Street Press, the small house that publishes my Kate and Kallie mysteries, and I have a great relationship with them, so I wasn't worried about their reaction to the insinuations against me. However, last night before bed I had emailed my editor, Jane Hall, to give her a heads-up. Might be a good idea to follow up with a phone call to reassure her things were under control, thanks to Brady's official warning to Brittany.

When we returned home half an hour later, I picked up my cell to call my editor and noticed I had a voice mail. "Hi, Teddie, it's Jane. I got your email—thanks. Can you give me a call back, please?"

I pressed the callback button, and Jane answered on the first ring. "Hello there, favorite author," she said. "Sounds like you've had a lot of excitement in Lake Potawatomi lately."

"Ya got that right." I kicked off my shoes and curled up on the couch. "It's been crazy. We've never had a murder in our entire history, and now to have two in one week—it's insane."

"I can imagine. And how are *you* doing?" I could hear the genuine concern in Jane's voice. Not only my editor, the sixty-something publishing veteran has also become my friend and mentor-slash-champion over the past few years. "Must have freaked you out that your signature scarves were used to strangle those women."

"Yeah, how creepy is that?" I shuddered.

"So bring me up to speed on where things stand now."

I filled her in on all that had happened, including having my scarves stolen and the likelihood that Annabelle Cooke had killed Tavish's ex Kristi and that her husband, Harley, had in turn killed Annabelle.

"So the husband's been charged in the murder of Tavish Bentley's stalker?"

"I don't think he's officially been charged yet. Our sheriff, Brady Wells, who is a good friend of mine, is waiting to hear back from the Illinois police. But it seems likely."

"That's good." The relief in Jane's voice was palpable.

"Why?"

"I don't want you to worry about it. A couple folks here just got a little nervous by the insinuations that beauty blogger made against you."

"Those *libelous* insinuations? She removed them immediately when confronted by the sheriff and Tavish's lawyer last night."

"Good. Good to hear."

There was an awkward pause. A pause I could not define. Was Jane upset that I hadn't called her last night? "I let you know about this as soon as I saw the blog—to keep Baker Street in the loop. I assumed legal would want to send the blogger a cease-and-desist letter or something."

"Uh-huh." Another awkward pause.

My heart sank. "Jane . . ." I swallowed hard. "You don't think I killed those women, do you?"

"No! You wouldn't hurt a fly. I told everyone here that. The only murder Theodora St. John would ever commit, I said, would be between the pages of a book." She chuckled.

I didn't feel like laughing. "Are you saying the powers that be at Baker Street actually gave a moment's credence to those ludicrous rumors that woman started?"

"No-o-o-o, not exactly." Jane expelled a heavy sigh. "It's just a different publishing climate today. Everyone's running scared and trying to protect themselves against bad author behavior, whether it's sexual harassment charges or fallout from things authors have said online or in public venues— that's why so many publishers are putting morality clauses in their book contracts these days."

Bad author behavior? "But I haven't done anything wrong—I've never even missed a deadline." And I was definitely not going to start now. In that moment, I determined to turn in *A Dash of Death* early.

"I know. That's what I told them. Quite forcefully, in fact," she said. "Trust me. I'm on your side. They're just a little concerned and reminded me of our morality clause, which says a book contract will be canceled in the instance of 'sustained, widespread public condemnation of the author.'" Jane sighed again. "The problem is that even though that blogger took down the post, thousands of people have since shared the rumor she started on Facebook and Twitter."

"It's not true, though." My stomach clenched. *I don't believe this is happening.*

Sensing my distress, Gracie jumped up beside me and slipped her cold nose and then the rest of her face beneath my hand. On autopilot, I stroked her head. "Are you telling me you're going to cancel my contract based on one person's innuendo and lies?"

"Absolutely not," Jane said. "I have complete faith in you. I am simply the reluctant messenger. The legal department— who will be sending you an email—wanted me to warn you that, in the case of libel, the burden of proof is, unfortunately, on you. You have to prove that the statements against you are false, but the husband being charged for the crime will take care of that, so don't worry. It will all work out. This is just a little blip. It will all get sorted." I heard a rustle followed by chewing and knew Jane had popped one of the Hershey's Kisses she always keeps in a bowl on her desk into her mouth. "Now let's talk about something more pleasant. Like that gorgeous Tavish Bentley. What's he like in the flesh?"

"He's great. Very nice and down-to-earth."

"Do I detect more than a professional appreciation?" Jane teased.

Normally I would have liked to dish with my editor and friend about the latest goings-on in my life, especially since the latest involved my budding romance—a first since Jane and I had been working together, and something I knew she would be thrilled to hear—but right now I had other things on my mind.

Like saving my job.

We chatted for a few more minutes and then I made an excuse to get off the phone, saying Gracie needed a walk. Upon hearing the w-word, Gracie sat up eagerly and wagged her tail.

"Sorry, Gracie-girl," I said, absently ruffling her fur after hanging up, "Mommy told a lie. Besides, we just came back from our circuit around the neighborhood." I headed to the kitchen with my dog on my heels and let her out into the backyard. Then I finished grinding the coffee beans, made myself a cup of French roast, and sat down at the kitchen table, thinking about what Jane had said. It was the last thing I had expected. I may not sweat the small stuff these days or expend energy on the negative, but this revelation from my publisher was far from small stuff. It was my profession. My passion. My dream. It had taken cancer to push me into finally pursuing that passion. Now that I was living my dream, I was not going to let anyone destroy it.

Chapter
Twenty-One

*H*ave *you heard anything from the Illinois cops yet about Harley Cooke?* I texted Brady.

Jane had said I needed to prove that the libelous statements made against me were false, and confirmation that Harley had killed Annabelle was all the proof I needed. While I waited to hear back from Brady, I decided to make a batch of peanut-butter blossoms. The combination of chocolate and peanut butter always soothes the savage breast. Although my breasts might have left the building, my sweet tooth remained.

My phone rang just as I finished putting the first batch in the oven. I set the timer, picked up the phone, and saw my Musketeer pal's name on the screen. "Hi, Sharon, what's up?"

"Do you have a few minutes?" she asked. "I never got to finish filling you in on my conversation with Melanie."

"That's right. You said she told you something about Tavish's ex-wife?"

"You might want to sit down for this one," Sharon said. "It's pretty juicy."

I grabbed a cup of coffee and pulled out a kitchen chair. "Okay, I'm all ears."

"Melanie said that Tavish's ex-wife Lucinda and Kristi had a knock-down, drag-out fight a couple months ago," Sharon said, breathlessly. "Apparently this Lucinda showed up drunk at Tavish's beach house one day when Melanie was there and started yelling at Kristi and telling her to get out of *her* house. Said she had found the house for Tavish, and it was *her* house and *her* husband, so Kristi needed to take her things and clear out then and there."

"Wow. What did Tavish do?"

"He wasn't home. It was just the three women—Kristi, Lucinda, and Melanie."

"What happened?"

"Apparently, Lucinda, the ex-wife, started yanking pictures off the walls and throwing them on the ground."

"Seriously?"

"I know, right?" Sharon said. "It gets even better. Kristi screamed at Lucinda and slapped her in the face, and then the two of them had the catfight to end all catfights, Melanie said, complete with hair pulling, kicking, and biting."

"Sounds like one of those not-so-real housewives shows. How did it end?"

"Melanie said she had to break it up and pull them off each other. She received a random punch in the face in the process, which left her with broken glasses and a bruised cheek," said.

"Ouch. Poor Melanie."

"I know. She finally calmed the two women down and called an Uber for the ex-wife, since she was in no condition to drive. Here's the clincher, though." Sharon paused for dramatic effect. "As Lucinda was leaving, she yelled at Kristi to watch her back. Said she was going to *get her* if it was the last thing she did."

"Whoa."

"Are you thinking what I'm thinking?" Sharon's voice squeaked the way it did whenever she got excited.

"You mean that maybe we got it all wrong and Annabelle didn't kill Kristi; Lucinda, Tavish's ex-wife, did?"

"Exactly. I mean, there's no proof Annabelle killed Kristi."

"You're right," I said slowly. "Only supposition." I had suspected, or rather assumed, that obsessive stalker Annabelle had strangled Kristi because she was jealous of her relationship with Tavish and wanted her out of the way. When Annabelle attacked me in front of Andersen's and warned me to stay away from Tavish because she had ownership rights, that had only sealed the deal for me. However, as far as anyone knew, Annabelle had never threatened *Kristi* outright. Unlike Lucinda, who'd told her she was going to "get her" if it was the last thing she did. And speaking of ownership rights, who would be more likely to believe they had *ownership* of Tavish Bentley than the woman who had married him?

The timer dinged. "Oops. Sorry, Sharon. I need to take the cookies out of the oven. We'll talk later." I returned my focus to my baking.

Two hours later, a light rap sounded on my back door. Char smiled and held up a white paper bag. "I picked up the hard rolls from Andersen's for the brats," she said, pronouncing it "brahtz" like every Dane.

"Thanks." Wanting to give Tavish a classic Wisconsin summer lunch—bratwurst, potato salad, baked beans, and watermelon—I had invited Char and Brady to join us as well. Brady loves his brats. He slathers them with mustard, ketchup, pickles, and onions, while Char and I prefer a more classic take—bratwurst and mustard.

As Char set the table, I sliced the watermelon. "So," I said casually, "you want to tell me the meaning of that look between you and Brady last night?"

"What look?" She affected an absorbed interest in lining up the water glasses with the knives.

"The one you exchanged when Tavish mentioned ending his engagement with Kristi."

"Oh, *that* look." She sighed and straightened her shoulders before turning around to face me. "Okay, you may not want to hear this, best friend, but I love you, so I'll tell it to you straight. Brady, who also loves you, is concerned that things are moving too fast between you and Tavish. His fiancée—ex-fiancée," she amended, "was killed less than a week ago, and it was only a couple weeks before then that they broke up. That's not a lot of time to get over a relationship before jumping right into another one, don't you think? Love doesn't end that quickly." She added, gently, "Are you sure Tavish isn't rebounding with you after the loss of Kristi?"

I started to respond, but Char held up her hand.

"And, by the way, those words come straight from Brady's mouth, not mine. You know he's always considered himself your older brother," she said. "He's not trying to butt into your business—although it sure seems like it." The corners of her mouth quirked. "He just doesn't want you to get hurt."

"And what about you?"

"I don't want you to get hurt either."

"Well, neither do I, so we're all on the same page," I said. "What you and Brady don't know is that Tavish wasn't in love with Kristi, he was just infatuated. Initially. Once he got to truly know her, however, the infatuation quickly wore off, hence the broken engagement."

Char scrunched up her forehead. "So he proposed to someone he wasn't in love with?"

I expelled a sigh. "No, to someone he was infatuated with. Tavish said the moment after he proposed, he realized it was a mistake." I fixed my eyes on her. "Haven't you ever made a mistake in the heat of the moment?"

"Me?" Char pretended mock offense. "Never." Then she spotted the see-through plastic container of cookies on the counter and did her usual Pavlovian response—like the dog in *Up* whenever anyone yells, "Squirrel!" She advanced to the counter in two long strides. "Ooh, are those peanut-butter blossoms?"

"Yep."

"Are you saving them for dessert?"

"Nope. We're having homemade banana-cream pie for dessert."

Char opened the container and grabbed a couple of cookies. As she bit into the first one, she moaned. "This is my favorite cookie of yours."

"I thought my lemon sugar cookies were your favorite."

"Well, yeah, among sugar cookies, but in the peanut-butter-and-chocolate category, this is the winner, hands down."

Gracie barked and ran to the back screen door, where I saw Tavish holding a grocery bag and Brady brandishing a six-pack of Pabst Blue Ribbon.

"We come bearing gifts," Brady said as they entered. Earlier he had texted that he still hadn't heard back from the Illinois police on the status of Annabelle's husband, but he'd send them an email following up.

"You didn't need to bring beer," I told him. "I already have some in the fridge."

"Ah, but is it Pabst?"

"Is the Pope Catholic? After all this time, I think I know your beer of choice, my friend."

"Well, you can never have too much beer." He winked and stuck the six-pack in the fridge alongside the other Pabst.

Tavish presented me with a gorgeous bouquet of roses and Gerbera daisies. "These are for you," he said shyly.

Char sighed. "Ah, I remember those romantic days. Seems like years ago." She inclined her head to her boyfriend. "Oh, wait, that's because it was years ago."

Brady popped open a beer and sat down. "I get you flowers every year on Valentine's Day and your birthday."

"Yep, you're as regular as Ex-Lax." Char ruffled Brady's hair and planted a kiss on the top of his head. "But I love you even if romance isn't your first language."

That's when it clicked that my best friend didn't share Brady's concern that things with Tavish might be moving too fast. She and Sharon had been trying to find me Mr. Right—or at least Mr. Right Now—for ages, and now that a man with romantic potential had shown up, Char didn't want to jinx it. Bless her.

Tavish removed two bags of chips from the grocery bag—Lay's Classic and salt-and-vinegar. "Brady said bratwurst requires potato chips, so I brought a couple selections. Although"—he jerked his head toward my childhood pal—"apparently salt-and-vinegar isn't the chip—or as we call it, crisp—of choice here, so I wanted to add my English contribution to the meal."

"Thanks," I said. "And ignore Brady; he's just a creature of habit." I added in a whisper, "And a little OCD to boot."

"I heard that," Brady said.

"I meant for you to hear."

As Tavish finished his first brat—minus onions—and was reaching for a second, he mentioned that Melanie had returned to New York earlier today. "I know she was quite eager to get back to Brandon," he said. "They're a great couple of kids. Brandon's a plumber and he's fixed many a clogged drain for me, which is lucky, because I'm rubbish at that sort of thing." He grinned. "Oh, and I saw the Hellmans at breakfast this morning. They apologized for their behavior last night, but I told them I was actually glad they'd drawn our attention to what Brittany was blogging or we'd not have known and been able to put an immediate stop to it." He delivered a warm smile to me that, before last night, would have given me butterflies in my stomach. Today, though, the knots in my stomach from Jane's phone call had strangled the butterflies.

I returned Tavish's smile with a feeble one of my own. I had decided not to say anything about what Jane had revealed about Baker Street's morality clause and the burden of proof against libelous innuendo resting with me. If everything went as I hoped, it would all soon be a nonissue. No need to ruin our lunch.

"And how's the job going, Sheriff?" I asked. "Any exciting crimes in Lake Potawatomi lately?"

"No. Thank God." Brady scarfed down the rest of his potato salad and took a swig of his Pabst. "Augie issued one parking ticket and one jaywalking ticket in the past couple days and that was it."

"Tell her who received the jaywalking ticket, though, honey," Char urged with a wicked gleam.

"Inappropriate," Brady said.

"Oh come on, it's a matter of public record. All right, I'll tell her." Char shot me a snarky grin. "Wilma Sorensen. She was cutting across the street at a clip to share the latest gossip with one of her blue-haired friends when Bea Andersen, who was turning the corner, had to brake hard to avoid hitting her. Well, Wilma screeched and carried on at Bea for nearly hitting her—threatened to sue, yada yada—but Augie saw the whole thing and wrote Wilma a ticket on the spot for jaywalking."

"So there's justice in the world after all," I said.

Tavish covered my hand with his. "Right always wins."

I hope so.

He stroked the back of my hand. "Since I'm extending my stay in Wisconsin, I would love to see more of your beautiful state. Would you be my tour guide, Ms. St. John?" he asked flirtatiously.

"Ooh, you should take him up to Door County," Char said. "It's gorgeous up there. Brady and I stayed at this great B and B out in the country that I know you'd love." She sent her boyfriend a seductive glance. "Remember, babe? Yummy breakfasts and this wonderful four-poster bed with eight-hun-dred-thread-count sheets and feather pillows."

Brady frowned at her, and I kicked Char under the table. She knew Tavish and I hadn't been intimate yet, and now here she was pushing us to stay overnight at a romantic B and B?

Tavish sensed my hesitation and held my eyes with his. "That sounds lovely, but it doesn't have to be an overnight trip. Anywhere you would like to go is fine with me. I'll leave that to you, since you're the native and I'm the stranger in a strange land."

"Good book," Brady said, changing the subject. "One of my favorites."

"Of course it is," Char said, wrinkling her nose. "It's sci-fi. What is it with men and sci-fi? I don't get it."

"And I don't get the Jane Austen fascination," Brady said. "Way too much talking and not enough action. Give me sci-fi and suspense any day. Right, Tavish?"

"Actually," Tavish said, with an apologetic shrug in Brady's direction, "I quite like Jane Austen, but then I'm English and it's in my DNA. Plus, she's brilliant with dialogue." He fas-tened his eyes on mine and quoted, "'It is not time or oppor-tunity that is to determine intimacy; it is disposition alone. Seven years would be insufficient to make some people acquainted with each other, and seven days are more than enough for others.'"

Take me, I'm yours, I longed to say. I settled for "Remind me. Is that *Sense and Sensibility* or *Pride and Prejudice?*"

"*Sense and Sensibility.*"

"That's what I thought."

Char fanned her face. "Now that's what I'm talkin' about."

Brady scowled.

I tore my eyes away from Tavish as I cleared the plates and brought the pie to the table. If we had been alone, I would have grabbed my Jane Austen aficionado in a lip lock, but I had company and there was my big brother to consider. We'd invited Sharon and Jim to join us, but they had a foursome checking in early and couldn't leave the B and B. I handed Brady a huge wedge of banana-cream. "Like Char, I'm not a big sci-fi fan either, but I loved *The Time Machine.*"

Tavish picked up my cue. "That's one of my favorites," he said, "that and Stephen King's *The Stand.*"

Brady nodded approvingly. "*The Stand* is killer."

"We appear to have gotten a bit sidetracked, however." Tavish forked up a mouthful of pie. "Teddie, we were talking about you showing me more of Wisconsin."

I would like to show you a lot more than that, especially after that Sense and Sensibility *quote. Now, however, I need to prove myself to my publisher and save my career.*

"I would love to be your tour guide," I said, "but I really can't take time off right now because of my deadline." Not with Baker Street's concerns of "bad author behavior" hanging over my head.

"I thought your book wasn't due for a few more weeks yet." Char licked the last trace of whipped cream from her fork.

That's what I get for being an open book and telling everyone everything. Except right now, I can't tell them what's going on with my publisher. I need to handle this on my own.

Tavish tipped his head to one side, a quizzical expression on his face. Was that a flicker of hurt I saw in his gorgeous hazel eyes? "I thought you were well on track to meet your deadline," he said. "Would a day or two make much difference? I always find when I'm nearing the end of the book that a couple days away gives me fresh eyes and renewed energy and focus for that final push."

Me too, I wanted to say. *Trust me, I would like nothing more than a romantic getaway with you.* My earlier hesitation about taking that next, intimate step had disappeared in the face of Tavish's *Sense and Sensibility* declaration.

"I—"

Brady's phone buzzed, saving me. "Sorry," he said, pulling his cell out of his pocket.

Char rolled her eyes. "Welcome to my world."

Brady read the text. When he finished, his face was grim.

"What's wrong?" Char and I said in unison.

"That was from the Calumet City chief of police. They released Harley Cooke. He has an ironclad alibi for the night his wife was killed. He was in a motel with his girlfriend—his pregnant girlfriend."

My stomach plummeted. "So that means Annabelle's murderer is still running around loose."

Chapter Twenty-Two

Lunch broke up right after that. Now that the Calumet City police were out of the picture, Brady jumped back into full investigative mode and so did I, knowing my career hung in the balance.

After Char and Brady departed, Tavish settled back in his chair and raked his hand through his hair. "It appears we're back to square one. With Annabelle's husband no longer a suspect, I can't begin to imagine who might have killed her."

"Me either. I don't have a clue." *But I'd better get one soon, before my publisher cancels my contract.*

I considered what Sharon had revealed to me over the phone earlier. "Tavish," I said slowly, "do you think there's a chance your ex-wife might have killed Annabelle?"

"Lucinda?" He gave me an incredulous look. "Why in the world would she do that?"

"I don't know." I shook my head, trying to figure it out. "I can't think of a reason that makes sense for Lucinda to kill your stalker. Unlike Kristi."

"Kristi?" Tavish stared at me. "Wait. Are you saying you think Lucinda, *not* Annabelle, might have killed Kristi? Lucinda lives in LA."

"So does Tom Rogers. That didn't stop him from coming out to Wisconsin."

Tavish waved his hand dismissively. "Tom followed Kristi everywhere. He was obsessed with her."

"Like Annabelle and Lucinda were obsessed with you."

"Annabelle was a stalker," Tavish said softly. "Lucinda is not." He tilted his head at me and knitted his brow. "Where is this all coming from, Teddie? Whatever made you bring up Lucinda?"

"I heard about the catfight between her and Kristi when Lucinda showed up at your house. *Her* house, she called it. *Her* husband." I placed my hand on Tavish's arm and fixed him with a steady gaze. "Lucinda threatened Kristi and told her to watch her back."

"I know," he said. "Melanie told me. So did Kristi." Then Tavish did something odd. He grinned. "Lucinda is quite territorial, particularly when it comes to real estate, and particularly when she's been drinking. She found my beach house and fell in love with it. Actually," he said ruefully, "I think she loved the beach house more than she did me. She hated losing it in the divorce. I bought her out, and she's been trying to get that house back ever since." He reached down to pet Gracie, who had sidled over to him. "Periodically, Lucinda would call or text me when she'd been drinking and say, 'You'd better watch your back, Bentley. I'm going to get it if it's the last thing I do.'"

It. Get *it*. She meant the house. Not Kristi. Melanie had apparently misunderstood what Lucinda said, or perhaps Sharon had misunderstood Melanie. Either way, it had gotten lost in translation.

"Lucinda didn't kill Kristi, and she certainly didn't kill Annabelle," Tavish said. "She had no reason to do so. Here, I'll show you." He pulled out his phone and scrolled through his texts. "Here it is." Tavish passed me his phone.

The photo showed a beaming Lucinda in a gauzy cover-up over a tiny black bikini on a sandy beach. Tavish's ex-wife was not alone. A handsome silver-haired man with ultrawhite teeth gleaming in a bronzed face encircled Lucinda from behind with his glistening, silver-haired arms.

"Who's that?" I asked. "Boyfriend?"

"Husband-to-be," Tavish said. "They're getting married next month."

"Oh."

"Notice what's behind them?"

I expanded the picture. A massive three-story shimmering cube of steel and glass facing the ocean filled the screen.

Not my style at all. Way too modern.

Yeah, but the view was killer. What do they say in real estate? Location, location, location.

"Read the text," Tavish said.

You can keep your beach house, Tav. I found a better one. Hasta la vista, baby.

"So . . . not Lucinda." *Guess I had better turn in my deerstalker hat.*

"Right," Tavish said. "I think your initial instincts were correct. I think Annabelle killed Kristi." He rubbed the back of Gracie's head and sighed. "Unfortunately, now that her husband has been cleared, we still don't have a clue who killed Annabelle."

"Nope." Then I remembered. I jumped up, opened the junk drawer in my kitchen, and began searching through it.

"What are you doing?"

"Trying to find the notebook I used when I interviewed Annabelle's family." I shoved aside the latest grocery store ads and takeout menus. "Ah, here it is." I pulled out the skinny notebook and began flipping through it, searching for the right page. "Tavish, did you ever meet any of Annabelle's friends or family at your signings?"

He thought for a moment. "Not that I recall. I think she was always on her own."

I consulted my notes. "Turns out Harley Cooke's younger sister is the one who first loved your books. She took her sister-in-law Annabelle along to your Chicago book signing two years ago. That was the first time Annabelle met you." I raised my head. "Does the name Jewel ring a bell?"

"Sorry." He shook his head. "I meet so many people at signings, they all start to run together after a while."

"Unless," I said, "they do something that makes them stand out from the crowd."

"Like showing up at every signing wearing bright pink and proceeding to make a spectacle of themselves."

"Exactly." I tapped my fingers on the notebook. "So we need to find out what kind of person this Jewel is and how she felt about her sister-in-law bulldozing in and co-opting her favorite author." I expelled a sigh. "This may require a return trip to Calumet City and another meeting with Annabelle's husband." I shuddered, remembering the odious Harley.

"That seems a bit farfetched," Tavish said. "Don't you think? Just because Annabelle's sister-in-law also liked my books, that would be no reason to kill her for turning into my biggest fan and a crazy stalker."

"You may be right." I puffed out another sigh. "I'm just trying to figure this out. I was sure Harley killed his wife—especially after meeting him. He certainly didn't shed any tears over Annabelle's demise. But then again, neither did her parents." *Poor, unloved Annabelle. Who would have wanted to kill her? And with my scarf, no less?* It didn't make sense. And it sure didn't look good for me. "But if nothing else, maybe Jewel can tell us more about Annabelle than Harley and the Grubbs did." I really needed to figure this out to save my career.

"I suppose, rather than a Wisconsin getaway, we could take a quick Illinois getaway instead." Tavish inclined his head toward me. "If you can afford the time away."

"I *knew* I hurt your feelings." I laid my hand on his arm. "I'm sorry. I would really love to go away with you for a couple days, but I heard from my—"

My phone blared out Journey's "Don't Stop Believin'." "Sorry," I said, "that's Brady. I should probably get it in case he has some news."

Tavish nodded.

"Hey, Brady, what's up?"

"Is Tavish still there with you?"

"Yep. He's right here."

Brady grunted. "Can you ask him to please check his phone? I've been trying to reach him."

"Okay. Anything wrong?"

"Just have him get back to me, Ted," he said curtly. "Gotta go." Brady hung up.

I stared at the phone in my hand.

"What was that all about?" Tavish asked.

"I don't know," I said slowly. "Brady said he's been trying to reach you. Asked you to check your phone."

"Oh, bugger. I set it on mute when I arrived so it wouldn't interrupt our meal." He pulled his phone from his pocket. "I neglected to turn it back on afterwards." Tavish scrolled through his texts. His face closed off as he tapped out a reply. "Right. I need to go to the sheriff's office straightaway."

"How come?"

"Brady wants to continue the questioning he started before Harley Cooke was arrested."

* * *

Gracie nosed my hand. *Where'd he go, Mom? Is he coming back? I like him.*

"I like him too, Gracie-girl." I stroked her fur absently as I considered Brady's summons. Of course he would call Tavish back in for questioning. With Harley cleared for Annabelle's murder, there weren't many other suspects in the running. Besides Tavish and me, that is, and we were both innocent. I knew that. Now I just had to prove it. For both our sakes.

The place to start was Jewel, Annabelle's sister-in-law. Although the easiest way to locate her would be through her brother Harley, I would prefer never to have to interact with that Neanderthal again. Instead, I did a search on my laptop for Jewel Cooke in Calumet City. Nada. Three Jewels popped up, but their last names were Lane, Johnson, and Murphy. I searched the greater Chicago area. Twenty-one Jewels surfaced, but none with the last name Cooke.

Use the little gray cells, my inner Poirot suggested. *She doesn't have to have the same last name as her brother.*

Doh. I pulled out the burner phone I use for all my research—I value my privacy and another author friend suggested it as a reader buffer—and called Jewel Johnson first.

"Hello?" a thin voice quavered on the other end of the line.

"Hi, is this Jewel Johnson?"

"Ye-e-es, but I'm not buying anything from telemarketers anymore. My son made me promise."

Son? Sounds too old to be Harley's sister, but in for a penny, in for a pound.

"No problem," I said quickly. "I'm not selling anything. Just doing a brief survey for our publishing company to find out the top authors people are reading today. May I ask who your favorite author is, please?"

"Well, I don't read as much as I used to—my eyes aren't so good anymore—but I always liked that lady who wrote those country romances. The ones with girls in bonnets on the front. Those were some sweet stories. You know the ones I mean?"

Unfortunately. After reading the single Amish fiction title Bea Andersen had pressed on me a few years ago, I'd had to down two cups of strong black coffee to cut the sugar.

The next Jewel preferred vampire novels. The sparkly kind.

Two down, one to go. I tapped in Jewel Murphy's number. "Hi," I blurted out when she picked up. "I'm not a robocall or telemarketer. I'm surveying readers to find out their favorite authors for a list our publishing house is compiling."

"That's cool," the youngish voice replied. "Go for it. I'm at work and bored."

Since this was the final Jewel in Annabelle's hometown, I crossed my fingers she would be Harley's sister. I did not relish spending my limited time calling all twenty-one Jewels in and around Chicago—not with needing to finish up *A Dash of Death*. To be sure, however, I added a couple more questions to the mix. "Great. For survey purposes, would you mind telling me your age, profession, and how many are in your household?"

"Twenty-seven," she said. "I work in a comic book shop, and usually my *household* is just me and my cat—which is how I like it—but recently my stupid brother and his pregnant girl-friend moved in."

Yes! I did an internal fist pump.

"That doesn't sound like much fun."

"Tell me about it." I could hear her slurping a drink. "The idiot got kicked out of his old place and they didn't have any-where else to go, so baby sister had to step up. Like always," she muttered, sotto voce. "I told them they could stay a month, tops, but then they're outa here."

"What's that old saying," I said, "'Guests, like fish, begin to smell after three days'?"

Jewel snorted. "That's a good one. I'll have to remember that—'specially if Harley's girlfriend keeps puking in my bathroom every morning and not cleaning up after herself."

My stomach roiled. "That's gross. Maybe her baby daddy should step up to the plate."

"Right? That's what I told him, but my brother's from another generation and totally sexist, so that's not happening." She slurped more of her drink. "So, what'd you wanna ask me about books?"

"Sorry, got sidetracked. Who would you say are your top three favorite authors?"

"James Patterson, Stieg Larsson, and Harlan Coben," she rattled off.

"Ah, you like suspense—is that your preferred genre?"

"For sure. I like stories with action and excitement." She released a sound that came off as a cross between a snort and a grunt. "The only excitement I'm going to get in this backwater burg."

"What about Tavish Bentley? His stories have plenty of action and excitement."

"Nah." Her voice went flat. "I used to read him, but not anymore."

"Why's that?"

"I lost interest and moved on."

"Any particular reason?"

Silence.

Oops, may have overplayed your hand.

"Who did you say you were again?" Jewel Murphy asked.

"My name's Olivia. I'm with a small publishing house that's expanding. We're doing market research to find out what are the most popular genres, and authors, among readers."

"Is Tavish Bentley one of your authors?" she asked. I heard the suspicion in her voice. "You seem really interested in him."

"Oh no, goodness me." I tinkled out a fake laugh. "He's much too big for our little house. If one of our editors could snag him, though, that would be quite a coup—to get an author of his caliber. He's got quite a following."

"I guess. I don't really pay attention."

"His newest book, *Her Blood Weeps*, is flying off the shelves and has already made it onto the *New York Times* best-seller list."

"Sounds like you're a big fan."

"Not as big as that lady who stalked him—the one who was recently killed." I adopted an innocent tone. "Annabelle Cooke? Isn't she from your town?"

"That does it," Jewel yelled. "Annabelle, Annabelle, Annabelle! I'm sick of hearing her name. I've got nothing to say about my dead stalker sister-in-law, and you damn reporters need to leave me the hell alone!" She hung up.

Mission more than accomplished. I'd found Harley's younger sister, who clearly had issues with both her brother and Annabelle. I also knew she worked in a comics shop. There couldn't be too many of those in Calumet City. Once I pinpointed the location, I could pay her a visit—in disguise, of course—and try to find out if she might be a likely murder suspect. This time, however, I would take along one of the Musketeers for backup.

The burner phone in my hand rang, and the number I had just called flashed on the screen. I let it go to voice mail. The voicemail without my name. All Jewel Murphy would hear as she listened to the recorded message would be a bland recording of the burner phone number in my voice.

Maybe that would ease her suspicions and give me a reprieve when I followed up in person. I would have to adopt a different persona, however. What that would be, I had no idea yet, but since lying was not my first language, probably best not to make it too farfetched or I would trip myself up. I tucked the burner phone away and picked up my cell to text Char. That's when I saw the old text she had sent the last time I went undercover to Calumet City, a text I'd overlooked in all the excitement of that day. *Guess what? I found someone who has it in for Tavish. Call me.*

Someone who had it in for Tavish? Enough to set him up to take a fall for murder? Now we were getting somewhere. I puffed out a sigh of relief. With two possible suspects to check out, it wouldn't be long before we found the real murderer and cleared Tavish's name and mine.

I texted Char. *You busy?*

Char: *Nope. The shop's dead at the moment.*
Me: *I'll be right over. I need your help.*

* * *

"Who has it in for Tavish?" I asked as I strode into the Corner Bookstore ten minutes later.

"Say what?" Char's ponytailed head snapped up from the book she was reading behind the counter.

"You were going to talk to some of your librarian friends and dig into Tavish's past to see if anyone might have a grudge against him? You texted you'd found someone."

"Oh yeah. I forgot about that after his stalker's husband got picked up."

I plopped down onto the stool opposite her. "Well, now that Annabelle's husband has been released, your boyfriend has returned to Tavish as his number-one suspect. I need to figure out who the real murderer is, so give me the scoop on this guy." I tucked a stray curl behind my ear. "Or girl?"

"Guy." Char set down her book, picked up her iPad, and began swiping the screen. "He's an author—well, a wannabe author. He accused Tavish of plagiarism after his third novel, *Blood-Soaked Flowers*, hit the best seller list." She handed me her iPad.

A younger Tavish with longer hair smiled out at me under the newspaper headline "Bestselling Author Found Innocent of Plagiarism." Scanning the news article from several years ago, I learned that a middle-aged Indiana man had accused Tavish of stealing his novel idea. Ronald Simms claimed that he had sent his manuscript, *Petals Dripping With Blood*— terrible title—to Tavish's agent, William Charles, three years before *Blood-Soaked Flowers* was released. Simms said the agent rejected his novel, but then took Simms's idea and developed it with his younger, more marketable client, Tavish Bentley, the new golden boy of publishing.

The article quoted William Charles of the Charles Agency saying that his client, Tavish Bentley, had been thoroughly vindicated. "Tavish is a talented writer and compelling story-teller," Charles said. "I'm not surprised someone else tried to ride the coattails of his success. Frustrated wannabes seem to come out of the woodwork whenever a new author makes it big."

I continued reading. The court had ruled that although the titles were similar and both books included the death of a woman in a garden, that was where the similarities ended. There were no verbatim passages, comparable characters, or even similar plot lines. Simms's book was a horror story about a serial killer who left dripping bloody roses atop his myriad female victims, while Tavish's tale of suspense involved an assassin who wound up having to kill a woman in a garden as collateral damage after she saw him kill his intended political target.

I swiped the screen. Another photo appeared—this one of a mousy middle-aged man with a bad sandy-haired comb-over in thick, black-rimmed glasses, scowling at the camera. The caption identified him as Ronald Simms, author of *Petals Dripping With Blood*. Simms was a poor loser. He responded to the judge's ruling by yelling, "I should have known. The rich always win. A poor guy like me didn't stand a chance. Forget David beating Goliath. That's just a fairy tale."

Tavish, on the other hand, against his agent's advice, had declined to seek financial recompense from Simms, who was having a hard time making ends meet. Instead, he simply got a cease-and-desist order against the Indiana author.

I passed the iPad back to Char. "Okay, so this Ronald lost his plagiarism suit, but that was several years ago and he didn't make any vindictive threats or anything."

"Not in print," Char said, "but Zoey, my librarian friend in Gary, said he's been nursing a grudge against Tavish ever since. Ronald Simms self-published a couple books—really bad ones, she says—and has spoken at local library author events where he repeatedly complains that *he* should have become the famous best-selling author, not Tavish Bentley. He claims the only reason Tavish has the success he does is because he stole his idea and resembles Colin Firth."

"Tavish does look a little like Colin Firth," I admitted, "but that's not why he's a best-selling author. Tavish is a wonderful writer. This just sounds like typical sour grapes from a jealous wannabe."

"Except when he's drunk," Char said. "Then Ronald Simms' gripes escalate into revenge fantasies and muttered comments like, 'Tavish Bentley will get his one of these days. I'll make sure of that.'"

My pulse quickened. "Is that right?"

Char pulled out a Red Vine from the stash she kept beneath the counter. "Zoey said that a couple weeks ago when Simms was in the library and learned that Tavish's latest novel had made it onto the *New York Times* best seller list, he lost it. She said his face got all red and a vein in his forehead popped out. He yelled that he was going to make Tavish Bentley pay and when he was finished Tavish wouldn't know what hit him. Then he stormed out."

"Now it's getting interesting."

"You haven't heard anything yet." Char's eyes gleamed behind her reading glasses. "Zoey has a friend who works with Ronald. She said he called in sick earlier this week, and when he returned Friday, he seemed smug and self-satisfied. Later, when people were talking about Kristi's death, followed shortly thereafter by Annabelle's murder and speculating about Tavish, Zoey said Ron Simms was positively gleeful and said, 'It took a while, but he finally got his.'"

Could it be? Did we have a viable suspect at last? "Wait a minute, let me think," I said, trying to put it all together. I ran through the chronology aloud. "Kristi was killed on Monday, Annabelle was murdered late Thursday or early Friday morning, and this Ronald was out sick until Friday morning?"

Char nodded.

"Are you thinking what I'm thinking?"

"I don't know." Her brow puckered above her glasses. "Am I?"

"Ronald Simms lives in Gary, Indiana," I asked. "Right?"

"Yep. He's a native son, born and raised. He's a Realtor—not a very good one, according to Zoey—and the treasurer of the chamber of commerce."

I tried to picture a map of the Midwest in my head. "My geography's a little rusty. Where exactly is Gary again?"

"Northern Indiana, near the Illinois border."

"You're kidding." I pulled out my phone and did a quick search. I raised my eyes to my best friend. "Gary is only twelve miles from Calumet City, which is just two hours from here." Oh. My. God. Ronald Simms could have driven to Lake Potawatomi late Thursday night, murdered Annabelle in the wee hours of Friday morning, and easily made it back to Gary in time for work that same morning.

But why would he have used one of your scarves? He doesn't even know you, my inner Sherlock pointed out.

Maybe because framing me would also hurt Tavish? The vegan reporter from the *Wisconsin Spectator* had linked me to Tavish after our first dinner at Caldwell's—the dinner that Annabelle had so loudly and publicly crashed. And several of the diners at the restaurant that night had posted photos of the confrontation on Facebook—photos that clearly showed me with the celebrity author. Some had even posed the question, "Tavish Bentley's new girlfriend?" as Sharon had pointed out to me with a huge grin. If Ronald Simms kept close tabs on Tavish, he would have read the article and seen the photos—photos that may have further fueled his revenge fantasies.

I shuddered.

Don't get ahead of yourself now. Don't forget Jewel.

I filled Char in on Harley's sister Jewel and my idea of going to see her—although she had now dropped far down the suspect list in light of this new Ronald information.

We looked at each other. "Road trip," we said in unison.

Before we left town, however, there was something important I needed to do—finish my book. All I had left to write now were the final few pages of the last chapter, and I could whip those out in an hour or two, since I knew exactly how it was going to end. Normally when I finish writing, I walk away from the book for a few weeks to let it—and me—rest. Then I return to it with fresh eyes and read it from beginning to end, fixing any plot holes and making any necessary tweaks or changes before sending it on to my editor. This time, though, I did not have the luxury. I needed to prove myself to my publisher.

Chapter Twenty-Three

The next morning, after hitting send on *A Dash of Death* and knowing I would likely be gone much of the day, I took Gracie for a long walk and asked Joanne to feed her later and let her into the backyard a couple of times while I was gone.

Char and I had spent hours strategizing and perfecting our plan the night before, with Sharon's help. We'd invited our third Musketeer to come along with us to do a full-on *Charlie's Angels* investigation, but mornings at the Lake House are always busy and Sharon had to make breakfast for a full house.

"If you're not back by five tomorrow, though, I'm sending out the cavalry." Sharon adjusted her mom's gray wig over my curls.

I didn't want anyone recognizing me from my author head shot as Darlene had the last time I'd tried—badly—to go incognito, especially since I'd become better known recently due to Brittany's beauty blog insinuations and the Facebook photos of Tavish and me at dinner. And I definitely didn't want Ronald Simms to recognize me. For this investigative trip, we'd decided that I would pretend to be Char's meek and aging mother who wouldn't garner a second glance from anyone. Unlike my mother. The idea was for me to be invisible.

"Magazines say once a woman turns fifty, she becomes invisible to society in general," Sharon opined, "but especially to men."

"I doubt that," Char said. "I think it's more like sixty. Jennifer Aniston is a year or two over fifty. She is definitely not invisible."

"Well sure, but she's *Jennifer Aniston*," Sharon said.

"Focus, girls, focus," I said. I checked out my image in the full-length mirror and didn't recognize myself. Baggy tan pants, nondescript oversized beige linen blouse, no scarf, green garden clogs, gray wig, and no makeup, save for the lines Sharon had penciled in around my lips and eyes. I looked like a mousy, boring woman in my late sixties or early seventies, someone who would easily blend into the background.

Sharon gave my drab outfit a final once-over. "Remember to slouch to hide your height, Teddie," she instructed.

"Yes, Mom." I slumped my shoulders and became even more invisible.

We had told Brady, Tavish, and Jim we were having a girls' night, and during that girls' night, while Sharon gave me my invisible makeover, we had all agreed not to tell the three men about today's fact-finding mission out of state. They would only object or try and do the protective-male thing, and this was something we two Musketeers could handle on our own.

Since Char, my pretend daughter and trip companion, didn't have her photo plastered on the back of any books and hadn't been to Calumet City or talked on the phone to Jewel Murphy, we agreed that she would take the lead in questioning the two possible suspects. I would stay in the background and observe how they reacted to Char's subtle probing. That would reveal which one was the killer—although I was now leaning toward the frustrated indie author.

The comic book shop where Jewel Murphy worked opened at eleven o'clock on Mondays, and we had found out she was working the early shift so determined to get there early. That would also give us plenty of time to make our one o'clock appointment with Ronald Simms twelve miles down the road in Indiana. Zoey, Char's librarian friend in Gary, had worked out our cover with her pal Linda, who worked in Ronald's real estate office and could not stand him. Linda had told Ronald we were a mother-daughter duo planning to move to Gary from Chicago and would like to look at houses Monday afternoon.

"He was practically foaming at the mouth when I set up the appointment." Char hung up the phone after talking to Ronald Simms and rubbed her hands on her jeans. "He was so slimy and obsequious, and that was just on the phone. Imagine what he's like in person." She made a face.

"Obsequious isn't bad," I said. "You can use that to your advantage."

* * *

As soon as we left Lake Potawatomi and hit the open highway, Char turned to me and said, "Remind me the usual motives for murder again?"

"Money, passion, and revenge," I said. Before I had begun writing my first Kate and Kallie murder mystery, I had spent time researching murder and the varied motives for committing one. I needed to understand what would drive someone to kill before I could write a believable mystery, and what I discovered was that generally—unless the murderer was a stone-cold sociopath who killed simply to display his or her power over others—the motives seemed to fall into one of the three overall categories of money, passion, and revenge. Crimes of passion were often committed in the heat of the moment, while money and revenge crimes were usually premeditated and more thought out.

"Well, if that's the case, then I think our realtor friend Ronald is a much more likely suspect than Annabelle's sister-in-law Jewel," Char said. "What would Jewel's motive be, anyway?"

"I thought possibly revenge for her sister-in-law co-opting her favorite author, but that seems pretty lame now," I admitted. "I guess I was willing to entertain any possibility to save my career." *And Tavish*, I thought, although I didn't say it aloud. I had finally told my fellow Musketeers when we got together last night what my editor had said about needing to prove my innocence to my publisher of the libelous accusations against me. After all, that's what friends are for.

"You've got to be kidding," Sharon had said. "That's ridiculous. So is a morality clause. What is this? 1950?"

"Hollywood had them back in the day," Char said, "and recently some publishers started using them as a safeguard against all the sexual harassment and sexual misconduct allegations that have been coming out against high-profile authors."

"I can understand that," Sharon said. "But what does that have to do with you, Teddie?"

"Bottom line?" I said. "If an author's reputation is tarnished, it can hurt sales. That's why I have to prove my innocence once and for all."

Pondering the concept of innocence as Char and I headed to Calumet City, I figured the only thing Jewel Murphy was likely guilty of was having lousy relatives. "I think you're right, Char," I said thoughtfully, "Ronald Simms is a far more likely suspect than Jewel. It's obvious he's bitter and been nursing a grudge for years after losing his plagiarism suit, and then, of course, there's Tavish's subsequent success. What's that saying? 'Revenge is a dish best served cold.' Ronald definitely had it in for Tavish, and what better revenge than pinning murder on his best-selling nemesis? It wouldn't get him any money, but he'd finally have his revenge."

Unconsciously, I raised my hand to play with my scarf, but then remembered I wasn't wearing one with today's disguise. I felt a bit naked without my signature accessory. "Let's pop in on Jewel anyway, since we're going to be so close. Then we can definitively eliminate her from our short list of suspects." I puffed out a sigh that lifted the bangs on my hot gray wig. "I sure wish we had a longer list."

"I hear ya, but I can't think of anyone in Lake Potawatomi who would kill two people they've never met before, can you?"

"Nope," I said, "except maybe Wilma Sorensen, just to get some new gossip going. She's been in her element since all this happened."

"Fred Matson's enjoying it too," Char said. "Keeps telling everyone it's the most excitement the town has had since Vern Jones caught that big-ass lake sturgeon a couple decades ago."

"Maybe Fred and Wilma should get together."

"Yabba-dabba do."

Pulling into a parking space in front of FreakaComics, I double-checked my gray wig in the mirror to be sure it was on straight. I noted with satisfaction that the age lines I had penciled in again that morning easily made me look like I was in the Medicare age bracket.

"Ready?" Char checked her phone. "The store just opened, so if we're lucky, Jewel won't have any customers yet."

"Yep. Let's do this."

The bell over the door jangled as Char pushed it open. Slouching in behind her in my innocuous beige, I clutched my oversized tote, trying to appear as unobtrusive as possible.

Inside the cramped shop, a riot of color assaulted us. Blood-red walls sported framed posters of Superman, Batman, Spider-Man, Captain America, Thor, Wonder Woman, X-Men, and a host of other superheroes. Beneath the posters, shelf after shelf of flimsy comic books sporting men, women, and other creatures with bulging biceps and colorful costumes beckoned. Rows of metal racks holding even more comic books, T-shirts, and cheesy superhero figures took up the center of the store.

A young tattooed woman behind the counter with straggly shoulder-length green hair looked up from her dog-eared copy of *The Girl With the Dragon Tattoo*. "Can I help you?" she asked, sounding as if that was exactly the last thing she wanted to do.

"I hope so," Char said. "I saw your store and just had to stop. My little brother loves Marvel comic books, especially Spider-Man, and his birthday's coming up, so I wanted to get him a few."

It was only half a lie. Augie did love Spider-Man comics, but his birthday was still seven months away.

The disinterested clerk, who I assumed was Jewel, waved her hand toward the rows of comics. "We've got lots of Spider-Man. Take your pick." She bent her green head back over her book.

"I'm sorry," Char said, with what sounded like genuine regret in her voice, "but I've never been in a comic store before, and it's a little overwhelming. Could you show me exactly where the Spider-Man books are and maybe even recommend a few you think he might like?"

The clerk set her book down on the glass counter top with a sigh and shuffled over to us in flip-flops, holey jeans, and a Captain Marvel T-shirt bearing a name tag that said Jewel. "How old is your brother?" she asked. "And what Spider-Man universe does he prefer?"

"Augie's twenty-six," Char said, "and I don't have a clue. I didn't even know there were different universes. Sorry. Are there maybe some new Spider-Mans you can recommend?"

"Excuse me, young lady," I interrupted, dropping my voice to a lower register so she wouldn't recognize it from my phone call the day before, "would you mind if I sit down and read my book while you're helping my daughter? My arthritis is killing me today."

Jewel barely looked at me. "Have a seat." She jerked her green head to two worn blue corduroy easy chairs nearby. "That's what those are for."

"Thank you." I plopped down with an exaggerated sigh, rummaged through my tote, and pulled out my book as I listened to the two of them discussing all things Spider-Man.

"I took my baby brother to the first Spider-Man movie with Tobey Maguire when he was eight," Char said. "That's what got him hooked."

"Good movie," Jewel said, "but I like the Andrew Garfield ones better."

C'mon Char, I willed my best friend telepathically, *don't go off on a movie tangent. Bring it back to the brother connection to get her talking about Harley. Then you can segue into Annabelle.*

"Augie liked those ones too, but I think the attraction for him was Emma Stone. He really had the hots for her." Char snickered. "Of course, he was eighteen, and you know brothers and their hormones."

"Do I," Jewel said. "My brother's forty-seven and his hormones are still all over the place. The dude can't keep it in his pants."

"Is he single or married?" Char asked nonchalantly.

Jewel shot a suspicious look at Char, who remained the picture of innocence and continued right on talking as if she were simply making casual conversation. "Augie's single," Char said, "but that's just because he hasn't met the right woman yet. He's a sweetheart. Some woman is going to be very lucky someday."

"Unlike the women in my brother's life," Jewel said, sotto voce. "One's dead and one's pregnant."

"Oh my goodness, I'm so sorry." Char fluttered her hands and acted flustered. "I mean, I'm sorry about the dead woman, not the one who's pregnant."

"Yeah, well, you lie down with dogs, you wake up with fleas," Jewel said dismissively. "Now let's check out these Spider-Man comics." She pulled several from the rack, and the two spent the next several minutes discussing the relative merits of one comic book over another. In the end, Char selected five.

As Jewel passed by me on her way to the register, I pretended to have fallen asleep and let my copy of *Her Blood Weeps* fall off my lap and onto the fake-wood floor. I startled awake at the loud thump. "Oops, must have fallen asleep." I strained forward to reach for the heavy hardcover at my feet and groaned. "Miss, could you get my book for me, please? I'm having trouble picking it up with my arthritis."

"Sure." Jewel bent down to retrieve it. Seeing the title and the author, she stiffened and extended the book to me with a curt nod. "Here you go."

"I just love Tavish Bentley, don't you?" I said in my lower senior voice. "His books are always so exciting."

"I guess. I haven't read any in a while."

"Oh, you just have to read this new one," I said. "It's so good."

Char rejoined us. "Mom, are you pushing *Her Blood Weeps* again?" She turned to Jewel and winked. "You'll have to excuse my mother; she's a Tavish Bentley evangelist. She thinks the whole world should read his books."

"I used to like them," Jewel said, "but my frickin' sister-in-law totally ruined them for me."

"How?" Char asked curiously, as we followed her to the register. "Ooh, is she one of those who gives away the ending before you finish the book? I hate that."

"Nah." Jewel rang up the comic books. "She just went a little cray-cray and got obsessive."

Char handed Jewel two twenties as the bell over the front door jangled.

"Hey, sis," a sickeningly familiar voice called out. "Can you loan me fifty bucks?"

Harley. I poked Char in the ribs and slouched even more. Turning off to the side, my heart hammering loudly, I affected an absorbed interest in a Wonder Woman action figure as Hulking Harley and the pregnant woman with him approached. I needn't have worried. Harley did not even notice me. The invisibility cloak worked.

"I'm. With. A. Customer." Jewel carefully enunciated each word so the Incredible Hulk might understand.

"Sorry," I heard Harley say to Char, "I didn't see you there." There was a pause, and I just knew he was checking my best friend out, but I also knew better than to turn around. The invisibility cloak might fade under scrutiny. Harley continued in what he must have thought was a seductive tone, "Although I don't know how I could have missed seeing *you*."

I wanted to hurl, and knowing Char, she did too.

"Babe," a plaintive voice whined, "I don't feel good. I think I'm going to be sick again."

"Well, go to the damn bathroom," he said. "You know where it is."

"And make sure you clean up after yourself," Jewel yelled after the laborious retreating footsteps.

"We have to be going," Char said, taking her bag of comics. "Thanks so much for all your help."

"Don't forget your change," Jewel said.

"Oh, right." Char released a nervous giggle. "Thanks."

"Aw, do you have to leave so soon?" Harley said.

"Yes, we have another appointment. Come along, Mother."

Keeping my head down, I slouched after Char.

"Hey!" Jewel called out after us.

Oh no. Did we blow our cover?

"Tell your brother to stop by in person next time," she said. "Maybe we'll hit it off. We're the same age and we both like Spider-Man."

"Will do," Char said. "You never know." She lifted her hand in a wave.

Before we reached the door, we heard Harley start in on Jewel again. "Can't you loan me fifty bucks, sis?" he asked in a wheedling tone. "I'll pay you back as soon as the insurance money comes in. You know I'm good for it."

Char turned the doorknob.

"What the hell?" Harley bellowed.

She froze.

"Go, just go," I urged.

"Turn up the sound," Harley yelled.

I sneaked a backward peek. Brother and sister stood transfixed by something on the flat-screen TV opposite them.

"Theodora St. John is one of my favorite authors," I heard Darlene Grubb's recognizable voice say.

Hearing my name, I turned slowly and regarded the TV screen.

"Why, she's even been to my house and signed my books personally." Darlene proudly held up my three cozy mysteries.

"So you don't believe the rumors that Theodora St. John is the Silk Strangler?" the local news reporter asked.

My breath hitched in my throat. *Silk Strangler?* I mouthed to Char.

She stared at me openmouthed.

"Of course not," Darlene said. "That's just a stupid rumor someone started on the Internet."

"You don't think she killed your daughter?" the reporter asked.

"Absolutely not," Darlene said. "I still think it was my no-good son-in-law."

Harley launched himself at the screen, bellowing an epithet.

"But Harley Cooke was nowhere near Lake Potawatomi when your daughter was killed," the reporter said. "There's proof he was in a motel outside Calumet City with his girlfriend."

"His *pregnant* girlfriend," Darlene said bitterly. "If you ask me, it's not too big a step from cheatin' to killin'. Man who cheats on his wife, what's to stop him from killin' her too?" She stared right into the camera. "Especially when there's a big insurance payout involved. One hundred thousand dollars."

"That bitch!" Harley roared. "I'm gonna kill her!"

Carefully I reached up to my full height and held the bell over the door still as Char silently turned the knob. Then we tiptoed out and made a run for it.

Chapter
Twenty-Four

"That was a close one," Char said as we left Calumet City in the rearview mirror. "That Harley sure is a piece of work."

"That's what I'm sayin'."

"You don't think he'll really go after his mother-in-law, do you?" she asked.

"I don't know."

"Should we warn her?"

"How? How in the world could we explain that?" I asked, playing drums on the steering wheel. "'Hi, Darlene, how are you? By the way, we were undercover in FreakaComics when your interview aired, and we heard your former son-in-law make wild threats at the TV screen.'" I yanked off the gray wig and rubbed my sweaty curls, then turned on the AC to blast away a hot flash. "Remember the last time I went undercover, how Brady got so mad and warned me to leave the crime solving to the professionals?"

"Yep." Char thought for a moment. "What if you texted Darlene from your burner phone and thanked her for standing up for you on TV, but also warned her to watch her back? Or . . ." She reconsidered. "I could just text Brady and tell him we saw Darlene's interview and are concerned because her son-in-law is volatile and maybe he might want to put a call in to his police pals in Calumet City and have them keep an eye on her or something."

"That sounds like a better plan. If Harley knows the cops are watching out for Darlene, he'll likely stay away from her. I'm guessing the last thing he wants is a return trip to jail." I sent her a warning glance. "When you text Brady, though, don't let him know where we are or what we're doing or we'll both be in big trouble."

"Ya think? I know how to handle Brady." Char's fingers flew across her phone. "Okay, done." She lifted her head and looked out the window, a pensive expression on her face. Then she shook her head and said briskly, "Well, we can definitely scratch Jewel off our list of suspects. One down, one to go."

Did she really believe that, or did she, like her boyfriend, have another suspect in mind? I took a deep breath and addressed the elephant hovering between us. "I know that Brady thinks Tavish killed Annabelle," I said softly, "and maybe even Kristi too, but he didn't. I know it."

"How do you know?" Char asked.

"Do you think I killed Annabelle?" I asked my best friend.

"Of course not."

"Why not?"

"Because I know you."

"And I know Tavish."

"Not really," she said gently. "You've known each other what, a week now?"

Adopting Kate Winslet's impassioned Marianne Dashwood voice, I repeated Tavish's earlier *Sense and Sensibility* quote. "'It is not time or opportunity that is to determine intimacy; it is disposition alone. Seven years would be insufficient to make some people acquainted with each other, and seven days are more than enough for others.'"

"You're going to hit me with Jane Austen now?" my former librarian friend asked. "Not fair." Then she grinned. "Okay, you made your point. Now should we check out this Silk Strangler stuff?"

"Yes, please. That's the first I've heard of that. I wonder where it came from."

"An Agatha Christie wannabe, perhaps?" Char pulled out her iPad and swiped it open.

"Maybe." I mused, "I must admit it has a certain ring to it. I like the alliteration. I just don't like it being attached to my name."

"Me either."

My phone buzzed with a text. "Can you see who that's from?" I asked Char. "It might be Joanne. I asked her to keep an eye on Gracie while we were gone."

Char picked up my phone from the cup holder between the seats. "It's not Joanne," she said. "It's Sharon." She read the text aloud: "'Tavish asked where you two went. I don't think he bought your shopping story. He kept asking questions. Finally, I improvised and told him it was a birthday surprise for him. That put a big smile on his face and shut him up.'"

Birthday? I slapped my hand to my forehead. "With all that's going on, I totally forgot Tavish's birthday is Wednesday. I promised to make him a Danish layer cake."

"It's only Monday," Char said. "You've got all day tomorrow to whip up a cake."

I slid a sideways glance to my non-baking friend. "It's a little more involved than just *whipping up* a cake. It's not like I'm using a box mix." I expelled a sigh. "And now I have to come up with a birthday surprise too."

"No problem," Char said. "We'll just throw him a surprise party. Piece of cake. Danish layer cake. Yum."

"Or"—my lips curved upward—"maybe we can deliver Annabelle's murderer. That would be a pretty nice birthday present to serve with the cake and ice cream."

Char high-fived me. "Oh yeah." She continued to search the Internet as I drove, mentally rehearsing my aging-mother lines before we met up with our next murder suspect. A colorful sign caught my eye. "'Welcome to Indiana, Crossroads of America,'" I recited. "Not long now and we'll be in Gary. Are you ready for your close-up, daughter of mine?"

"Crap," Char said.

"What?"

"The Silk Strangler is all over the Internet."

I sucked in a sharp breath. "You've got to be kidding me." I looked at her out of the corner of my eye. "Attached to my name?"

Char nodded miserably. "And Tavish's."

I stared dumbly at the road ahead. I would not have been surprised to see the rug just yanked out from under me fly by. "May as well kiss my writing career good-bye. Talk about upending their morality clause." I slapped the steering wheel. "What the actual hell?"

"This is why I hate social media," Char said. "All it takes is one person to post something spurious on Twitter or Instagram, someone shares it, and boom, before you know it, it's all over the place."

"Sounds like Lake Potawatomi."

"Except we have less than three thousand people. The Internet's reach is a bit longer," Char said wryly. "It can destroy a person's reputation in one tweet. Look at Lindsay Lohan, Charlie Sheen . . . Aunt Becky."

I slumped in my seat. "I'm starting to know how Thelma felt," I said. "Wanna be my Louise? We're already in the car."

"Nah, I'm not ready to go over that cliff yet." Char gave me her stern librarian gaze. "Now you listen to me, Teddie St. John. You have overcome far worse things." Her eyes filled. "Life-threatening things." She dashed the back of her hand against her eyes. "This is just gossip. It will blow over. Tomorrow they'll be talking about the most recent royal family feud or the latest shenanigans between those real housewives."

"You're right." I reached over and touched my best friend's arm. "Sorry." I sat up straight. "Okay, pity party over. So tell me what they're saying. I need to be prepared for when I talk to Jane. Better the devil I know than the devil I don't know."

"They're all speculating on who the Wisconsin Silk Strangler might be," she said. "It's pretty evenly divided into two camps. Some suspect Tavish, others are convinced it's you, and a few think it's some frustrated mama's boy that women have always rejected." She raised her right hand in a fist imitating Anthony Perkins's downward slasher-in-the-shower motion as she emitted the repeated violin screech from *Psycho*.

"Nice," I said. "Now can you try and find out who first coined that Silk Strangler expression? Was it Brittany the beauty blogger?"

Char shook her head. "I checked her first thing, and she's been noticeably quiet on the issue. I guess between Brady and Tavish's lawyer, they really put the fear of God into her."

"Or at least the fear of having to cough up big bucks that she doesn't have." Something niggled at the recesses of my memory. Hadn't I recently heard something similar where someone didn't have the money to pay for their bad behavior? Tuning out Char, I cast my mind back. Then I remembered. "Ronald Simms," I breathed.

"What about him?" Char turned to me, a questioning look on her face. "I've got my fake story straight for when we meet him after lunch, not to worry."

"I'm not talking about that. Remember in the newspaper article about the plagiarism suit, it said that Tavish, against his agent's advice, declined to seek financial damages, basically because Tavish is a decent guy and knew Ronald Simms didn't have the money?"

"Yeah." She frowned. "So?"

"So the lawyers got a cease-and-desist judgment against Ronald Simms years ago that legally prevented him from slinging mud at Tavish," I said, "but . . . what's to stop our friend Ronald from starting a rumor about Tavish online now using a fake name and hiding behind the anonymity of the Internet?" Entering the city of Hammond, I pulled into the parking lot of a burger joint and turned off the engine. Twisting in my seat to face Char, I said dryly, "It wouldn't be too hard for the man who titled his book *Petals Dripping With Blood* to come up with a provocative nickname like the Silk Strangler."

"You may be onto something there. Let me check it out." Char started tapping her iPad again.

"Can you check it out inside, please? I'm starving." I opened my car door.

"Not so fast, *Mom*. Aren't you forgetting something?"

I scrunched my eyebrows. "I don't think so."

Char's eyes slid to the gray wig on the armrest console between us.

"Oh." I clapped the hot hairpiece back on my head, pulling down my visor mirror to make sure I looked more like Sophia in *The Golden Girls* than crazy Doc from *Back to the Future*.

After the server left with our order for cheeseburgers, fries, and Cokes, we both began searching for the originator of the Silk Strangler. As I checked my phone, Char swiped through her iPad and began tapping away.

"Gotcha!" Char crowed moments later. Turning her screen my way, she displayed the amateurish done-on-the-cheap website of a male writer.

"Don Juan?" I said wryly. "Sounds like someone's overcompensating."

"Keep reading."

I scanned the basic black-and-white site, which featured the author's name at the top in bold Olde English seventy-two-point font. The text used the same Olde English font, but scaled down to twenty-four-point and dripping blood. I read aloud, "'Don Juan is the popular author of several erotic horror novels, including *The Seventh Street Slasher*, *The Poisoner and the Postman*, and'"—my eyes flew up to meet Char's—"'*The Silk Stocking Strangler*.' You got him! Well done, you."

"Check out the author photo."

The bad postage-stamp picture tucked away in the bottom right-hand corner of the webpage showed a washed-out man with thick jet-black hair—obviously a rug—of indeterminate age squinting at the camera. "So?" I said.

"Enlarge it."

I spread my index and middle finger across the screen. Not so indeterminate. The man's deeply lined face and creased forehead came into focus. He had to be in his mid to late sixties, easily. "Wow. Is that who I think it is?"

"Yep," Char said. "Ronald Simms, the one and only."

"Well, this is going to be quite an interesting afternoon."

As we ate our lunch and continued to check out Don Juan Ronald, we discovered that DonJuan39 (as if) frequented dating sites and mystery writers' chat rooms. In one of those rooms, responding to a woman who'd said she thought Tavish Bentley's *Her Blood Weeps* was his best book yet, he posed the question: "Would you still be a fan if the author you so admire turned out to be the silk strangler? Seems rather coincidental that two women within the orbit of a certain *New York Times* bestselling author died within the same week, in the same town—both strangled."

The Tavish fan angrily replied, "Those women were both strangled with scarves belonging to the scarf-wearing mystery author who lives in that SAME town. Talk about coincidental." That sparked a firestorm, which soon blazed in earnest with mystery fans lining up, taking sides, and taking the fight to Twitter.

"Well, at least we know where it all began," Char said.

"And where it's going to end." I drained my Coke and stood up. "Let's do this."

"But I haven't finished my pie," she whined.

"I thought you said you didn't like it."

"No." Char crammed the remainder of the pie in her mouth. "I said it couldn't hold a candle to your chocolate-cream, but that doesn't mean I should let it go to waste."

I shook my head. My best friend has never met a dessert she doesn't like. The annoying thing is, as she always reminds Sharon and me, she has a great metabolism and never gains a pound. Her daily jogging helps.

Back inside the car, I adjusted my knitted knockers and tugged my bra back down into proper position. Since I no longer have real boobs to hold the silky undergarment in place gravity-wise, my bra has a tendency to wander. Sometimes that baby rolls up like a window shade all the way to my shoulders. "Down, girls," I told my yarn boobs. "I can't afford to have you give my identity away." After making sure everything was back in its proper place, I patted the gray wig on my head. "How do I look?" I asked Char.

"Boring. Unmemorable. Invisible."

"Good. The last thing we need is for our self-published Don Juan author to recognize me like Darlene did."

Char gave a mock sigh. "It must be a curse being a celebrity."

"It is. I can hardly walk down the street without someone wanting my autograph." I waved my hand in a sweeping dismissive gesture. "And the paparazzi? Don't even get me started."

Actually, I cannot imagine anything worse than being rich and famous and leading a clubbing, jet-setting party life where strangers follow you around and you lose your privacy and any kind of normal existence. I'm a homebody. The only club I want to be part of is a book club. My idea of a party is having friends over for a home-cooked meal and playing Pictionary. Since leaving behind my cubicle-drone existence to follow my bliss, I am now quite happy living a quiet life in Lake Potawatomi writing my lighthearted mysteries, baking, gardening, and spending time with those I love, especially my sweet Gracie-girl. Lake Potawatomi has everything I need. Except kringle, and that's just a few miles up the road.

"What about me?" Char asked, breaking into my hometown reverie.

"What about you what?"

"How do I look?"

I surveyed my best friend, taking in her long red hair freed from its usual workday ponytail, creamy skin sprinkled with freckles, ivory slacks, and emerald shirt that brought out the green of her eyes. "You look great. Ronald will be so busy trying to impress you that he won't even realize he's tipped his hand until we're safely back home."

Driving the last few miles to Gary, we went over our plan a final time to make sure we were both on the same page. Ten minutes later we pulled into a tired strip mall off the main drag that included a shuttered used bookstore, dry cleaner's, Chinese restaurant, and Ronald Simms's small real estate office.

"You ready?" I asked Char.

"Ready as I'll ever be. Let's nail this bastard."

I grabbed my tote-bag prop and adopted my slouching posture as Char pushed open the glass door that read "Simms Realty—Where We Help You Find There's No Place Like Home!"

"Why hello there, ladies!" The man from the postage-stamp picture jumped up from his seat behind a large oak-laminate desk, sucked in his paunch, and hurried to greet us. "Come right in. Welcome to Gary." His brown suit pants were shiny with age and his short-sleeved once-white button-down shirt had seen better days. Sticking out his hand to Char, he blinked and gave her a smarmy smile. "Ron Simms at your service."

While the real-estate agent focused on Char, I subtly checked him out. The onyx toupee had replaced his sandy comb-over from the newspaper photo, and judging from his constant blinking, he now wore contacts in place of his thick nerdy glasses.

"Carol Johnson," said Char, shaking his hand. The man barely came up to her eyebrows. "And this is my mother, Betty."

Ron's hand lingered a moment too long in Char's-slash-Carol's, his blinking eyes never leaving her face, so I broke the spell. "Pleased to meet you," I said, thrusting out my hand. Even slouching, I towered over him.

Reluctantly Ron Simms relinquished my best friend's hand and shook mine, hardly giving me a glance. Up close, his lined face revealed him to be more likely in his seventies than his sixties, which made his ill-fitting charcoal-briquettes-colored hairpiece even more ridiculous. Patting my gray hair, I suppressed a giggle as the thought flashed through my mind, *Guess this is what you might call a meeting of the wigs.*

Char shot me a warning look behind Ron's back as he ushered us over to two chairs in front of his desk. He offered coffee, but when I saw the omnipresent Mr. Coffee and the red plastic supermarket container, I declined.

The Realtor resumed his seat behind his desk. His chair must have been on stilts, because he suddenly appeared much taller. "I understand you ladies live in Chicago at present and are considering a move here to Gary," he said in a jolly salesman–type voice.

"Yes," Char said. "I work from home as a medical transcriptionist, and Mom, of course, is retired. We're both fed up with all the noise and craziness of the big city—not to mention the crime—and want a more small-town feel, yet still with the advantages of living in a city." She leaned toward Ron and continued in an animated tone, "I've read articles over the years about how Gary had a declining population with a lot of abandoned buildings and houses, but that the city's been turning around lately and you can find older houses quite reasonably priced."

"That's true, that's true," Ron said. "Our city on the beautiful shores of Lake Michigan has been undergoing a revitalization in the past couple years. There are plenty of lovely vintage properties available. Is it just the two of you?" he asked flirtatiously, staring hard at my pretend daughter. "Or is there a Mr. Johnson?"

"There was, but he's dead," I said bluntly.

Ron's pasty face blotched red. "I'm sorry. I beg your pardon."

Char kicked my foot beneath the desk.

"Oh, that's okay," I said. "My husband died years ago, and Carol here is divorced, so since both of us are now footloose and fancy-free—as fancy-free as this stupid arthritis allows me to be"—I grimaced and rubbed my knee—"we decided to pool our resources and get a nice place together."

He beamed. "Well, that sounds great. I have several houses available to show you. Tell me again exactly what you're looking for, and I can narrow it down to meet your needs."

"At least a three-bedroom, two-bath, since I need a home office," Carol/Char said. "Depending on the price, though, four bedrooms might be nice, wouldn't you agree, Mother?"

"Sure. That way I could have my own wing—bedroom, bath, and maybe a sitting room to entertain guests. When it gets right down to it, though, all I really care about is having my own bedroom and my own toilet." I chuckled. "I get up several times a night to go the bathroom." I winked at Ronald. "You know how it is when you get to be our age."

His already thin lips thinned even more.

Oops. Better shut up and let Char do the talking. I waved my hand. "But I'm not fussy. I'll let you two pick which houses we visit today." I reached in my tote bag. "While you're doing that, I'll just sit here and read my book." Curious to see if Ronald Simms's reaction would mimic Jewel's, I pulled out *Her Blood Weeps* as Ron took a drink of coffee.

He made a garbled sound halfway between a choke and a splutter.

"Are you okay?" Char asked solicitously, leaning toward him.

"Fine," he said in a strangled voice. His eyes blinked rapidly and his fingers tightened on his coffee cup, the knuckles white. "Just went down the wrong way." His face splotched an angry red, and his scraggly sandy eyebrows drew together in a thunderous scowl beneath his coal-black rug. Ron coughed and slammed his cup on the desk.

Forgetting my arthritis act, I jumped up and set Tavish's book facedown on the laminate desk. "Here, let me get you some water." As I filled a mug with water from the water cooler just out of his line of vision, I observed Ronald Simms unobtrusively. No longer coughing, he regarded the book on his desk with a venomous glare. His eyes darkened and his chest heaved. All at once, he reached out and gave the hardback book a vicious shove. It slid off the desk and fell to the ground with a heavy thud. The Realtor then shot out of his chair, rounded his desk, and delivered a swift kick to Tavish's latest book. Then, to my astonishment, he proceeded to jump up and down on the best-selling novel, letting loose a stream of expletives in the process.

"Hey," Char-slash-Carol said, leaping up from her seat, "what are you doing? Stop that! Are you crazy? That's my mother's book."

I stared at the grown man turned toddler—and possible murderer—throwing a tantrum. Cautiously I approached with the glass of water. Ronald Simms looked up at me midfit, his eyes wide and wild, his breathing ragged. "I hate that sonofabitch," he ranted. "He has everything. *Everything*. That should be me!" Spittle formed on the sides of his mouth, and his chest heaved with rage.

"Calm down," Char said. "You need to chill out before you have a heart attack or something."

He stared at her through blinking, unseeing eyes. "What?"

"Deep breaths," I said, adopting a mother-knows-best role. "You need to take a deep breath and then exhale."

He gulped a mouthful of air.

"That's it. Now exhale."

Ron blew out his breath. A fetid mix of coffee and cigarettes hit me full throttle.

Stifling the urge to step back, I said calmly, "And again."

He inhaled another lungful of air and released it. More coffee-and-cigarette breath slapped me in the face, but his breathing returned to normal and his eyes lost their glassy appearance. He puffed out a sigh and stepped off the mangled book on the ground. "I'm sorry," he said, running a shaking hand through his toupee, unwittingly causing it to list to one side. "I don't know what came over me."

I extended the glass of water to him. "Drink this."

He glugged the water down, tantrum spent, and returned to his seat.

Char sat back down in her chair and looked across the desk at the deflated real-estate agent. "You want to tell us what that was all about?"

Ron sighed and recounted the plagiarism tale we had read in the paper, only with embellishment. "I wrote my story first," he said. "It took me eight years to write." Pulling a book off the credenza behind him, he held it up with pride. *Petals*

Dripping With Blood, the lurid title screamed above a cluster of yellow roses garishly dripping bright-red blood over the body of a voluptuous woman in white. He proffered the book to Char, who accepted it gingerly. "I poured blood, sweat, and tears into this baby," Ron said, "and then along comes Mr. Good-Looking Young Author with a British accent, and *his* book, using *my* idea, becomes a best seller. It's not fair!" he whined, starting to get worked up again. "Money and looks always win out over the little guy like me."

To avert another tantrum and God only knew what else, since this might be Annabelle's murderer, I nodded to the credenza behind him. "Are those more of your books? It looks like you've written several."

He nodded proudly. "Four published so far, and another one almost ready to go to the printer." He lined up the remaining books in a row on his desk next to *Petals Dripping With Blood*: *The Seventh Street Slasher*, *The Poisoner and the Postman*, *The Silk Stocking Strangler*.

"Wow," Char said. "That's impressive." She lifted her thick red hair off her neck and twisted it to one side, where it draped across the front of her green top in striking contrast. "Do you come up with all the titles yourself, or does your publisher?"

"I do," Ron said, puffing out his chest as he blinked at my best friend's voluminous tresses.

"Very creative." I picked up *The Seventh Street Slasher* and repressed a shudder at the cover, which showed yet another voluptuous woman in white dead on the ground, only this time with a massive man holding a knife over her dripping blood. "Great alliteration."

"Thank you." Ron leaned forward. "I'll tell you a little secret." He smirked. "I'm not only the author, I'm the editor and publisher as well."

"Really?" I said, interjecting the requisite amount of admiration. "That's amazing. You're a one-stop shop. Sounds like a lot of work, though. How do you manage to do all that and sell houses too?"

"When you love what you do, it's not work."

Preach.

Char casually picked up *The Silk Stocking Strangler* from his desk. "This sounds really familiar." Her eyebrows met in a puzzled frown. "I've seen this title somewhere before, and recently, I think . . . but I don't remember where. Online, maybe?"

"Could be." Ron got a cagey look in his ever-moving eyes. "I sell all my books online. That's probably where you saw it."

Char/Carol tipped her head to the side, considering. "I don't think so . . . it wasn't on Amazon or anything . . . Wait! I know. I think it was a tweet somewhere."

"That's possible," he said, affecting a nonchalant tone. "People are always tweeting about books they like and recommending them to folks."

My pretend daughter shook her head. "I don't think that was it." She pulled out her smartphone. "Let me see if I can find it."

"I think we should get going and start looking at those houses you want to see," Ron said, slipping back into professional Realtor mode. He stood up and waved the sales flyers he had printed for us. "There's a few that are exactly what you're looking for, including a couple of four-bedrooms that are a steal." He blinked and released a knowing chuckle. "I think it might become a battle between mom and daughter over the one you pick." Then he caught a glimpse of his crooked hairpiece in the wall mirror opposite his desk. His face flushed, but I acted as if I hadn't noticed anything, busying myself by bending over and pretending to tie my shoe while surreptitiously watching Ron through my lowered lashes. He quickly raised his hand and tugged his rug back into place. "Shall we go, ladies?"

Chapter
Twenty-Five

"Hang on," Char said, her head still bent over her phone. "This will just take a minute."

"You might as well sit back down, Ron," I said with a little laugh. "When Carol gets something stuck in her head, there's no stopping her. It won't take too long, though—she's a whiz at finding things on that phone of hers." I picked up the battered *Her Blood Weeps* and stuck it in my tote.

Ron's face flushed red. "I apologize for destroying your book, Betty; my behavior was inexcusable. I must have lost my mind there for a moment."

Is that what happened with Annabelle too? Or was that more deliberate?

He pulled a twenty from his wallet and held it out to me. "This should cover it."

Really? When was the last time you were in a bookstore? I kept that thought to myself, though. Thanking him, I pocketed the twenty.

Ron hurried over to his credenza and picked up a copy of *Petals Dripping With Blood*. Grabbing a pen, he scribbled something on the inside cover. Returning to me, his blinking eyes shining, he held out the book and said, "To fully make amends, here's an autographed copy of my first novel. A first edition, no less." He beamed.

"You don't have to do that," I protested. *Seriously—you really don't have to do that.* Char made a gagging motion behind his back.

"It's the least I could do."

"Well, thanks." Taking the book from his proffered hand, I started to slip it into my tote, but he stopped me. "Aren't you going to read the inscription?"

"Of course." I opened the book and read aloud, "'To Betty, may you never find any petals dripping with blood at your new home in Gary. If you do, let me know and I can arrange to find your Realtor a property six feet under. Ha-ha!'"

Like you did for Annabelle.

Ron chortled. "Pretty funny, huh?"

"Hilarious. Have you ever considered writing humor books instead of horror?"

His eyes lit up. "Actually, I have," he said, missing the sarcasm completely. "Everyone laughs at the funny stories I tell at our annual independent Realtors' convention. I've thought of putting the stories from all the years together into one collection and calling it *Gags and Giggles From the Real Estate Home Front.*" He giggled. "What do you think?"

"That's a good one," I said weakly as I tried to communicate with Char telepathically: *Come on already. I can't take much more of this.*

"Found it!" Char exclaimed. "It *was* a tweet. She read aloud, "'Spill the tea. Which mystery author is the Silk Strangler? Could he be tall, dark, and English? Or is *she* tall, flat, and closer to home? Hashtag Tavish Bentley. Hashtag Theodora St. John.'" She deliberately avoided glancing my way, and while Ron was intent on my make-believe daughter, I took the opportunity to slouch even more, grateful I had had the foresight to wear my knitted knockers as part of my disguise.

Char-as-Carol offered Ron an innocent look. "It sounds like someone appropriated the title of your book, and this time I don't think it's Tavish Bentley." She widened her eyes. "You should sue them for plagiarism, stealing your title that way."

His pasty skin turned even chalkier. "I don't think so. I have already been down that road once. All it brought me was a lot of trouble," he said bitterly.

"You're probably right," Char said. She adopted an I-just-remembered-something act. "Oh, and guess what? When I Googled Silk Stocking Strangler, your website came up, Ron." She batted her eyes at him. "Or should I say *Don Juan?*"

His face turned pink. "Authors need to have a unique name to stand out . . . I thought that pseudonym might attract a lot of female readers."

I'll bet you did, Ronny-boy. What else were you hoping to attract? Then it hit me. How could I not have seen it before now? The realtor-slash-author's erotic horror book covers showed the man had an obsession with men murdering women—having power over them. Every single one of his book covers showed a dead woman on the ground, usually wearing white, and usually with a large murderous man looming over her. Ronald Simms might come across as a meek, mild-mannered, ineffectual old man, but clearly the guy had issues—mother ones, perhaps?—and was acting out frustrated fantasies of killing women in his novels. Visions of Anthony Perkins murdering Janet Leigh in the shower filled my head, complete with the screeching-violins background music.

Oh. My. God. Maybe we've been looking at this all wrong. Maybe Annabelle hadn't killed Kristi in a jealous rage after all. Maybe Ron Simms had. Kristi was young, beautiful, and voluptuous—just like the women on Ron's book covers, I realized to my mounting horror. The realization pinned me to my seat. The more I thought about it, the more it made sense. Killing Kristi would not only satiate the wannabe Don Juan's erotic horror fantasies, it would also give him his long-awaited revenge on Tavish—effectively killing two birds with one stone, to use a cliché. Something that's frowned upon in fiction. That meant . . . we were alone in the same room with a murderer. At least this time I wasn't alone. I had brought one of the Musketeers along for backup, and Sharon, our third Musketeer, knew where we were and would sound the alarm if we weren't home by five. That was still several hours away, though. A lot could happen between now and then.

Returning to the conversation, which our likely Silk Strangler hadn't even realized I'd checked out of a while ago, I studied Ron intently and caught him staring at Char with lust-filled eyes as she chattered on. Unaware that I was watching—and on to him—the author-slash-murderer licked his lips.

We need to get the hell out of here. Now. No way are we getting in a car with Ron Simms and letting him take us to empty houses, more than likely in the middle of nowhere where we'll be alone and vulnerable and no one can hear us scream. Who knew what weapons he might have stored in his house-of-horrors traps? Likely more than scarves—although thankfully I hadn't worn one today. I gnawed at my lower lip. How to let Char know, though—what reasonable excuse could I use to get us out of there? As I considered the best course of action, I recognized the two things I had going for me were that Don Juan didn't know I was onto him *and* that he thought I was an old lady. He didn't have a clue about my Wonder Woman moves.

I'll start by playing the arthritis card like I did on Jewel at the comics shop, I mused, *only really lay it on thick this time and pray madly that Char will follow my lead. If that doesn't work, I'll just get up close and knee the bastard. I'll have the element of surprise on my side, as I had with Kristi's ex Tom. Besides, Ron Simms is much older and smaller than Tom. I can easily incapacitate the nasty bugger.* Confident of my plan, I once again tuned back in to the conversation.

"I've really enjoyed talking with you about my books, Carol," Ron was saying, "but we really should get going now and see those houses."

"Sounds good," Char-slash-Carol said. "I'm eager to see what you have for us."

No, you're not, Char. You're really not.

Ron fumbled with his keys. "Shall we all go in my car? Although . . . thinking about it, it's a bit small for all three of us." He turned to me, laying the phony solicitousness on thick. "Betty, would you be more comfortable following Carol and me in your car instead? I wouldn't want you to feel cramped and uncomfortable, especially considering your arthritis."

Hell to the no, I thought. I smiled sweetly at him. "Nah, that's okay. Let's all go together in one car. I'll be fine. Besides"—I released a rueful laugh—"I'm directionally impaired and get lost all the time. I don't know this city." Then I adopted a frightened-old-woman demeanor, making my voice all tremulous and quavery. "Wh-what happens if I can't keep up with you and you lose me?"

Char sent me a curious look behind Ron's back, but played along like the quick-thinking daughter she was. She patted my arm reassuringly. "Don't worry, Mom, we'll stay together. Right, Ron?"

"Whatever you ladies want." He handed Char one of the flyers. "I thought we'd start with this one first. It's an old Victorian with four bedrooms, two baths, and a powder room. The entire house has been totally remodeled. It sits on a corner lot at the end of a quiet street and backs up to an open field— very pretty and peaceful. Almost feels like you're living in the country."

Of course it does, you sick puppy. In the country, no one can hear you scream.

"Sounds great," Char said. "It's gorgeous." She passed me the flyer. "Look, Mom, it's even blue, your favorite color."

"Beautiful," I said, playing along. "I can't wait to see it."

He made a little bow. "After you, ladies."

As Char stood and picked up her purse, I pushed myself up from the chair. "Ow!" I exclaimed, grabbing my left knee and immediately plopping back down.

"What's wrong?" Ron asked.

"My rheumatoid arthritis." I rubbed my knee and grimaced in fake pain. "It's really acting up. I must have aggravated it when I jumped up earlier to get your water."

"I'm sorry, Mom," Carol/Char said. "I should have thought about that and not spent so much time talking with Ron here. I was really enjoying our conversation, though." She flashed him a smile before returning her full attention to me. "Do you think you can walk it off? That helps sometimes."

"I can try." Easing myself slowly back up from the chair, I hobbled a few steps, moaning and contorting my face in mock pain the whole time. "I don't think that's gonna work this time, honey," I said to my counterfeit daughter. "I think I need to sit back and stretch out my leg."

"How about some ice?" Ron asked. "Will that help? We've got an ice pack in the freezer. My colleague keeps it there for her bad back."

"It might," I said in a pathetic voice.

"Great." He hurried over to the ancient white refrigerator in the back corner of his office and opened the freezer door. "You can stretch out on the sofa here and put the ice on your knee and just rest and take it easy while Carol and I go look at houses."

Giving a quick headshake to Char while the Silk Strangler's back was turned, I jerked my eyes to the front door and mouthed, *We need to leave. Now!*

Ron shut the freezer door and scurried over with the ice pack. "Here you go," he said, offering it to me.

"Thanks, Ron, but I don't think that will work," Char said regretfully, making it up as she went along. "When Mom is in this much pain, her doctor recommends alternating between heat and cold."

"That's right," I said, running with it. "What I really need is a long hot bath and my heating pad. Twenty minutes with the heating pad, twenty minutes with ice, and repeat."

"I'm really sorry," Char said to him, "but I'm afraid I'm going to have to take my mother home."

"But we didn't even visit one house," he whined.

"I know," she said, "and I'm really sorry about that, but it can't be helped. I need to get her home. I'll put the seat down in the car so she can stretch out."

Ron frowned, and I could see his fiendish little brain beneath his toupee trying feverishly to come up with another way to keep us there. I knew his real quarry was Char. I was just collateral damage. He snapped his fingers. "I've got it. I have a heating pad at my house. It's just a couple blocks away. I can run home, get it, and bring it back here. Or if you'd rather, Betty, you can just stay at my house, stretch out on the couch with the heating pad, and watch TV while Carol and I go look at houses." He beamed at the two of us. "Problem solved."

Desperate much?

"That's so kind of you, Ron," I said weakly, "but when I feel like this, I just want to be home in my own bed with my sweet little doggy next to me for comfort."

"I understand." He smiled, but it didn't reach his eyes. "I'm the same way when I don't feel well."

"I'm so sorry about all this," I said as I struggled to my feet. "I feel terrible for wasting your afternoon. Can we reschedule for one day next week?" Then I heaped it on thick. "I really want to see that blue Victorian."

"Of course." He pulled his planner off his desk. "Carol, what day would be good for you with your work schedule?"

"Ohhhh," I cried out, doubling over and clutching my knee to lend verisimilitude to my fake-pain act. As I did, I felt my wig shift. *Oh no, please don't let him notice.*

Char quickly stepped in close beside me and laid my head on her shoulder, giving a discreet tug to my wig in the process. "It's okay, Mom," she said in a soothing voice, "I'm going to take you home now." With her arm around me, she carefully ushered me to the door, saying over her shoulder to the foiled Realtor, "I'll call you tomorrow to reschedule."

"My tote," I whispered.

"Ron," she said as she opened the door, "would you mind bringing my mother's bag?"

Following us outside, Ron waited while Char got me situated in the passenger seat before handing my tote to me through the open window. "Here you go, Betty," he said in a voice tinged with concern yet underlain with anger. "I hope you feel better soon."

"Thank you," I murmured, acting spent—although it wasn't much of an act. "And thank you so much for your book. I can't wait to read it."

Liar.

Carol buckled her seat belt and gave Ron a brief wave out the window. "Thanks again for everything. We'll talk tomorrow."

He returned her wave, and Char slowly backed out of her parking space. Flipping my visor mirror down, I caught Ron's eyes narrowing as he looked at our license plate. Checking his wave, he balled his hand into a fist.

"You want to tell me what the hell that was all about?" Char asked through a clenched smile as she pulled into the street.

"Later," I said sotto voce. "He's still watching and he saw our license plate. He knows we're not from Chicago, and he's not happy." As soon as we turned the corner, however, I said, "Burn rubber. We need to put as much distance as we can between Don Juan and us."

Char pressed her foot on the accelerator, and we sped out of Gary. Once we were out of the city limits, she said, "Now are you going to tell me why we had to leave so fast?"

"Because I'm pretty sure Don Juan is the Silk Strangler. And not only did he kill Annabelle, I think he killed Kristi as well."

*　　*　　*

Continually checking behind us to make sure Ron Simms was not following our car as we flew toward home, I yanked off my hot, itchy wig. Then I filled Char in on how I had arrived at my conclusion that the Realtor was likely the Silk Strangler and responsible for the recent deaths of the two women in our small town.

"You may be right," she said thoughtfully. "His extreme reaction to Tavish's latest book clearly shows how much Ron hates him. And not only that, his slimy book covers really

263

creeped me out—his books are clearly the product of a fevered imagination."

"Which reminds me . . ." I reached into my tote bag and pulled out *Petals Dripping With Blood*. Opening the book, I started skimming through it.

"Well?" Char asked after a few minutes.

"The writing's absolute crap. It reads like something a horny seventh-grade boy wrote—one who is flunking English. Our Ronny needs to go to a Fiction 101 writing seminar or invest in some how-to books." I made a face. "No one *says* anything. They all shriek, scream, sob, shout, exclaim, or cry out, and do not even get me started on all the exclamation marks. He vomited them onto every page."

Char snorted. "What a surprise to learn that Ron's a lousy writer. I'd never have guessed from those amazing covers." She slid me a sideways glance. "How about the actual content, though? Is it horror porn?"

"Oh yeah," I slapped the book shut and threw it in the back seat. I wanted to throw it out the window, but that would be littering. "It's full of testosterone-fueled men and helpless—but of course always voluptuous—Marilyn Monroe types in peril from sadistic rapists and serial killers. It's misogynistic as all get out. The man who wrote this really hates women." I shuddered.

"Enough to kill them?"

"I think so, but I'm not a psychologist. We'll let the experts puzzle that out." I grimaced. "I really need a shower after reading that, but I'll have to settle for hand sanitizer." I pulled out the plastic travel-sized bottle I always keep in the glove box and squeezed a liberal amount into my palms. Then I Lady Macbethed my hands.

Two hours later when we pulled into my driveway, Brady and Tavish were sitting on the back step waiting for us.

Char swore under her breath.

"We're in for it now," I muttered, unbuckling my seat belt and taking a deep breath as I climbed out of the car.

"Nice outfit, Ted," Brady said. "Not your usual style though. Bit old for you, isn't it?"

"A girl's gotta change it up every now and then," I said, grateful I had left the gray wig in the car.

Tavish didn't say anything, but he had an odd expression on his face as he regarded me. I couldn't tell if it was concern or disappointment. Maybe a mixture of both.

Char stood next to me in solidarity. All for one and one for all.

Brady fixed us with a piercing stare, his lips set in a thin line. "You two just came from Calumet City, didn't you?"

"No," we chorused. It wasn't a lie, technically. Calumet City had been the first stop on our journey, not the last.

"What makes you think that?" Char asked, feigning innocence.

"Because," Brady said in a clipped tone, "Darlene Grubb's interview only ran on the local Illinois TV station. The only way you could have possibly seen it was by physically being in Calumet City at the time."

I held up my hands. "Okay, you got us. We did go to Calumet City earlier. But that's not important now." I waved my hand in a dismissive motion. "What is important is that we found the person who killed Annabelle and likely Kristi too."

Tavish sucked in his breath.

Brady expelled a loud sigh. "For the last time, Harley Cooke did not kill his wife."

"I'm not talking about Harley." I looked directly at Tavish. "I'm talking about Ron Simms."

Tavish's eyes widened. "Ronald Simms? The man who accused me of plagiarism years ago?"

I nodded and reached into the car to pull out *Petals Dripping With Blood*. Handing the book to Brady, I told the two of them how we'd gone to Indiana to see Ron Simms, and how he'd flown into a jealous rage upon seeing Tavish's *Her Blood Weeps*. I then recounted the rest of our visit with the Realtor-slash-author and linked the title of one of his horror-porn books to the rumors he had started online about his nemesis Tavish being the Silk Strangler. I ended with my explanation of how Ron had been off sick from work during the time frame when Kristi and Annabelle were murdered, and laid out the chronology of how he could have easily gotten to Lake Potawatomi and killed both women and at last gotten his revenge on Tavish.

Brady let out a long low whistle. "That's a pretty fantastic story, Ted. Do you have proof of any of this? Or is this all just wild imaginings on your part?"

Char jutted out her chin at her sheriff boyfriend. "I can show you the Twitter trail about the Silk Strangler that leads directly back to Ron Simms, or as he calls himself online, Don Juan."

Tavish had remained silent during my entire recitation, listening thoughtfully to what I had to say and contemplating it, but now he spoke up. "Don Juan? As in the great lover?"

"Yep," I said, giving him a wry look, "from a man who is anything but, based on what we learned and saw firsthand." I turned to Brady. "As far as proof goes, the only *proof* I have is the Twitter trail Char uncovered about the Silk Strangler and the creepy books Ronald Simms wrote. I'm not a cop or a private investigator. That's above my pay grade. I leave that to you and the professionals."

Brady threw back his head and howled with laughter.

A little later after Brady and Char left, just as things were starting to get interesting between Tavish and me, Mom showed up. Thankfully, she didn't use her key and just barge in this time. I had divested myself of my old-lady disguise in favor of a casual navy cotton boho dress and multicolored scarf, which Tavish was admiring as he slowly unwound it. Helping him remove the scarf, I dropped it on the floor. We were snuggling on the couch when the knock came on the back door and we heard my mother's voice call out, "Teddie?"

Picking up my scarf, I quickly wound it back around my neck before answering the door. "Hi, Mom. What's up?"

"I was wondering if I could borrow some—oh hello, Tavish, I didn't know you were here," she said innocently as he joined us in the kitchen.

Sure, Mom. You didn't see his rental car parked out front.

"Hello, Claire," Tavish said. "Lovely to see you again. Actually, I was just going. I still need to pack."

"Pack?" My mother's plumped lips turned down in a pout. "You're not leaving us so soon, are you?"

"No, I just have to go to New York for a couple days to take care of some business." Tavish gave me a gentle peck on the lips right in front of my mother and God and everyone. "I'll see you Wednesday," he said, his eyes lingering on my lips. "I'm really looking forward to my Danish layer birthday cake." Tavish ruffled Gracie's fur as he left. "'Bye, Gracie. Take good care of your mum until I get back." He bounded down the back steps, whistling.

"Tavish's birthday is Wednesday?" Mom said. "Are you having a party for him?"

So, of course, I then had to invite her as well. It's called etiquette. The woman before me taught me well.

Mom asked where I'd been all day, so I filled her in on our out-of-town adventures, relieved to inform her that suspicions now centered on Ronald Simms as the likely killer of both Kristi and Annabelle. I saw the relief in her eyes.

"Imagine anyone thinking you could strangle those women," she said. "Ludicrous. Why, you can't even kill insects. Even as a child, you would always carry spiders and ants outside and set them free."

Was that a note of pride I heard in her voice?

Just when I think I have my mom all figured out, she goes and says something like this. Between my parents, my dad was always the more emotional of the two—getting misty-eyed at Hallmark commercials, at his first sight of the Grand Canyon, and every time he listened to his beloved Simon and Garfunkel's "Bridge Over Troubled Water." He wept when his mother died. And when Atticus had to be put down. And the day I told them I had breast cancer. Mom, on the other hand, has always been more stoic (some might say cold) and is not one to wear her heart on her sleeve. That's why I was shocked when I overheard her crying and ranting the night before my mastectomy. The three of us were going out to my favorite Racine restaurant for dinner that evening, and I'd arrived early and let myself in the house, unbeknownst to them.

"I can't believe tomorrow they're going to cut my daughter's breast off!" I heard Mom sob from their bedroom. "It's barbaric!"

I tiptoed to the end of the hallway to hear better, careful not to make a sound.

"No," Dad soothed her. "It's necessary."

"It is not," Mom yelled. "Teddie could have had a lumpectomy—the doctor said so."

"The doctor also said it was her choice," Dad said evenly, "that it was up to Teddie to decide. This is her body and her decision, and we need to honor that and support that."

"I'm scared," Mom said in a tremulous tone I'd never heard before.

"I know you are," Dad said. "I am too. But we need to be strong for our girl."

The sound of muffled crying followed.

Blinking back tears, I tiptoed back down the hall. Quietly I made my way through the living room and into the kitchen. There I took a moment to compose myself. Then I loudly opened and shut the back door.

"Hey, where are you guys?" I called out. "You ready? I'm starving."

Chapter
Twenty-Six

After sifting together the flour, baking powder, and salt, I set them off to one side and began creaming the butter for the yellow cake that would be the foundation of Tavish's Danish layer birthday cake. I added in the sugar in quarter-cup increments and creamed the butter and sugar together until the mixture was light and fluffy. Then I beat in the egg yolks one at a time, humming as I did so, and stirred in the vanilla extract. Next, I beat in the flour mixture a little at a time with the milk. In a separate bowl, I beat the egg whites until stiff peaks formed and gently folded them into the batter. After pouring the batter into the two greased and floured round cake pans, I slid the pans into the oven and set the timer.

Gracie, who had been waiting patiently, having learned not to interrupt me while I did my meticulous measuring-and-mixing baker's dance, sidled up to me, wagging her tail and staring up at me with a beseeching gaze.

"Yes, Gracie-girl, you know I'm a sucker for those big eyes." Opening her doggy-biscuit jar, I tossed her one of her favorite peanut-butter-flavored biscuits. She likes to have me throw it;

that way she can pounce on it and play with it for a while. Gracie seized the biscuit and darted under the kitchen table.

Pouring myself a cup of coffee and nibbling on my "biscuit"—a peanut-butter blossom Char had missed—I reflected on the events of the last couple of days. I had not been lying when I told Brady I had finished my sleuthing into Lake Potawatomi's two murders. I had done what was necessary to discover and draw attention to another suspect—a much more plausible suspect than Tavish or me—and to hopefully end the speculation against us in the process. Now the ball was in the professionals' court.

Brady had talked to the chief of police in Gary, Indiana, and he said the moment he mentioned Ronald Simms's name, the chief told him there had been complaints made over the years against the Realtor—ones of a sexual nature. Turns out Ron had served a year in the county jail after being charged a second time as a peeping tom. He was also currently the subject of an active investigation, the details of which the chief was not at liberty to discuss. Brady had mentioned the tight-lipped investigation to Char, who had then let it slip to me—confidentially, of course. When she told me about the current investigation in Gary, we looked at each other and said, "Kristi and Annabelle."

Tavish had left the day before for New York to meet with his publisher and lawyer to discuss the prospect of bringing legal charges against Ron Simms for maliciously suggesting in print that Tavish had strangled his ex-fiancée and his stalker Annabelle. However, he would be back in time for his birthday dinner tonight—a birthday dinner I was making.

271

Meanwhile, as the professionals were focusing on the Realtor-slash-author, I had been focusing on my two favorite things: writing and baking. I called my editor to let her know there was a promising new suspect in the two murders, but she had more important things on her mind.

"First, I received *A Dash of Death* and loved it," Jane said. "Your readers will too. It is delightful. And speaking of readers . . ." She paused before adding excitedly, "Your books have been flying off the shelves, ever since that whole Silk Strangler speculation went viral! We have already had to go back to print *twice* on *Death by Danish* and *The Macaroon Murders*. Now the powers that be want to rush *A Dash of Death* into production immediately so we can release it as soon as possible and capitalize on all that publicity. They're over the moon and think it has a good chance to become a best seller."

I listened to Jane in a daze, unable to take it all in. *A best seller?* One of *my* books? "But what about the morality clause?"

She snorted. "Sales trump morality. *You*, Theodora St. John, are Baker Street's hottest author right now. You can bet Baker Street is going to ride that gravy train all the way to the bank, and so should you," she advised. I heard the familiar rustle of a Hershey's Kiss being unwrapped. After Jane finished the bite-sized chocolate, she said, "We'd like you to write a new Kate and Kallie mystery ASAP. Think you can get me a proposal and first chapter or even just the first few pages by the end of the week?"

"*This* week?"

"That's the one."

"I—I don't know," I said, taken aback. I had only just finished *A Dash of Death* and was looking forward to a breather, especially after the added stress of the two murders. I always took a break for a few weeks after finishing a book to relax and putter around the house and garden, spend time with friends and family, take fun day trips, and have a life again—a life not consumed by a looming book deadline. Besides, last night when Tavish had called me from New York, I had finally accepted his offer to show him more of my beautiful state. We planned to head up north to Door County Friday—just the two of us for a long weekend, returning Monday. "Let me check some things and I'll get back to you soon," I told her.

"Soon, as in tomorrow?" Jane pressed. "It doesn't even need to be a full-length proposal—just a short synopsis and the first few pages."

"I'll do my best." I hung up the phone, bemused by all that my editor had said. What a shock to find out that my first two books were enjoying a resurgence and attracting new readers— although I confess it didn't sit well with me that most of those readers were simply curiosity seekers drawn to my books by online gossip.

Who cares why *they're reading them*, my pragmatic self pointed out. *Don't be so particular. At least they're reading them. You'll likely gain some new fans in the process, and that's a good thing. As is that larger royalty check you'll be receiving.*

As I thought about Jane's request for a new Kate and Kallie mystery, I had to smile. Only this morning I had been scratching down ideas for the next adventure of my crime-solving duo. I was having trouble deciding on the title, however. As a genre writer, I usually come up with the title first and then write the story to fit, but this time I couldn't make up my mind among three options. Time to call in the cavalry.

I sent a group text to Char and Sharon:

Me: *Help. Which title do you like best for my next K&K mystery: Drowned in Dark Chocolate, Suffocating in Soufflé or Choking for Cherries Jubilee?*

Char: *Suffocating in Soufflé. No contest.*

Sharon: *That's a tough one. I like the sound of Suffocating in Soufflé but you know how I love my dark chocolate. I say Drowned in Dark Chocolate.*

Me: *Thanks, guys.*

Sharon: *Hold on a minute there, Sparky. Is everything on track for tonight? Do you need us to come early to help?*

Me: *No thanks, I'm good. Char and Brady are coming at five to do the decorations and Tavish won't be here until six-thirty, so just make sure you're here by six and park a block away.*

Sharon: *Will do.*

The kitchen timer dinged. *Must take the cake out of the oven. C-ya later.*

Removing the cake pans, I set them on the counter to cool. Then I checked my to-do list. I had invited Tavish over for dinner tonight for his birthday—a dinner he was expecting to be a romantic dinner for two but was actually going to be a surprise birthday party instead. I had tried going the romantic route, but my friends wouldn't let me.

"You've got plenty of time for romance on your trip, Ted," Brady said. "No way are you depriving the rest of us of your fabulous Danish layer cake and that killer frosting."

"What Brady *meant* to say is that we would love to celebrate with the birthday boy as well," Char said.

"Yeah, that too," Brady added.

So it was decided that Brady, Char, Jim, Sharon, and my mother would all celebrate Tavish's birthday with me tonight at a surprise birthday party at my house.

In addition to the requested cake, the menu included Caprese salad, chicken marsala—one of Tavish's favorite dishes, I had learned—mashed potatoes, and sautéed green beans almandine. Sharon and Jim were bringing the wine, Char and Brady were taking care of the decorations, and Mom had insisted on bringing an appetizer, which made me more than a little nervous, since my mother doesn't cook.

While the cakes and the almond-custard filling cooled, I made the raspberry filling, combining the sugar and cornstarch in a small pan and then adding in the thawed frozen raspberries and juice. Once the filling became thick and clear, I set it off to one side to cool completely. Then I began making the yummy buttercream frosting—my favorite—eager to get to the licking-the-bowl ritual I usually share with Brady. He's a big bowl licker too. Whenever I make buttercream frosting, he has me save the remnants for him.

* * *

Dressing for the party a few hours later, I decided to wear the green batik dress with swirls of teal and fuchsia that I had worn on my first date with Tavish. Topping it off with my fuchsia silk scarf, I returned to the kitchen to discover my mother waiting for me, a proud grin on her face and a brown paper package resembling a pizza box in her hands.

"Whatcha got there, Mom? A birthday present for Tavish?"

"Of a sort," she said. "It's my appetizer contribution for tonight."

Oh no, I thought. *Please don't let it be one of her awful health-food snacks like tofu wrapped in kale or those terrible brown-rice cakes that taste like sawdust.*

"Thanks," I said, casting a wary glance at the box. "So . . . did you make it?"

Mom tinkled out a laugh. "Certainly not. You know I hate cooking and baking." She peeped at me over her readers. "And you and I both know that I'm a terrible cook. However, I do excel at shopping." She opened the package and set it on the counter with a flourish. "Voilà! For your dining pleasure, I present sausage rolls from England."

"Wow. That's great," I said, peering at the tan-colored pastry bites encompassing savory sausage meat. "Tavish will love them." He had recently mentioned he was missing English food—including sausage rolls—and Mom must have heard and paid attention. "Where'd you find them?"

"An online British specialty store. I ordered them Monday and asked for express shipping so they'd get here today." She frowned. "I think they have to be nuked in the microwave or something before you serve them."

"No problem. I'll take care of it."

* * *

I scanned the dining room one last time to make sure everything was all set. The antique walnut table gleamed with my grandmother's sparkling crystal and china. The whimsical decorations were all in place—Char and Brady had woven Union Jack bunting through the arms of my bronze chandelier, strung a Happy Birthday banner across the buffet, tied a bouquet of colorful balloons to the back of Tavish's chair, and filled my trifle bowl with musical blowout noisemakers—Brady's offering. And Jim had set up a bar with wine and whiskey on the buffet.

"Everything looks great," Sharon said as her other half poured my mom a glass of Chardonnay. "Tavish is certainly going to be surprised. Although"—she frowned—"I hope he won't be disappointed to find us all here—he said earlier how much he was looking forward to your romantic evening tonight."

"He'll get his romantic evening on their getaway up north," Brady said, grabbing a handful of cashews from the nut bowl on the sideboard. "A little delayed gratification is good for the soul."

Char arched an eyebrow at him. "Is it now? I'll have to remember that."

Leaving my guests to talk quietly among themselves, I returned to the kitchen, where I stirred the chicken marsala simmering on the stove and checked that everything else was ready: Russet potatoes chopped and in a pot of water waiting to be boiled, check. Green beans washed and trimmed, ready to be sautéed, check. Sliced tomatoes, mozzarella, and basil leaves on a platter in the fridge awaiting a last minute sprinkling of olive oil, check. Yeast rolls risen and ready to pop into the oven, check. Danish layer cake iced and decorated in the fridge, check.

A noise behind me made me turn from the stove to see Brady with his head in the fridge. "I'm sorry, Brady. As I already told you, there's no leftover frosting. I got stressed with all the preparation busyness and totally forgot to save the bowl scrapings for you. My bad."

Brady shut the refrigerator door and faced me. "I see how it is now," he said with an exaggerated sigh. "Another man waltzes into your life and I get the boot. I never thought you would do that to me, Ted. I expected better of you, especially after all these years."

Gracie raced into the kitchen, barking, as a car pulled into the driveway. "Oh my gosh, he's here!" My eyes flew to the clock above the sink. "Fifteen minutes early. Get back to the dining room," I hissed to Brady, putting my finger to my lips, "and keep everyone quiet."

Brady crouched down so Tavish wouldn't see his silhouette through the closed yet thin curtains and crab-walked quickly and stealthily out of the room.

A car door slammed, and Gracie barked anew and wagged her tail. Moments later a brisk knock sounded at the back door. *This is it. Don't give it away.* Tamping down my nerves, I arranged my features into a calm yet welcoming smile as I opened the door. "Happy birthday!" I said to a massive bouquet of yellow-and-pink roses, white tulips, and Stargazer lilies.

Tavish poked his head around the bouquet. "For the lady of the house."

"They're gorgeous," I said, breathing in the heady scent, "but it's your birthday, not mine. You shouldn't be bringing me flowers."

"I will always bring you flowers," Tavish said, leaning in for a kiss. As our lips met, I wished—not for the first time—that I had stuck with my original plan of a romantic dinner for just the two of us.

Gracie barked at Tavish's feet, circling around him in her excitement. He ended the kiss with reluctance and bent down to pet her, but she zoomed toward the dining room, continuing to bark and shooting backward glances at him.

"Someone's certainly excited tonight," Tavish said. His eyes met mine with a flirtatious gleam. "I know the feeling."

"Let me just put these on the table," I said, hurrying toward the dining room and beckoning the birthday boy to follow. "There's wine, if you'd like." As I approached the doorway and the hidden group within, Tavish came up behind me and snaked his arms around my waist. He kissed my neck. "Mmm, you taste good," he said, nibbling my ear. "Shall we skip dinner and have dessert first?" he asked in a seductive tone.

"Surprise!" everyone yelled as my face flamed.

*　*　*

Char pushed back her plate and groaned. "I'm stuffed. I can't eat another bite."

"I know how you feel," Mom said, patting her nonexistent stomach.

"Everything was delicious, Teddie," Sharon said. "You've outdone yourself."

"She certainly has," Tavish said. "That's the best dinner I've had in I don't know how long. It's been ages since I've had a home-cooked meal."

"How quickly they forget," I teased. "What about that Wisconsin lunch I made you just a few days ago—the one where you scarfed down multiple brats?"

Tavish made a quick recovery. "Ah, but that was a barbecue—entirely different."

"Teddie inherited her cooking ability from her father's side of the family," my mother interjected. "My husband was a wonderful cook." I glimpsed the hint of tears in her eyes. "And his mother made the most amazing desserts. That woman could bake anything." She chuckled softly, remembering. "I gained ten pounds when we first started dating. I, on the other hand, can't even boil water."

"Perhaps not." Tavish returned her smile. "But you are quite a splendid shopper. Those sausage rolls were scrummy. Thank you so much for that lovely, unexpected treat."

Mom basked in his praise.

"Well, I don't know about the rest of you," Brady said, "but I've been waiting all day for the treat Ted's got in the refrigerator, and I'll bet Tavish has too." He turned a pleading gaze to me. "Can you put the poor man out of his misery and bring him his birthday cake already?"

"Aw, honey," Char said, "I love how you always think of others first."

Surveying the table, I asked, "What do you say? Are you ready for cake?"

"Yes, please," Tavish said.

Jim licked his lips. "To paraphrase Marie Antoinette, let us eat cake."

"I thought you'd never ask," Brady said.

Char and Sharon pushed back their chairs and collected the empty dinner plates. "We'll help." They followed me into the kitchen.

Pulling the birthday cake out of the fridge, I set it on the counter.

My Musketeer pals gasped. "Oh my goodness," Sharon said, "you've outdone yourself. That is the most gorgeous cake I have ever seen. Tavish is going to love the decorations."

Char nodded in agreement. "I'll say. Is there anything you *can't* do, Wonder Woman? You can be really annoying sometimes. If I didn't love you so much, I would hate you."

"Spreadsheets," I said, as I stuck the candles on the cake. "I can't do spreadsheets. Or taxes, or algebra, and geometry . . . any kind of math. That's why I'm a writer."

"A really good writer," Sharon said. "I still can't believe the news about your book sales. That is so exciting! Will you still talk to us when you're a best-selling author?" she teased.

"If you're nice. Otherwise I'll act as if I've never seen you before in my life."

After we finished singing "Happy Birthday" and Tavish blew out the candles, Jim asked Brady, "Have you heard anything more about that pervert Ron Simms? Have the Gary cops dug into his whereabouts on the nights the two women were killed and found the proof they need to get him off the streets?"

"Murder is off the table tonight," I said firmly.

"Ya got that right." Brady drooled as he looked at the Danish layer birthday cake. "The only thing on the table I want to dig into is Ted's cake."

All at once, Gracie growled and zoomed toward the kitchen, where she began a frantic barking. Brady started to get up to check it out, but I told him to stay and eat his cake. "It's probably just the neighbors. Or a skunk. Gracie hates skunks."

I joined my Eskie in the kitchen, where she continued to bark in earnest at the window. "What is it, Gracie-girl?" Pulling aside the thin curtains, I searched the darkness, but didn't see anything. "Well, whatever it was, you scared them away. Good girl." I patted her on the head and gave her a dog biscuit, then returned to the others.

After everyone had their fill of cake—Tavish and Brady both had two pieces, while Mom had a sliver—Tavish followed me into the kitchen with the empty cake plates. Sharon, Char, and Mom all tried to stop him, protesting that Tavish was the birthday boy and should not do cleanup, but he insisted.

"Leave him be," Brady said, waving his hand. "Can't you see the guy wants a few minutes alone with Ted?"

"That was the most scrumptious cake I've ever had," Tavish said. "I especially loved the decorations. However did you make those tiny books along the base?"

"I piped them on with three different pastry bags to get the multiple colors and then just staggered the heights so it looked like a bookshelf of books." I rinsed the plates and began loading the dishwasher.

"That's amazing," Tavish said. "*You're* amazing." He stepped closer to me. "Thank you for such a wonderful birthday, you talented, marvelous girl." He tilted my chin up and gave me a long, lingering kiss. I forgot all about the dishes and everything else until a voice intruded.

"All right, you two, break it up," Brady said. "Otherwise I might have to arrest you for excessive PDA." He grinned as we reluctantly broke apart. "Tavish, there's something called port in the dining room. The guy at the Milwaukee Trader Joe's told me it's an English after-dinner drink, so I got you a bottle. Shall we try it? How about you, Ted?"

Gracie flop-botted to the back door and sent me a distressed look.

"Oh my goodness, I totally forgot." I grabbed Gracie's leash from the hook. "I'm sorry, baby," I said to my anxious dog. "Mommy will take you for a walk right now."

"Can't you just let her into the backyard?" Brady asked.

"Not in the dark. She's been skunked too many times."

"I'll come with you," Tavish offered.

"No way, birthday boy," I said. "Go start on your present from Brady. We'll be right back." I flashed him a smile, my heart full.

He smiled back. A smile full of yearning and promise.

Gracie yanked on the leash. *Hurry up, Mom!* As I opened the back door, she bounded down the steps, almost yanking the leash from my hand. Two doors down, she did her business on Joanne's lawn. Once I disposed of the evidence, Gracie scampered down the sidewalk. She glanced back at me, a Mel Gibson look on her face that yelled *Freedom!*

"Okay, girl, you deserve a proper walk, but we can't go too far. We have guests waiting."

Her canines gleamed in a happy grin as she trotted down the street. As we neared the Corner Bookstore, I stopped. "Okay, time to go home." A strange noise sounded in the alley. Gracie growled. Probably a rat. I shivered. Char had seen one when she took out the garbage recently. "No, Gracie." I tightened my grip. "We're not going there. Mommy hates rats."

Then I heard the noise again. An odd choking sound. Could something be hurt?

Gracie uttered a loud growl and barked, tugging on the leash and racing toward the alley, barking furiously all the way, as I followed at a fast clip. Entering the alley, I saw a dark shape on the ground. A dark shape in a skirt. A woman? We raced over to her. The woman was lying on her side, her dark hair obscuring her face. Dropping to my knees, I gently brushed her hair from her face.

"Oh. My. God. Melanie?" When had she returned? My heart caught in my throat at the sight of the familiar features, the Harry Potter glasses askew. A creamy silk scarf wrapped around her neck gleamed in the moonlight against the ubiquitous black clothing. My scarf.

"No!" I screamed. "No!" I cradled the young woman in my arms, rocking back and forth. Dimly, sounds penetrated my anguish. I heard Gracie barking and the sounds of running feet.

Melanie shuddered and coughed, her eyes fluttering open briefly.

"Oh my God, you're alive!" Tears streamed down my face. "Thank God you're alive." I lifted my head and yelled, "Help, somebody, we need help over here!"

A shocked voice behind me burst out, "What the hell—Melanie?"

Relief coursed through me. Tavish. He must have decided to join us on our walk. He dropped down beside me and touched Melanie's shoulder. Her eyes had closed again. I shifted her gently into his arms, knowing his presence would be of more comfort.

"You're going to be okay, Melanie," Tavish said soothingly as a siren blared nearby. "Help is on the way."

Melanie coughed. Her eyes fluttered open again, wide and frightened, and she started to thrash.

"You're okay, sweetheart," Tavish soothed, "you're okay. It's Tavish. I'm right here."

Running feet pounded behind me. I touched Melanie's shoulder and gave her a reassuring smile. "You're safe now. Don't worry."

She flinched and burrowed her head into Tavish's shoulder. "She did it," Melanie said in a muffled voice. "It was Teddie. She strangled me." Then she passed out in her boss's arms.

Tavish stared at me dumbstruck.

Chapter
Twenty-Seven

Late the next morning, Mom and my fellow Musketeers paid me a visit at the jail, bearing gifts—cherry-cheese kringle, a thermos of freshly brewed coffee, and my dog. Gracie released a joyful bark when she spotted me, racing over, wagging her tail madly, and pressing her nose through the iron bars of my cell.

"Gracie-girl!" I crouched down and slid my hands through the bars to pet her, touching my forehead against hers—which she'd managed to squeeze through the bars—as I did.

My mother stared trembling and went white-faced at seeing me in the tan jail uniform. "Brady Wells," she yelled in the direction of the sheriff's office, "get in here!"

A wretched-looking Brady, sporting dark circles under his eyes, appeared in the doorway.

"Unlock this cell so my daughter can hug her dog properly," Mom demanded, two angry spots of color staining her cheeks.

"I can't let the prisoner out of the cell, Mrs. St. John," Brady said miserably.

"No, but you can let us in," Char said, gently placing her hand on her boyfriend's arm.

"It's against the rules."

"What, you think maybe we've hidden a file in the kringle so Teddie can break out of jail or something?" Sharon snarked. She extended the flat kringle package to the ganged-up-on sheriff. "Feel free to search it."

"Honey, I promise there will be no jail break," Char said, "and we won't tell a soul that you bent the rules. We just need to have a little girl talk with Teddie. You can stay here the whole time and keep an eye on us."

Brady rubbed his forehead. Then he sighed, unlocked my cell, and opened the door to admit my visitors. Gracie immediately jumped into my arms and covered my face with wet kisses. "Okay, but keep it brief. I don't want to lose my job."

"Of course, sweetie," Char said, dragging the lone visitor chair into the cell as Gracie and I continued our happy reunion. "We won't be long."

Brady returned to his office.

Mom encircled me—and Gracie—with her arms, giving me a tight hug. When she released me, her eyes were bright. Our three Musketeers then shared a group hug.

"I thought you could use a picker-upper," my mother said. She cut four large slices of kringle with a plastic knife and passed them around on paper plates she extracted from her purse.

"No kale smoothie today?" I teased.

"Nope," she said. "Some days only kringle will do."

"Welcome to the dark side."

"Speaking of the dark side," Char said, "sorry we got here so late. We had an important stop to make first."

"Oh?" I sipped my French roast gratefully—a marked improvement on the jail's coffee.

"We went to the hospital," Sharon announced, "to see Melanie."

"How is she?" I asked. "Is she okay?"

"She's fine," Char said. "Just a little bruised. They'll probably release her later today. Her boyfriend and parents are on their way from New York and will be arriving anytime."

"That's good," I said. "After such a traumatic experience, she needs her family."

"Yep," Sharon said from her seat beside me on my jail bunk. "Family's important." She slid a glance to my mother, who was sliding the kringle back into its package. "You should have seen your family in action. Your mom rocked."

"She did?"

"Oh yeah," Char said, high-fiving my mother, whose cheeks had pinked. "Your mom brought Melanie this huge bouquet of flowers and was kind and solicitous—asking her how she was doing after such a terrifying ordeal. Melanie mumbled that she was fine, but she couldn't look your mom in the eye. Me or Sharon, either. Right, Blondie?"

"Right," Sharon said. "She just kept staring down at the bed and plucking nervously at the sheets."

"Did she say what she was doing back in Lake Potawatomi?" I asked.

Sharon and Char exchanged a glance. "She wanted to surprise her boss on his birthday," Sharon said. "She had a special present she wanted to give him in person. She flew into Milwaukee early last night and rented a car. When she got to the Lake House, she learned Tavish was at your house celebrating his birthday, so she decided to walk over and surprise him. That's when she was attacked."

Char picked up the story thread. "And that's when your mother fixed Melanie with a penetrating gaze and told her to come clean." Char adopted Mom's no-nonsense tone of voice from childhood when she caught me in a lie, repeating my mother's words from the hospital: "'Melanie, I want you to look me straight in the eye and tell me that you saw my daughter strangle you with her scarf. Can you do that?'"

"Really?" I stole a glance at Mom, who was busy applying hand sanitizer to her French manicure.

"Oh yeah," Sharon interjected. "Your mom's eyes never left Melanie's face. She said to her calmly and deliberately, 'Isn't it true that someone came up behind you, in the dark, someone you never saw, who slipped Teddie's scarf over your head and began choking you, and then Teddie and Gracie stumbled on the scene and scared the strangler away?'"

Char continued the chronicle of events, "Your mom then laid her hand on Melanie's and told her fear can make people do crazy things. She said she knew what it was like to be fearful of someone new coming in and changing things. 'It's easy to view that new person as a threat when they have your boss's ear. Especially after they figured out you told your boss's stalker where to find him, even though it was for PR reasons. What if this new person—Teddie—decides at some point to tell your boss to fire you or to stop being friends with you? Then what?'"

Sharon interjected. "Then your mom said, 'Accusing my daughter isn't going to make her go away, Melanie. Teddie's no threat to your job or your friendship with Tavish, but you need to understand and accept that your boss likes Teddie and vice versa. Teddie and Tavish are going to be in each other's lives, so you'd better get used to it.'"

"You said that, Mom?"

She nodded, her eyes bright.

"Melanie began to cry then," Char said, "and"—her voice rose in triumph—"she admitted that she lied."

"She did?"

"She certainly did," Mom said, wrapping up the play-by-play. "Her exact words were, 'I never saw the person strangling me. They ran off when they heard Teddie's dog bark. If it wasn't for Teddie and her dog, I would probably be dead.'"

I snuggled Gracie close to me. "You hear that, Gracie-girl? You saved a life."

A phone shrilled in the sheriff's office.

"That will be Melanie," Char said. "She wanted to call and confess to Brady while we were at the hospital, but the nurse came in and shooed us out, said they had to do some final tests and paperwork, but Melanie promised to call and officially confess as soon as they were finished."

Moments later we heard Brady slam down the phone and bark at Augie to go to the hospital to take down Melanie's official statement.

My childhood friend appeared in the doorway, a look of anguish mixed with relief on his face. "Ted, I'm so sorry,"

Brady said as he let me out of my cell. He hung his head. "I knew you didn't do it, but—"

"It's okay, Brady. I know. You had to arrest me. It's your job. Don't worry about it. I'm fine. Although"—I paused—"you really need to get some current magazines in your cells. That *People* was from last December."

*   *   *

Red geraniums nestled beside delicate columbines and black-eyed Susans while slender stalks of lavender swayed in the breeze as Gracie and I strolled to the park. A fine summer rain began to fall, causing some we passed to duck back inside, but not me. I've always loved walking in the rain, especially when I need to think, and I definitely needed to think after all that had happened in the past twenty-four hours.

Spending time behind bars can do that to a person.

I didn't blame Brady for arresting me and putting me in jail. Two women had been strangled in our little town—both with scarves that belonged to me—and an attempted strangulation had been made on the life of a third woman, again with one of my scarves. When Melanie hysterically called me out as her attempted murderer, Brady *had* to arrest me. I would have done the same in his position.

I didn't blame Tavish either. I could see the shock, confusion, and disbelief in his eyes when he looked at me after Melanie's accusation. But what was he to do when his distraught employee and young friend, whom he'd known so much longer than me, sobbed in his arms after the attempt on her life and identified me as her strangler?

Upon hearing the news of Melanie's confession, a contrite Tavish immediately called and wanted to come over, but I told him I needed some alone time and promised to get together with him later. Right now, I needed to decompress. Mom drove me home from jail, passing several townsfolk on the way, including Wilma Sorensen, who gave me the stink eye. I waved my fuchsia scarf at her.

Once we were home, Gracie cuddled up next to me on the couch as I checked my phone. My voice mail was full, and the number of text messages—several from reporters, friends, extended family, and Tavish—was too overwhelming to deal with now. There was one important call, however, that I needed to return. I called my editor and gave her the good news that my accuser had lied and I had been released.

"I never expected anything less," Jane said.

Promising her a brief synopsis and the beginning of *Suffocating in Soufflé* by the end of the day, I hung up and took a long hot shower, scrubbing off the jailhouse grime. Although Brady kept a neat and clean jail, it was still jail. Somewhere I'd never expected to spend the night. As I toweled off and put on my happy clothes—a sunny yellow cotton boho dress and my Monet water lilies scarf from the Museé D'Orsay—I decided to view my jailhouse experience as behind-the-scenes research for a future Kate and Kallie novel. Now I would be able to paint a realistic and accurate picture of what it was truly like—not only physically, but also emotionally and psychologically—for my protagonist to find herself behind bars. How many mystery authors could say that? Ha! I straightened my shoulders and shook my wet curls.

Atta girl, Mom. Gracie gave me a proud look.

When I walked into the kitchen, Mom was waiting with a fresh cup of coffee.

"Thanks for getting Melanie to spill the tea, Mom."

"You're welcome, but you're using that slang incorrectly."

"I thought it meant tell the truth."

"No, actually it means to gossip, usually about something scandalous," Mom schooled me. "Cheryl at book club told us it comes from the southern custom of women getting together for afternoon tea and gossip."

I took a long drink of coffee. "Well then, all of Lake Potawatomi must be spilling the tea about me today."

* * *

Come on, Mom! Gracie urged me on. *We need to make up for that lost time while you were in the joint.*

I flapped my scarf at my face to cool down a sudden hot flash. Those suckers strike without warning. "Okay, Gracie-girl, settle down, there's no rush. The park's not going any-where." I smiled at elderly George and Kathy Henderson from church as they approached, walking their Maltipoo Honey on the sidewalk. Honey and Gracie are pals. They always do the butt-sniff dance and banter when they see each other.

Kathy Henderson paled, her wide eyes fastening on my scarf. George put his arm protectively around his wife and hurried across the street, Honey yapping all the way.

Gracie tilted her head at me, a confused and hurt expression in her soulful eyes.

"Sorry, girl." I squatted down and stroked her head. "Mom's a little persona non grata at the moment, but this too shall pass." *Sooner rather than later, I hope.*

When we arrived at the park, it was empty—no kids playing hide-and-seek behind the trees, no dogs chasing Frisbees, no couples on a morning stroll. The rain must have chased away all the usual visitors. Holding back my Monet scarf, I bent over the drinking fountain near the facilities for a drink. All at once, Gracie began to bark furiously. My lip smacked the metal bubbler as she yanked on the leash, throwing me off-balance. I tasted blood.

"Hey there," I heard a familiar voice say.

I whirled around, touching my tender lip, to see Tavish's assistant exiting the women's room. Talk about awkward. I reminded myself that the poor girl had been traumatized— nearly becoming another one of the Silk Strangler's victims. A little jail time was nothing compared to that.

"Melanie. Good to see you. How are you feeling today?" I glanced around. "Is your family with you?"

Gracie continued to bark and strain against her leash. "Gracie, stop that," I scolded, pulling her back. I noticed Melanie had added a pop of color to her standard black uniform—a red scarf loosely draped around her neck. Likely to hide the bruising. She stopped a few feet away, maintaining a safe distance from my dog, who continued to bark.

I pulled on Gracie's leash and tried to make her heel. "Gracie, stop. What is wrong with you? I'm sorry," I said, "I don't know why she's acting this way."

"I do." Melanie had an odd expression on her face. "I knew you'd come here to walk your dog. I've been waiting for you." Her eyes had a slightly feverish look to them.

Ah, she's come to apologize and she's nervous. "Are you okay, Melanie?"

"I will be once I take care of some unfinished business."

"What's that?" I asked gently.

"Getting rid of *you*, Nigella Lawson," she said. "For good this time." She fingered the scarf at her neck. "I thought I'd finally managed to break your hold on Tavish with your arrest, but I should have known my self-induced attempt at strangulation wouldn't hold up against your hick town posse."

Wait. What? My fingers tightened on Gracie's leash. "You strangled *yourself*?"

"Piece of cake." Melanie yanked the ends of her scarf taut, tightening the looped portion around her slender neck. "I had to pull the scarf tight enough to choke myself and look believable, but not as tight as Kristi's so that I too shuffled off this mortal coil." She casually flicked a piece of lint from her scarf.

I stared at her, unable to take it in. "You—you killed Kristi?"

"Easy-peasy." She snapped her black-polished fingers. "The klepto bimbo was already wearing your scarf she'd stolen. When I saw that, I realized I could get both of you out of Tavish's life in one fell swoop." Melanie smiled with satisfaction. "All I had to do was sneak up behind Kristi, grab her scarf tight, twist hard, and hold."

Bile rose to my throat as I listened to Tavish's assistant nonchalantly detail the murder of his ex-fiancée. Melanie's crush on Tavish was much more intense than any of us had realized. Something in her twisted recounting didn't make sense, though. "The day Kristi died, I wasn't even in Tavish's life yet," I told her. "I'd only just met him."

"Yes, but I watched him with you. You'd already piqued his interest with your fluffy little book and your baking," she said with a disdainful sniff. "Tavish loves his sweets, so you scored some serious brownie points with your *scrummy* cookies. When I heard him say he wanted to compare writing notes later, I knew I needed to stop things before they started. Then when I saw Kristi out back with your scarf around her neck, it all clicked. I knew I could—excuse the cliché—kill two birds with one stone."

Melanie leaned forward, causing Gracie to bark anew and me to take a step back. "Since your scarf strangled Kristi, you should have been arrested for her murder, which would have gotten you out of the way and effectively ended Tavish's interest in you." She glared at me, her eyes glittering behind her Harry Potter glasses. "I didn't know the sheriff was such a good buddy of yours. That's when I knew I had to step up my game with Annabelle."

I looked at Melanie with mounting horror. The woman was a stone-cold killer. She showed not even a hint of remorse over ending the lives of two women. "Why Annabelle?" I asked faintly. "Tavish wasn't interested in her—he had a restraining order against her."

"True, but since your sheriff friend wouldn't arrest you for one murder, I figured he'd have no choice when *two* women were strangled. With *your* scarves, in your town." Melanie played with the ends of her red scarf and smirked. "Annabelle was so obsessed with Tavish, she didn't notice that the entire time she was following him, *I* was following her—until the night I found her asleep and snoring on one of her stakeouts." She gave me a maniacal grin. "Your scarf effectively cured her snoring."

I shivered as all the pieces fell into place. "You broke into my house." Gracie growled and I pulled her closer, making sure not to break eye contact with Melanie.

"Cute place, but way too cluttered. You need to do some Marie Kondo–ing." Her eyes flickered to Gracie. "I tried to get you started, but I see the sleeping pill I gave your fur ball didn't do her any harm. Pity."

You sick, twisted psycho. My fists clenched, and I had to refrain from smashing them into Melanie's face. I knew I could take her down—I'm bigger and stronger than she is—but I wasn't sure what kind of weapon she might have on her to carry out her latest murderous plan. *I will* not *become Melanie's third victim. I am not a victim. I am a survivor. I need to come up with my own plan. Fast. Keeping her talking is a good start.*

Slowly I unclenched my fists. "How did you manage to get into my house without Gracie barking her head off and alerting my mom or the neighbors?"

Melanie flicked her hair. "Like any good assistant, I did my research. I learned that the neighbors closest to you are all over sixty-five and that they love their bingo. Once I discovered it was bingo night at the Elks Lodge, I simply waited until your mother and all the other old geezers had left for the hottest game in town before I made my move. After that it was a snap." She snapped her fingers, causing Gracie to emit another bark and Melanie to grimace. "Cotton ball here is sure a noisy-ass dog, but that hunk of meat quieted her down real quick." She sent me a twisted grin.

It took everything I had not to punch her lights out. Time to change tack. "How long have you been in love with Tavish, Melanie?"

Melanie's face softened as she pushed her glasses up, a dreamy look in her eyes. "Since I started working for him and discovered what an amazing, incredible man he is. There's no one like Tavish."

"What about your boyfriend?"

The shine dulled. "Boring Brandon who never reads anything other than plumbing manuals? The literary giant who never heard of Jane Austen or the Brontë sisters?" Melanie snorted. "The cultural savant who only knows Michelangelo and Leonardo as Ninja Turtles?" Her upper lip curled with contempt. "Yeah, he's a real Renaissance man. Every girl's dream. When we first started dating, I thought he was cute and sweet. A really nice guy. Everyone loves Brandon. Including my parents. Brandon *is* a really nice guy," she acknowledged. "But he also doesn't have a single cultural bone in his entire body. His idea of a great vacation is going to sporting events. Or camping. I *hate* sports. And I despise camping."

While Melanie talked, I had been covertly scoping out the park, looking for signs of someone arriving. The rain had stopped, so people would soon venture out again. I tried figuring out the best avenue of escape. Sprinting to the nearby restroom and hitting 911 as I ran? Furtively slipping my hand into my back pocket and pressing Brady's number in my favorites?

Then I heard the silence. Crazy-girl had stopped talking. As I returned my attention to Melanie, I saw her closing in on me.

Gracie growled and bared her teeth, effectively halting her advance. "It's okay, girl, it's okay," I soothed my canine daughter, keeping my eyes on Melanie. I glimpsed something out of the corner of my eye. Someone approaching, thank God. Tavish. A wave of relief washed over me.

"Your mom told me where I could find you," Tavish said, as he came up alongside me. He sent a warm smile to his psycho assistant. "Mel, brilliant to see you up and about. How are you feeling, dear girl?"

He doesn't know. How to tell him his friend and employee was a total nut job?

"I'm feeling great now that you're here." Melanie beamed out her crazy love at her boss.

Danger, Tavish Bentley, danger. I nudged his arm and tried to warn him discreetly and telepathically. Then I blurted out, "She's the Silk Strangler. Melanie killed Kristi and Annabelle, and I'm next on her list."

Tavish's head swiveled from me to Melanie, his mouth a large O. "What?"

"I did it for you, Tavish," Melanie said. "I did it so we can be together as we're meant to be."

He stared at her, his face bleached of color. "You killed Kristi?"

"She was trying to get you back after you'd broken up with her. She told me as much at the bookstore."

"That was *you* I heard in the restroom with Kristi that day," I said.

Melanie ignored me. She had eyes only for Tavish. Bright shining eyes burning with a fanatical passion. "I love you, Tavish. I've always loved you and I know you love me too."

I used her distraction to make my move, lunging forward to grab at her scarf.

"Not so fast, Nigella." Melanie whipped out a gun from the back of her waistband and aimed it at me.

Gracie snarled and tried to surge toward the crazy woman threatening her mom, but I held her back.

Melanie held the gun steady on me. "Should I shoot you"—she swiveled the gun and pointed it at Gracie—"or your rotten little dog first?"

Get away from her, you bitch, I screamed in my head, moving in front of my canine daughter to shield her.

"Put the gun down, Mel," Tavish pleaded. "Please. You do not want to do this. This is not who you are. You need help."

"No, what I *need* is you and to get the hell out of this stupid town. Let's go back to New York where we belong, Tavish," she implored, "and put all this behind us. Let's forget we ever came here."

"I can't do that," he said gently. "I'm sorry. I care about you, Mel. I want to help you. I promise I will get you the best help available. Will you let me do that?"

Maybe I can rush her and grab the gun, I thought as Tavish tried to reason with his assistant and talk her down. *She wouldn't expect that. I would have the element of surprise.*

You would also be dead, my common sense countered. *Check out her stance and the way she's holding that gun in her hand. This is not her first time at the rodeo. She knows how to use that bad boy.*

"Give me the gun, Mel," Tavish said, holding out his hand. "Let Teddie and Gracie go. They have nothing to do with this. It's between you and me."

"You and me?" Melanie released a bitter laugh. "There is no you and me," she said. "You *care* about me, but you don't love me. Even after all I've done for you." She waved the gun, her eyes wild and unfocused. "Well, if you think I'm going to let Nigella here have you, you're wrong. If I can't have you, nobody can." Then before either of us could react, she quickly turned the gun on the object of her affection and shot him.

As Tavish crumpled to the ground, Gracie broke free of her leash and charged at Melanie, who swung the gun toward her.

"No!" I roared, head-butting Melanie in the stomach. The shot went wild. She fell, and I grabbed her wrist and slammed it on the ground to jar the gun loose from her hand. Gracie sank her teeth into Melanie's ankle.

"Ow!" she shrieked. "Get your damned dog off me!" She attempted to stand. Remembering the weapons training Dad had taught me in high school—which I had never used before now, since I hate guns—I grabbed the pistol and hit Melanie in the head with it, knocking her out. Then I sprinted over to

Tavish, telling Gracie to stay and guard the unconscious woman.

Sirens screamed nearby, and I could hear shouts and running feet, but my only focus was the motionless man on the ground whose shirt was drenched in blood. Tavish lay on his back, his hand clutched to his bloody chest, unmoving.

"Tavish, Tavish!" I yelled, the tears coursing down my cheeks as I pressed my hands tightly on his chest to stop the bleeding. "Tavish, can you hear me?"

His eyes flickered open. "Can you keep it down, please? How's a guy supposed to sleep with all this noise?" He sent me a weak smile. "That's the second time you've come to my aid, Wonder Woman. I owe you." Tavish's eyes fluttered shut.

Chapter Twenty-Eight

I set the Victoria sponge cake on the counter, next to my dad's favorite fifties fruit-cocktail cake. Since getting home from the hospital this afternoon after Tavish was safely out of surgery and resting, I had thrown myself into a baking frenzy. As I baked, I thought long and hard. Gracie, sensing my pensive mood, stared up at me from her bed in the corner, concern etching her furry features.

"It's okay, Gracie-girl," I said as I mixed the batter for my carrot-cake muffins. "Don't worry. Everything's going to be okay."

Things had started heading toward okay when Brady called to update me on Melanie. After Brady took her to the Lake Potawatomi jail and tried to question her about the two murders, Melanie had had a complete breakdown. She was now in an upscale Milwaukee sanitarium asking every person in sight—including her parents and boyfriend—if they'd seen her husband Tavish and when he was coming to take her home. Melanie's psych stay was paid for by the generous insurance policy her boss provided. That same boss had also instructed his lawyers to provide the woman who had shot him with the legal services she would need at the appropriate time.

Definitely one of the good guys.

Then Brady told me about Ron Simms. Turns out the Gary cops had caught the creep taking some shady bondage porn pictures of women—including a few underage teen girls—at the empty houses he was selling. The blue Victorian featured prominently in the pictures the police confiscated. I shuddered, remembering how the perv had looked at Char and how hard he'd been trying to entice her to the blue house. Thankfully, Ronald Simms would not be enticing anyone to any houses for a long time.

By the time I pulled the muffins out of the oven, I realized what I had to do.

Wearing the turquoise-embroidered coral cotton dress Mom had bought me topped with the turquoise scarf from Tavish, a basket of iced carrot-cake muffins in my hand, I quietly pushed open the door of Tavish's hospital room an hour later, not wanting to wake him.

No worries there. Jim, Sharon, Brady, and Char were clustered around Tavish's bed, laughing and joking.

"Welcome to the took-a-bullet club, brother," Brady teased. "Now next time you write about your hero getting shot, it will be more authentic and have even greater verisimilitude."

Char cast him an admiring look. "Listen to you with your big words."

"My girlfriend's a librarian," Brady said. "I gotta step up my game to keep her interest."

She planted a kiss on his cheek. "You'll always have my interest, baby." Then Char saw me. "Look who's back bearing gifts."

"Hey, Ted," Brady said, sniffing the air, "whatcha got there?"

Tavish's eyes locked on mine, a huge smile spreading across his face.

Char jumped up from her chair. "Never mind, Brady. That's for the man in the hospital bed." She picked up her purse. "Come on, guys, let's get out of here and let these two have some time alone."

My friends said their good-byes and headed to the door. Sharon lingered, fussing with Tavish's blanket. "Take it easy, now," she said, "and you make sure you do what the doctors say." She bustled after the others, blowing me a kiss as she left.

"Alone at last," Tavish said.

I set the muffins down on his bedside table and scooted the hospital chair closer to the bed so I could hold his hand. "How are you feeling?" I asked.

"Like I've been run over by a lorry." He smiled wryly. "Luckily, it's just a flesh wound," he said, quoting Monty Python. Then his smile faded. He stroked my hand. "I'm so sorry for all this and for what Melanie put you through."

I squeezed his hand. "And I'm sorry I jumped in to protect Gracie from a bullet yet didn't do the same for you."

"You had no idea Melanie would shoot me." Tavish gave a dry laugh. "*I* had no idea she would shoot me. I've heard of employer-employee conflict, but that takes the cake."

"Cake. That reminds me." I inclined my head to his bedside table. "I brought you some carrot-cake muffins. I also made my dad's favorite fruit-cocktail cake, and I thought you might enjoy a taste of home, so I baked a Victoria sponge cake too—both waiting for you at my house."

Tavish eyed me with a bemused expression.

"I bake when I'm stressed or upset," I explained.

"My sweet tooth thanks you," he said. "I look forward to eating them all—although perhaps not all at once." He lifted his hand to caress my cheek and flinched in pain.

"Careful. Do you want some water?"

Tavish shook his head and fastened his hazel eyes intently on mine. "Today was supposed to be our romantic getaway," he said with regret. "Every time we try to be alone together, we're thwarted at every turn."

"Maybe the universe is trying to tell us something," I said softly.

"Like what?"

I hesitated. "Maybe that we should just be friends."

"*What?*"

"Just kidding." I bent down and gave Tavish a kiss. A long kiss. A kiss full of promise. Then I sat back and regarded him thoughtfully. "You know that line from *Sense and Sensibility* we keep quoting? The one about seven years being insufficient to make some people acquainted with each other, while seven days are more than enough for others?"

"Yes . . ."

"Well, I realized that Marianne Dashwood is the one who said that line, and she said it about Willoughby in the early days of their budding romance—a romance that did not end well. Let's be honest, Tavish," I said gently. "We really don't know each other all that well. Things have been moving so fast between us. Two weeks ago I hadn't even met you. If you don't mind, I'd like to slow things down a bit and spend more time getting to know you."

Tavish eyed me speculatively. "As I recall, Colonel Brandon is your favorite Austen hero," he said.

I nodded.

"And it was slow and steady Colonel Brandon who got the girl in the end, not the dashing impetuous Willoughby."

"That's right." I smiled.

"Well then, Willoughby be damned," Tavish said. "How do you like your pianoforte, Ms. St. John?"

"Actually, since I'm a Wisconsin girl, I'd prefer an accordion." I winked at him. "We really love our polka music here."

Recipes

Grandma's Norwegian Fattigman Bakkels

Pronounced "futtymon buckles." *Fattigman* means "poor man." Traditionally made at Christmas. Grandma wrote a note about my dad at the bottom of her recipe: *This is my son Georgie's favorite cookie, so I make them a few times a year, not just Christmas.*

9 egg yolks and 3 whole eggs
12 tablespoons sugar
12 tablespoons whipped cream
¼ teaspoon cardamom
1 teaspoon lemon juice
2 tablespoons brandy
1 lump of butter the size of a walnut
Pinch of salt
About 4 cups flour (not too much, now)
Powdered sugar
16 ounces lard *or* 4 cups vegetable oil (my grandma always
    used lard, but I prefer vegetable oil)

Mix and cream well together all ingredients except the flour, powdered sugar, and lard. Keep the dough cold to be easily handled. Then add enough flour, a little at a time, to make a soft dough (be sure not to use too much flour).

Heat the lard or oil in the bottom of a heavy pot.

Roll out the dough very thin and cut into diamond shapes. Cut a slit through one end of the diamond and gently pull the other end through. (Invest in a *fattigman* cookie cutter—available at most specialty baking stores—to make cutting faster and easier.)

Deep fry at 370 degrees, turning occasionally. Don't fry too hard or keep the grease too hot. You want a nice golden color.

Remove with a slotted spoon and drain on paper towels or brown paper, then roll lightly in powdered sugar.

Lemon Sugar Cookies

3 cups flour
1 teaspoon baking powder
1 teaspoon salt
¼ teaspoon baking soda
1 cup butter, cold—cut into cubes (Grandma's original recipe called for "fat," but I've updated it with butter)
3 eggs
1 cup sugar
1 teaspoon vanilla
1½ tablespoons fresh lemon juice
½ tablespoon lemon zest (add more for extra flavor)
¼ cup Demerara sugar (or sugar in the raw)

Sift together all dry ingredients except the sugars. Cut in the butter as for pie crust. Beat eggs lightly with the sugar. Add to dry mixture and mix well. Add vanilla and lemon juice.

Chill a few hours. Scoop into balls and roll in Demerara sugar. Place sugared dough onto baking sheet and bake at 375 degrees for 8 to 10 minutes or until golden brown.

Carrot Cake Muffins (or mini loaves— makes six mini loaves)

2 cups sugar
3 cups flour
2 teaspoons baking powder
2 teaspoons baking soda
2 teaspoons cinnamon
1 teaspoon salt
⅔ cup canola oil
½ cup applesauce
4 eggs
2 cups shredded carrots
1 cup crushed pineapple with syrup
1 tablespoon vanilla (yes, tablespoon)
1 teaspoon orange extract

Sift together all dry ingredients. (If you don't have a sifter, use a fine-mesh strainer.) Then add the rest of the ingredients and mix until moistened. Beat 2 minutes at medium speed.

Pour into greased and floured muffin tins, or several small greased and floured loaf pans. (If you're planning to give away as gifts, use disposable aluminum loaf pans.)

Bake at 350 degrees for 35 minutes. Let cool before frosting.

Cream Cheese Icing (optional, but oh so delicious)

2 tablespoons butter
6 ounces cream cheese (two 3-ounce packages)
4 teaspoons vanilla
4 cups powdered sugar
Secret ingredient: 1 teaspoon almond extract

Cream butter and cream cheese together; add in vanilla and almond extract. Slowly add in powdered sugar.

Frost cooled carrot cake loaves and enjoy. (For a fun, decorative touch, pipe an orange icing carrot atop each loaf—don't forget the leafy green top!)

Laura Jensen Walker

Quick and Easy Fruit Cocktail Cake

A modern-day "fruitcake" favorite from the 1950s, only so much faster and easier to make (and definitely more moist).

1 #2 can fruit cocktail
1 egg
1 cup sugar
1 cup flour
1 teaspoon baking soda
¼ teaspoon salt
¼ cup brown sugar

Drain fruit cocktail well. Beat egg in a bowl.

Sift together sugar, flour, baking soda, and salt. Add beaten egg and fruit cocktail to sifted mix.

Pour batter into greased and floured 8-inch square cake pan. Sprinkle brown sugar over top.

Bake at 350 degrees for 40 minutes. Cool slightly, top with whipped cream,* and serve.

*A childish scrawl (my dad's) at the bottom of the recipe card read: *Canned whipped cream from the fridge is the best because you can squirt it in your mouth first. Yum!*

314

Danish Layer Cake

A favorite among Danes in Lake Potawatomi and Racine, Wisconsin

Almond Custard

Making the almond-custard filling from scratch is a difficult, time-consuming process. If you don't have the time or inclination to make homemade custard, use either Bird's custard mix (available at specialty stores) or vanilla pudding. (Make sure to add ½ teaspoon of almond extract to whichever shortcut "custard" mix you choose.)

After much trial and error over the years, I've learned it's best to make the almond-custard filling first, before the cake.

3 cups milk
¼ cup sugar
¼ teaspoon salt
3 eggs, beaten slightly
1 teaspoon vanilla
½ teaspoon almond extract

The custard is baked in 4 or 5 custard cups (or ramekins) in a water bath. You'll need a 2-inch deep roasting pan, filled with enough water to go halfway up the sides of the ramekins. For safety, place the roasting pan and an empty ramekin on the oven rack, then fill the roasting pan with hot water. Remove the empty ramekin. Very gently, slide the roasting pan in and close the door. (Whenever you slide the pan, be very careful not to slosh the water.) Preheat oven to 325.

Scald milk with sugar and salt.

While continually whisking the eggs, pour milk very slowly into beaten eggs, starting with just a few drops at a time and ending with a slow steady stream. Add vanilla and almond extract.

Strain into custard cups or ramekins. Very carefully set the cups/ramekins into the roasting pan water bath.

Bake about 30 minutes until a sharp-pointed knife inserted halfway between the center and the side of the ramekin comes out clean. Be careful not to overbake.

Cool the custard completely before spreading between cake layers.

Yellow Cake

You can either make yellow cake from scratch or use a box mix, depending on time and preference. I prefer homemade but have used a box mix in a pinch.

1¾ cups cake flour
2 teaspoons baking powder
2 tablespoons cornstarch
½ teaspoon salt
1 cup butter
1⅔ cups sugar
6 yolks and 2 egg whites, separated
1 tablespoon vanilla extract (yes, tablespoon)
¾ cup milk

Preheat oven to 350. Grease and flour the sides of two 8-inch round pans. Line the bottoms of pans with parchment.

Sift together flour, baking powder, cornstarch, and salt. Set aside. (If you don't have a sifter, use a fine mesh strainer.)

Cream butter first for 2 to 3 minutes, then add in sugar in ¼-cup increments and cream the two together until light and fluffy. Beat in egg yolks one at a time, then stir in the vanilla. (Turn off the mixer to stir in the vanilla.) Starting and ending with the flour, alternately beat in flour mixture and milk, a little at a time, mixing just until incorporated.

In a separate bowl, beat egg whites until peaks form, then gently fold into batter.

Pour batter into prepared pans. Bake in preheated oven for 25 minutes. (Use a toothpick to check for doneness.) Cool 15 minutes before turning out onto cooling racks.

Raspberry Filling

Raspberry preserves or jam can be used for the filling instead if you're in a hurry.

¼ cup sugar
2 tablespoons cornstarch
10- to 12-ounce container frozen raspberries (thawed; do not rinse)
Juice from half a lemon

Combine sugar and cornstarch in a small pan. Add berries and juice. Cook over medium heat until thick and even, stirring constantly. Cool completely.

Buttercream Frosting

If you have a sweet tooth like me, buttercream is best. If you like a less sweet topping, go with whipped-cream frosting.

Although there are several shortcuts or substitutes you can use for the rest of this delicious yet time-consuming dessert (for example, a box mix yellow cake, Bird's custard or vanilla pudding, and raspberry jam or preserves), *do not use* horrible canned buttercream frosting. It tastes awful and will ruin the entire cake.

1 cube butter (half a cup), softened
1 teaspoon vanilla

3½ cups powdered sugar
Pinch of salt

Cream butter and vanilla with mixer on medium speed for about two minutes. Blend in sifted powdered sugar with a pinch of salt. Add lots of love and that's it. (Add a little cream or milk if frosting is too thick. Be very careful not to add in too much milk.)

Whipped-Cream Frosting

Never *ever* use Cool Whip—too artificial tasting.

½ pint heavy whipping cream
2 tablespoons sugar

Beat cream and sugar together until peaks form.

Assembly

Cut each cake horizontally in half. Spread bottom layer with almond-custard filling first, then the raspberry filling (atop the custard). Repeat between layers and frost with buttercream or whipped-cream frosting.

Oatmeal-Raisin Cookies

1 cup butter (room temperature)
¾ cup white sugar
¾ cup brown sugar (firmly packed)
¼ cup molasses
2 eggs
2 teaspoons vanilla extract
1 teaspoon orange extract
2 cups all-purpose flour
1 teaspoon baking soda
1 teaspoon salt
1½ teaspoons ground cinnamon
½ teaspoon ground nutmeg
3 cups quick-cooking oats
1 cup raisins (or dried cranberries if you prefer)
Optional: turbinado sugar

Cream together butter, both sugars, and molasses. Beat in eggs, one at a time, then vanilla extract and orange extract.

In a separate bowl, combine flour, baking soda, salt, cinnamon, and nutmeg.

Slowly mix dry ingredients into creamed mixture. Stir in oats and raisins or dried cranberries.

Cover and chill cookie dough for at least an hour.

Preheat oven to 375 degrees.

Line cookie sheets with parchment paper. Using a melon ball scoop, drop slightly rounded balls of dough onto cookie sheets. Slightly flatten cookies with the back of a tablespoon. (As needed, dip the spoon in flour or turbinado sugar.)

Optional: Sprinkle a little turbinado sugar atop each cookie.

Bake for about 10 minutes (depending on the size of the cookies) until lightly golden. They're best when they're slightly undercooked. Cool on wire racks—if you can wait that long.

Acknowledgments

Writing a book is a solitary activity; getting it published is not. I am deeply grateful to my editor Faith Black Ross, Terri Bischoff, Melissa Rechter, Madeline Rathle, and the rest of the Crooked Lane team. Thank you for taking a chance on this debut mystery author! Heartfelt gratitude to my agent Chip MacGregor for always believing in me and never giving up; and to those friends and family who read and commented on my manuscript at various stages, especially Cindy Coloma, Jennie Damron, Cathy Elliott, Cheryl Harris, Dave and Dale Meurer, Eileen Rendahl, Annette Smith, and Marian Hitchings (with extra thanks to fellow breast cancer sister and survivor Marian for the "Boobsey Twins.") A huge shout-out to Kim "Kimmie" Orendor, my longtime journalism pal and big-hearted friend who read pages as fast as I sent them and gave me immediate and encouraging feedback. You rock, Kimmie. Special thanks to the lovely and amazing Catriona McPherson, Eileen Rendahl, James L'Etoile, Erica Ruth Neubauer, Connie Berry, and Zoe Quinton for so kindly and generously welcoming me into my new mystery-writing family and for their ongoing encouragement and

Acknowledgments

support. And finally, to Michael, my creative Renaissance-man partner who is a far better cook and baker than I'll ever be, thanks for testing and tweaking all the recipes. My sweet tooth thanks you too.

Thanks to my fun and beloved aunts Sharon and Char who began my lifelong love of mysteries by bringing home copies of Trixie Belden from Western Printing (with additional thanks to Aunt Sharon whose bingo playing jaunts to the Potawatomi casino inspired the name of Teddie's small town.) Thanks also to my sister Lisa and cousin Heidi who confirmed my remembrance of "yous guys" and other Racine-specific vernacular. Heartfelt gratitude to all my Wisconsin relatives—including my LaPoint cousins and those childhood sleepovers—for happy memories of growing up in Racine. (The delicious kringle and Danish layer cake didn't hurt either.)

324